CHAOS THEORY

Rich Restucci

SEVERED PRESS
HOBART TASMANIA

CHAOS THEORY

ISBN: 978-1-925342-57-4

For my brother. You've missed so much…

F is for fire that burns down the whole town.
U is for uranium… bombs!
N is for no survivors when you…

The FUN song, as sung by Plankton before being rudely interrupted by SpongeBob

I GOTTA SAY SOMETHING

There's still a government. I don't think this, or believe this, I know this.

I know this because they want me. They want me badly. I didn't kill anyone of great importance. I don't possess nuclear launch codes or have a stocked underwater base. I haven't come up with a cure or a vaccine.

They don't want me because of who I am. They want me because of what I am.

I am the vaccine.

Somebody needs to know this, so I'm putting it here.

It was early on, back when people were still fighting instead of hiding. I was travelling on a prison bus in a caravan on the back roads of New Hampshire when we were attacked. We weren't attacked by *them*, we were attacked by *us*. Another group of survivors with guns and vehicles who desperately wanted our guns and vehicles.

Bullets flew and people died. The attackers fell back when they realized that we weren't going to lie down and die so they could have our stuff. Some of us did lie down and die, but not on purpose. Didn't stay down though. Got up in short order and tried to kill everyone, attacker and defender. We had good guns, which is why we were able to fight off the bad guys. We were prison guards, cops with their families, and the prison doctor. And prisoners. Fourteen inmates that the guards decided not to leave in cells when they bugged out. They didn't take all of us, but they took the guys that they thought would help them and not kill their families.

Yup, I was a prisoner. Three left of a four year stint. What I did isn't important as it was a lifetime ago in another world.

Three of our seven vehicles, including the bus, were rendered useless in the attack, but we were able to scavenge two of the attacker's trucks. I was working on a Ford F150 extended cab, trying to see if I could save the radiator for a third vehicle, when a bloody hand snaked out from underneath the truck and grabbed my pant leg. I wasn't expecting it, and as I said, it was early on, so I wasn't used to things grabbing me.

I looked down, and another hand grabbed my leg. The hands pulled, and rather than me sliding under the truck, the thing pulled itself out from under. Now, as I'm sure you know, these things are damn fast when they're close to you, but this particular attack happened in slow motion. I remember it like it was yesterday instead of almost a year ago.

The man, who had been peppered by small arms fire I would later find out, pulled his mouth to my leg. He didn't just go for the bite, like they always do, but he actually reared back with his mouth open. I remember he reared because he hit the back of his noggin on the bumper of the F150, and it made a thud that I thought would have really hurt. I thought it was quite funny.

Until he bit me.

He shot his face forward and latched his jaws around my lower leg, and bit down. Hard. I was an inmate, and we had to wear denim jeans at all times, prison rules. This guy bit right through them and into my leg. Not the meaty part, but the front right, sort of between my shin and my calf. Either way it friggin hurt. I let out a yell and jerked back, but the dead SOB didn't let go. He was on me like a snapping turtle, dug in like a tick. He must have had trouble with the jeans, because he didn't just rip out a chunk like a bite out of a cheeseburger, he just kept gnawing, and I fell on my ass. One of the cops heard me yelling and ran over. He shot the guy in the back, but that didn't do anything, so he pistol whipped him.

The guy let go of me and I scuttled away like a crab. He started to crawl toward the cop and the cop ventilated his cranium. I remember that too because the dead guy's head once again smacked into the bumper with the same thud.

Everyone came running at that point. Whether it was to help, or just to see, I'll never know. The cop reached his hand down to me to help me up, but drew it away quickly when he saw my bloody leg.

Then he pointed the gun at me and screamed for the doc, who was standing right next to him. The doc put on some blue gloves and looked me over. I'll never forget those gloves, or the look on his face when he looked me in the eyes. His face said it all, with sort of a sad revulsion, and helplessness.

Infected.

He stood and whispered to the cop, who nodded with the same look on his face. I glanced around at the people who were standing and looking down at me. Mothers, wives, kids, cops, and my former room-mates. Most of them had the same look, but others had looks of relief. I don't know if the relief was because I was a prison inmate and I was going to die, or that there was one less mouth to feed. Didn't matter, I was dead and everybody knew it.

I finally pulled my pant leg up and looked at my wound. There was a semi-circular bite pattern that was already beginning to bruise. And blood. There was some blood, but not much. The dead guy had most definitely broken the skin though.

It's amazing how you can try to rationalize yourself out of your own doom. I thought that it was only a tiny bite, barely broke the skin. Maybe the jeans prevented any of the dead guy's death from getting in me. Maybe he wasn't even infected with the same stuff, but this was something different. A hundred other get out of jail free cards ran through my mind in the space of a nanosecond, but what brought me back to reality was the gun pointed at my face.

The cop told me I was infected. I sat there and came up with the only thing I could think of to prevent that inevitable lead headache. I told the cop I could fix the truck.

And I did. I fixed the hell out of it.

When that baby was purring like a cream-fed kitten, the cop, who no longer had his gun drawn, told me to come with him. He and this other guy, and inmate called Dave, or Don, or Dan… began with a D but I can't remember now, they brought me behind this little shed thing that reminded me of an outhouse. I remember it had this gray antenna and some solar panels on it. I can't remember that convict's name, but I can damn well remember those blue solar panels with the white spots on them. They took me behind the little structure, and the cop tells me that the best thing for everybody would be to shoot me. Nobody gets better, it's a bad way to die, and I would be adding to the enemy. Blah blah blah.

I told him I wanted every damn second, and he said he understood, but I couldn't come with them. I was infected after all, and more than a liability, a potential catastrophe. Me, a catastrophe because I got too close to a dead guy. It was unfair, but I did the only thing I could: I acquiesced. I told them to leave me. The cop, who incidentally I had never seen prior to the morning we bugged out of the prison, gave me some food and water, and said thanks and that he was sorry.

Another guard, I had saved his kid earlier from one of those things when we stopped for a piss break, said he would leave a gun and some ammo on the road a half mile up after they left. He didn't trust me enough to give me the weapon now as I might shoot somebody. I was a con, and don't think it didn't occur to me. I thanked him and the convoy left me standing on the solid yellow line in the center of the road in southern New Hampshire.

I saw the guard's pickup stop a bit down the road, so I went to see if he left me a gun. He did. An old fashioned wheel gun with half a box of .38 shells. There were twenty six rounds. Twenty six rounds between me and probably two hundred million dead people wanting to taste my important bits.

It didn't take them long to find me either.

HUNGRY HIPPOS

I still haven't found out why some of them can run, or can't, depending on how you look at it. The Runners are still alive, the slow ones aren't. That's all I know. That's all anyone knows. Except they're *fast*. Everybody knows that.

Damn fast.

Did I mention that I waved as the convoy pulled away, leaving me to die, quite literally, in the middle of the road? Nobody waved back.

So with gun in hand, I followed the convoy at a modest three miles per hour or so. Within two hours, my leg hurt so badly I wanted to cut it off. Ten steps later I had to sit down.

It was unseasonably warm for November in New England. I remember that too. I also remember a couple of vehicles drove past me as I sat there agonizing in the New Hampshire sun, but nobody stopped. Better for them that they didn't I guess. I was wondering how long I was going to hang out there before I got sick when nausea hit me like a major league fastball and I started to puke. It didn't creep up on me, it grabbed my insides and kicked the hell out of them until my coffee and ramen noodles had been deposited on the median strip of the highway. The noodles looked like worms in the vomit, so that got me to keep with the void diet and I kept going.

I could see movement on the road about a half mile out. It wasn't a car, but in my state my vision wouldn't focus, so I couldn't tell exactly what it was. I decided I should make all haste and vacate the area and tried to stand. I was thinking it wasn't so bad when the dizziness hit and I swooned and promptly passed out.

You would think that waking up to a living dead thing staggering toward me at top undead speed while only a mere thirty feet away would scare the ever loving crap out of me, but I was serene. As serene as I could be with what felt like a horde of demons hacking at my leg from the inside and a shirt covered in stinking, partially digested stuff.

Arms outstretched, the thing came straight at my mostly prone form, and I was still woozy. She was hungry. I could see in her dead eyes that I looked like one of those delicious cooked roadrunners that the coyote always fantasized about. She was drooling and foaming, and bloody and dead, but the most important thing to me at the time was her proximity.

At ten feet I snapped out of it, but that was when her undead-burst-of-hustle kicked in.

You've seen it. Hopefully not up close, but you've seen it. They stagger and lurch, sometimes they stumble, but they always get up. In a group or singly, they're very slow until they get within arm's reach, then they're like cheetahs. It's like they save all their speed for a last ditch, one second surge. True survivors, those of us that no longer fear but respect the abilities and shortcomings of the dead, have learned to wait for that surge before making a critical move. You do this because all the speed and balance that the dead have is aimed in one direction and that direction is at you.

'Course it doesn't help you at all if you're on your ass in a puddle of puke.

She was a blur of death and teeth as she came at me, lunging. Most people will say that the dead fall to their knees when they are attacking something on the ground but that's not really true. Their knees don't hit first. Her mouth came at me as fast as it possibly could, and it was open. I put my forearm up to stop her, but that was a panic move. Seriously, lie down on the ground and have somebody fall on you. Make it a ten-year-old kid if you have one handy, and stick your forearm up to try to stop the impact.

Nope.

Little Billy or Sara or insert-kid's-name-here is going to plow through your feeble barricade like a freight train.

This lady was no ten year old either. She was a lot of woman, and I don't mean her personality.

Bitch fell right on me teeth first. I thought the puke stank, but this woman was *ripe*. The plague was new, so I don't know how she could have smelled like a week old dead thing that had fermented in the sun, but she did. Actually, maybe that's what she was. She bit me just below the collar bone and I yelled. She pulled her head back and I screamed, because her mouth was no longer empty.

Something else you probably already know, but hey this is for posterity: Once they lock their hands on you, they aren't letting go. She slurped that nibble of my shoulder down with a bloody piece of prison purchased t-shirt as a garnish, but she multitasked, and latched her mitts on to my shirt and pants. She finished my shoulder, and leaned in for another morsel, but I was having none of that.

This lady outweighed me by fifty pounds, and I'm a big guy. She was not big boned. I rolled her sideways, and pushed for all my infected ass was worth, which was damn little at that point, but hey, it was *my* ass.

She wanted my nose next, and pulled as I pushed. It's amazing what you remember and forget in certain circumstances. I can't remember her hair color, or what she was wearing, or even what her dead face looked like, but I remember she was fat. Fat and *strong*.

We continued our tug of war with me as the prize for a few seconds until I heard shuffling footsteps over our struggle. I dared a furtive glance toward the new sound, and lo and behold, fat dead lady's twin sister was coming for brunch. She wasn't really her twin, but she was every bit as big.

The tide had definitely turned in favor of the dead folks, and I desperately needed a weapon. Like a gun or something. I wanted to smack myself in the head with my palm for forgetting the pistol, but I would have had to let her go, then the fat lady would get to sing.

Pinned lady started snapping. She chomped so hard that one of her teeth flew out and hit me in the cheek. The other dead lady was about fifteen feet away, so whatever needed to be done had to happen fast or I wouldn't spend the next few hours dying in agony, but the next few minutes.

I seriously considered that. Should I just let the New Hampshire heifers finish the job now? I mean it would hurt. Like, agony on a level I don't want to comprehend. But then again, not an hour previous I told that cop that I wanted every second. Although that was before I knew for sure I was infected. The puking and passing out, plus the look of the leg bite were both indicative of infection. Spot on. I mean I knew before, I just didn't want to believe. So yeah, I was infected. And nobody gets better.

But being torn to pieces by a duo of tubbies? Seriously? I could always shoot myself if the pain got too bad later. If I started puking up important pieces of me instead of my breakfast, or if I saw a living person and pictured them wearing those little bootie thingies you put on a turkey's drumsticks, I could always opt out then. Also, for some reason, the Scorpions *Winds of Change* just shoved its way into my thoughts. Didn't even like that song.

So in the end, after all of those thoughts, which took, perhaps, point five seconds, I decided I wanted to end things my way. I gave a herculean shove and smashed my hefty hanger-on into the street. Her head banged off of the asphalt, and it must have stunned her because she blinked in rapid succession. Her grip didn't slack, but she stopped snapping and pulling. I did it again, and this time I looked for the revolver, which was right next to her flabby right arm. I grabbed the gun and put it to the side of her head. She stopped blinking and looked into my eyes, almost pleadingly.

I can't imagine how many people went out like that in the first couple of weeks. Not knowing or believing a loved one was one of them, and then just getting gnawed on by your kid or your grandma. This dead woman, who had already dined on a portion of me, however small, raised her eyebrows and frowned, jutting out her bottom lip slightly. She looked sad, and I blew her head off. I wasn't going to be one of those dumb people I just mentioned. No gloomy-looking dead fat broad was going to get the better of me.

Except she already had. Bitch bit me.

The undead will let go if you disable their brain. Doesn't make any sense to me either. All of their systems are shut down except their core nervous system. They don't breathe, there's no heartbeat, they don't poop, and they feel no pain. They can hear and see, but I don't buy that they can smell because they don't breathe. Although they make audible sounds, so they must draw in air to push it past their decaying vocal cords. If that's the case then maybe they *can* smell. OK, I'm on board with the smelling thing. As of now.

Now now, not then now.

So she let go of me and I rolled off of her and aimed at number two, who had gotten significantly closer during my hasty tussle with number one. I couldn't focus for shit though, and missed my first two shots. Well, I mean, I hit her, just not in the head. She did the same face plant on me, but I blasted her on the way down. She hit me hard, but I was able to push her off before she chomped down.

I rolled left, or maybe it was right, it was a while ago. She was on her face, the back of her melon now spread out on fatty number one. It was gross. Them lying there with holes in them that I had put there. I would have tossed them again, but I was shit out of cookies.

I had never shot anyone before. No, I wasn't *that* type of criminal.

I sat up, and I can remember looking at them lying there. They were pathetic. They had probably been eating pie (double portions) at a church lunch a couple of days before, and I had smoked both of them. I felt like I had just won a seal clubbing contest.

That was when that little dude who runs stuff in your body jerked the adrenaline shut-off valve extra hard. My leg and shoulder wounds decided to remind me of our acquaintance. That same little guy, who was probably giggling maniacally, next launched an all-out ballistic missile attack on my pain receptors.

And yet I stood. The sound of the last shot was still ringing in my ears when I started my trek north. My plan was to find someplace nice to swallow a bullet, because I did not fancy being eaten, and I didn't want to be one of them. Either way, I would be part of the living impaired soon enough.

TRAILER TRASH

So the Runners. We all know they're fast. We all know they hate us and want to tear into us. They eat us. But do they drink? I mean if you forced one to fire down a handle of Stolies, would it stagger like its dead buddies? And that's something else…if they aren't dead, why don't the dead ones eat them? If you put nine Runners and one uninfected human in a room with a dead one, the dead one will come straight at the live guy. I've seen it. Well, not as an experiment, but I've seen that type of scenario. That would be a crappy experiment for the dude in the room with all those infected types. Downright cruel.

By nightfall, the heat of the day had been replaced with a biting wind. I had decided that I would slog into the woods and end it in a pretty place if I had the stones. It had gotten cold fast though and I had a fever. Have you ever had a fever and been subjected to cold? You might not remember what it's like if it's been a while. It sucks. I needed a place to crash pretty quickly, and a beat up old silver airstream trailer about a mile into the woods looked damned inviting.

I got in the trailer easy enough. It was state of the art. In 1963. It had holes in the walls and roof that had been poorly patched, and there were indeterminate stains all over. It was heaven. The wind howled outside and I told it to screw off. I found some ratty old blankets near the bed in the back of the trailer that were undoubtedly knitted by Betsy Ross herself. I clutched the revolver tight to me as I shivered, and then realized what an idiot I would be if my shaking caused me to shoot myself in the nuts or something. I put the gun on the moldy mattress next to me to avoid a .38 caliber vasectomy. If I died tonight, it would be with my twig and berries un-perforated.

I bundled up and waited for the sickness to get worse before I pulled the trigger. It got way worse. Other than one particularly vile experience I had with some scallops and tequila in Boston's North End, this was the worst night of my life. I got sicker and sicker and finally, when I thought enough was enough I picked up the gun. I just couldn't be one of them. I couldn't.

Could I? How bad would it be? Would I just go away and be replaced with something else? What would happen to my soul? The part of me that was nobody else, where would it go? Then it hit me. What if it didn't go anywhere? What if every dead bastard out there held a normal person screaming to be let loose of a rotting fleshy prison, totally aware, but unable to stop this...this *thing* from committing the most heinous acts in history while it wears their skin.

Fuck that.

I put the gun my temple with a shaky, fever-ridden hand. The trigger was cold against my hot finger as I slowly squeezed. Then I released. I couldn't do it. Those stones I mentioned earlier were nowhere to be found. Packed their bags and took off for parts unknown with no forwarding address or cellphone number.

I couldn't kill myself because I didn't have the balls I almost shot off earlier. Ironic.

I checked my leg and shoulder and they were horrible looking. Black lines radiated from both of them, my veins had grabbed the infection and were spreading it around inside me quite effectively. I stunk like the fat ladies who had tried to ingest me too. It was awful, so I did the only thing I could think of. I went to sleep.

Have you ever totally ruined yourself with booze and drugs on a two day binge? By 3:15 AM on the second night, you're thinking you should quit, but your buddies are still raging so you keep going right alongside them. Eventually your body can't take anymore, and that little guy we spoke about before pulls the master switch and you shut down completely. Oh how you hate yourself when you finally wake up. You feel like somebody did something revolting in your mouth and *everything* hurts. Head, stomach, eyes, ass, everything.

I had none of that. I was fine.

It was very cold when I woke, and my shoulder and leg ached, but I wasn't sick. Immediately, I remembered the whole being trapped in the dead guy thing, and I felt for a pulse. I was alive. F those scientists and military douches. NOT everybody dies from being bitten. I was living proof, and I was bitten by *two* different infected, and their combined weight was that of five!

I didn't die. I didn't die. I must have said that out loud a hundred times while sitting up looking at my leg. The wound looked like when Billy Rickles (that little shit, I hope he got infected and did die) had bitten me in the first grade. It was a full on upper and lower teeth mark, but that was all. No black lines, no pus, no festering stink. Same for my shoulder, although there was a patch of skin missing there. I needed to fix that up or I could get an infection.

I broke out laughing when I thought that. Actual hysterics. That's when I realized I needed to pee. The trailer had a bathroom, and I opened the little sliding partition, finding the toilet. My stream could have cut steel. It was like I had been hoarding urine for three days. This is when I noticed something out of place in the old trailer. Brand new toilet paper. I furrowed the old brow at that one, but whatever. I was so happy at not being dead, or sort of dead, that I howled at the roof of the trailer while I shook off the big guy.

And something howled back.

It was a caterwauling scream, the hybrid shriek of a mountain lion and Death himself. The boys (my nuts) had returned briefly from their hiatus, because I felt them shrink up into my stomach. That scream sounded again, and if I could have pissed myself I would have.

Whatever it was started smashing against the trailer, hammering for all it was worth on the side. The whole damn vehicle shook. I zipped up quickly, thankfully missing the good stuff, and grabbed the wheel gun. I checked the cylinder, all six rounds were there.

Pointing the gun at the flimsy door to my aluminum deathtrap, I waited patiently. Actually, I was so scared my nuts had come back and then left again. Twice. But I waited nonetheless.

The screaming and pounding ceased, and after a few grunts, all became quiet. I then turned into the smoking hottie in the horror movies that you are always yelling at not to open that or go there. I slowly parted the threadbare curtains over the sink in the airstream.

The first thing that grabbed my attention was that it had snowed. Flurries were still falling, but there was at least three inches of the white stuff blanketing the world. The second thing I noticed was footprints in said precipitation. Or I should say boot prints.

Now being from Massachusetts, I have seen some fauna. Hawks, squirrels, sea gulls, weasels, deer. I even saw a fisher cat once. Mean S.O.B. too. Said animal did not have the intelligence to strap on a pair of Timberlands though, and I was fairly certain that even the animals up here in New Hampshire didn't parade around in shoes either.

Options on the species boot-wearing critter were limited.

I waited for at least an hour. It had stopped snowing, but the footprints were mostly covered. I peeked out the curtains one last time before I cautiously opened the door and peeked out of that as well. Nothing.

I took a furtive step outside, panning the .38 around. More nothing. I took two steps out the door and into the snow and realized that all this nothing was scaring the piss that I no longer had right out of me, so I spun around and made for the trailer door. I dunno who was doing all that yelling, but I no longer needed to find out.

I should have looked up.

On top of the airstream, with his ass on his heels in a crouch and staring right at me was the culprit. His head was cocked to the side, but only momentarily as he threw it back and screamed the scream of the damned. Then he launched himself off the trailer like a leopard pouncing on a gazelle. Gazelle = me for the slow people.

BLOOD ON THE SNOW

Now I know you've been wondering why I've brought up the Runners twice previously, but only in a sort of an aside. They have been surreptitiously absent from this gripping tale. That's because Runners are *different*. Some people use the word "zombie" for the dead folks that have taken over, but that term is incorrect. Look up your Haitian voodoo.

I'm going to call them zombies from here on out too, even though the term is crap.

Runners are as different from those walking pus bags (zombies) as you are from a can of spam. There are commonalities mind you, but they are most definitely not the same. I was talking about commonalities in the types of infected, not between you and spam. Although, come to think of it, I don't know you, so maybe you're as dumb as spam, and you're probably fashioned out of meat like spam. God is fickle.

Anyway, the point is that the thing hurtling at me velociraptor style, was most assuredly a Runner. It was my first Runner, so you should consider that a particularly terrifying moment for me. Previously, I mentioned I had deposited what most would reflect on as an extremely manly and hard-hitting piss. I did this while flexing my un-infected pecs and standing over a filthy toilet containing Heaven knows what. So this is twice I had no urine to spare, because damn, my bladder let go with a bunch of nothing.

As it leapt gracefully through the cold pre-December air, I couldn't help but notice that the thing looked like a mountain man. Scraggly beard, dirty clothes with a green military jacket, obviously fabricated the same year as the Airstream for a tour in Vietnam. It had scratches on its cheeks, above the whiskers. The eyes are what I remember most though.

People use descriptive terms like 'inhuman' to designate the infected, but you can't really understand what that means until you've seen a Runner, or, more to the point, until you see a Runner who sees you. When you look into their eyes, you can tell that they are no longer human. To me, being human isn't defined by anatomy, but by humanity.

That is to say, many emotions. When you look at a human being, you can generally tell how they are feeling even if they try to mask it.

There was no masking this thing's emotion. It only had one, and that was pure, unadulterated hatred, all of which was directed directly at yours truly. I'm not sure if it wanted to eat me, as would its dead cousins, but I am downright positive it had intentions on evisceration. If I let this thing have its way with me, it would be wearing my small intestine as a necklace forthwith.

All of these considerations were contemplated in the time it took for the thing to spring from the roof of the trailer and impact my left shoulder. It was slippery in the new fallen snow and we both went down scrambling, both of us fighting for my life. The .38 went off, and I swear to Christ the bullet took the zipper of my prison issue Wranglers with it. Yeah, after all I wrote before, now was the time I shoot off my dick. I didn't have time to check if my little pal and I were still friends, because the Runner rolled and looked at me while on its hands and knees. Its eyes narrowed and it tried to attack again, but its boots slipped in the snow and it fell on its belly.

Snarling in rage and frustration, (two more of my least favorite emotions), it fought for purchase in the snow and tried to scrabble on all fours toward me. That was all the impetus I needed, so I shot it in the face. The creature's head snapped back, and whatever was inside his noggin sprayed out on the slush behind it in a conical shape.

I flopped on to my back and looked at the sky, thinking how ridiculously lucky I was. Then I remembered my penis, or possible lack thereof, and had a wee (he he) bit of a panic attack. I checked and everything was where it should be, thank all that is holy, but I would need some new pants. And I don't mean because of the zipper.

Eventually I got cold and sat up. I gave myself a once over, just to make sure I hadn't been scratched. I was less scared of bites and scratches now, but why take the chance?

I seemed to be unscathed and was somewhat overjoyed. I used said joy to fuel a search of the dead hillbilly. He had dog tags. Maracek, John J., 016626262, O+, Lutheran.

I remember every single letter and number on that dog tag, but I have no idea what my cell mate's last name was. His first name was Benny. I lived with him for just over a year.

The only thing in Mr. Maracek's nylon bi-fold wallet was a grainy picture of a kid on a swing. The photo was torn in half, excluding whoever had been pushing the cute little blonde girl. The only other things on poor Johnny were a G-Shock watch, a dented Zippo lighter with some type of military sigil I didn't recognize, and a bite mark resembling the one on my leg on the meaty part of his hand.

I took Mr. Maracek's jacket because the temperature was starting to drop. New England weather. I also pilfered the watch and the lighter because those were items I could use. It was then I realized how thirsty I was. I had left my meager food and water stores in the trailer in the small pack that I had been given by the prison convoy. I reached down and grabbed a handful of snow, wolfing it down. It was delicious and so cold it hurt my teeth. I strapped the watch on and pocketed the lighter. Checking the watch, I could scarcely believe my eyes. The date told me it had been three days since I split up with the convoy. I had slept for three days, and if John J. Maracek had been skulking out here all that time, that meant I had been sleeping in this trailer while he skulked, probably pawing at the door here and there. The Airstream was probably his anyway.

To sound like a New Englander: Wicked wake-up call, kid.

The flurry flakes were getting larger and more frequent as I stared into the sky. The temperature would drop another twenty degrees by the time the sun went away, so I searched the perimeter, for what I don't know and I hid out in the trailer. I wanted to wait out the storm before I went trudging through the snow to God knows where.

It took two days. The snow fell for two damn days. It wasn't a blizzard or anything, but it put close to two more feet of the white stuff down. There was some split wood in the trailer with more logs outside, and a pot-bellied stove sat close to the mattress so I was able to keep warm thanks to the Zippo. A thorough search of the trailer revealed some photographs of that little blonde girl, so I was able to deduce that the Airstream had in fact belonged to John Maracek. Or he was squatting, not that it mattered.

My search also added a beat-up machete, a hunting knife with sharpening stone, a double-bladed Collins axe, and some sundries to my cache of survival crap.

When the snow stopped, I looked out the window. John's carcass, complete with ventilated melon and cranial spray, was covered with snow and I could no longer see it.

I also scanned for footsteps, of which there were none.

I had been wondering if the gunshot a couple of days before would have brought anybody knocking, but no one seemed to come. I was about a mile off of the highway, the entire forest was blanketed with snow, and I had food and supplies for a month and weapons.

I was safe.

On day four of my New Hampshire exile, I grabbed the axe and went out to split some of the cut fire wood. I still had plenty, but half of what had been inside before had been burned away. Getting to the stack I noticed something scary. Fresh trudge prints. I hadn't been to this side of the trailer in a while, so I knew they weren't mine. The prints came from the woods right up to the window of my new home, then they went back into the woods.

I packed my stuff and left.

The intentions of whomever or whatever had peeped on me were unclear, so it was time to go. I figured I would find a farmhouse, or something more defensible, and wait out the winter in solitude. Pack on my back, machete and knife strapped to my sides, gun in my pocket and axe on my shoulder, I looked exactly like Mr. Maracek. Especially since the trailer had yielded no razors and I was wearing the dead guy's jacket. I looked like a total badass.

What an idiot.

Three hours into my journey, I realized I had no idea where to go. Everything was covered in snow, so I couldn't even find the road. Badass? How about dumbass. Rather than turn around and follow my footprints back to the Airstream, I figured I was committed and should keep going. I certainly should have been committed. I was friggin crazy.

Six hours later the skies began to darken. Not only was it getting dark, but it looked like another storm was on the way. Terrific. I soldiered on, until I saw smoke. Now the whole point of me being in that trailer was that I wanted to be alone. If I'm alone, then nobody can kill me to take my stuff, or die in their sleep and eat me in mine. The smoke was a conundrum: do I risk all that I just listed and join up with the smokers, or go in the opposite direction and probably freeze to death?

Admittedly, I needed someone's help. I was cold and it was getting late, so I moved toward the smoke. It took about fifteen minutes to find the source and I walked into a clearing that stretched endlessly in both directions. I climbed an embankment, cautiously peering over to find out what the smoke was.

If I wasn't so cold and tired, and if the sky wasn't full of clouds, I would have been able to tell that the smoke was all wrong. It wasn't smoke from a campfire or fire place, it was the greasy black smoke of burning vehicles. A prison bus, as luck would have it, and a large Deuce and a half truck had collided, and there was no way it had been an accident. Bullet holes peppered both vehicles and bodies littered the ground. Some of the bodies had been torn to pieces and some were whole.

My old friends were there too and some new folks I was soon to be acquainted with. Almost every one of them staggering about, covered in blood and worse.

All of them but one. He was simply walking around, looking for something. One of the zombies (there I said it) staggered too close to him and he screamed and threw it to the ground, punching it with giant haymakers as it tried to stand. The other dead folks just looked at the scene for a second, continuing with their meanderings in short order.

For reasons still unbeknownst to me, the guy stood, whipped around and stared right at me. He hooked his hands into claws, threw his head back and screamed long and loud. He was wearing a police uniform.

Every single dead person looked at him when he screamed, then they all turned their collective gaze on me. As one, they came plodding toward me, but I didn't hang around for drinks and a cigarette, I ran like a little girl. I ran back toward the woods, all my stuff clanking against me. I was not the epitome of stealth and the snow was two feet deep at least. It was hard going and I got tired quickly.

I paused and leaned against a pine to catch my breath. I saw the cop bounding through the snow, chasing me like I had just snatched a purse. I knew I couldn't out run him, so I pulled the machete and waited, heaving.

The thing coming at me was grunting and growling from exertion and hatred, no trace of the cop who had not shot me when I had been bitten left in him. My back was to a copse of trees, and I raised the machete high in anticipation of his death charge. I heard a *twang*, felt something moving past my face, and suddenly the cop had an arrow sticking out of his chest. The Runner had a comical expression of surprise on his features, just before he collapsed, clutching at the thing stuck in him.

I turned around but all I could see were the trees. Until one of them moved.

Do you remember your seventh grade science teacher? He was probably a little bald guy with glasses who had trouble picking up textbooks with his pipe-cleaner arms. My teacher was the polar opposite of yours. Mr. Sheldon. Mr. Sheldon was six foot eight and four hundred pounds of solid muscle. This was the kind of man that would make professional wrestlers piss themselves at the thought of a bout with him. He had tree trunks for arms, and legs the size of…well…tree trunks.

So when I tell you that the man I was looking at was bigger than Mr. Sheldon, I want you to store that in your memory bank. Guy was a house. I have no doubt that he could have played football against the New York Giants and won. By himself.

He was holding a camouflage compound bow, which was dwarfed by his giant frame and massive hands, and he was looking at me. He cocked his head to the left to look past me and pointed behind me.

My former friends, the ones who had left me to die because I had been bitten, were coming through the snow a few hundred feet behind. I swallowed hard and turned to face the giant. With a simple nod of his head, he beckoned me to follow, and he moved into the woods with a grace that belied his size.

So I followed, the cries of the dead not far behind.

HERE THERE BE GIANTS

A tree house. The guy lived in an A-frame tree house with antennas and satellite dishes and solar panels on the side. I mean, who lives in a tree house? Squirrels and giant dudes I guess. We climbed a ladder with a hinge in the center, and he folded it up when we got through his trap door. The place was hardly Spartan, with real windows, running water and power but hand-made furniture. There was a forty-two-inch flat screen on a birch table and an assortment of DVDs. A laptop sat on a bench in a corner.

He indicated I should sit down in a rough-hewn stick chair. I did. I had to move two books that were on the chair; *Principles of Quantum Physics* and *String Theory, a First Look*. He took off his gear and sat down, letting out a sigh. He opened a small fridge and passed me a Bud Light. It was cold. He took one for himself, popped the top and took a swig. His swig was twelve ounces, and he tossed the empty into a trash can. Swish. He moved to a book case, searched for a moment and pulled out a notebook. Scribbling something quickly, he passed it to me. *My name is Ship, I don't speak. What is your name?* He took off his balaclava, and I picked the string theory book back up. His picture was on the back. Dr. Ship Parish. Good looking guy. Solid features, dark hair with little flecks of gray just starting to creep in over the ears.

I was stunned. Who the hell names their kid Ship? That's just downright cruel. Can you imagine what the other kids said to him in the third grade? On the flip side, what person in their right mind would pick on this guy? He was a cross between Stephen Hawking and the Hulk. Not that stupid, crappy gray Hulk either, the green one that kicked ass. Yes, I've read a comic or three, and believe it or not, convicts root for the good guy too, it's human nature.

I asked him if he was a genius, and he told me via notebook that was a relative term and smiled. The notebook also revealed that he was born with no vocal cords. I guess when they were cooking him, they missed one ingredient and made up for it with extra muscle and brains. The notebook continued to tell me things about him and we traded information for a few hours.

Ship was from California. Grew up near San Francisco, attended the California Institute of Technology, then traded one tech school for another and graduated from MIT with a double doctorate in physics and quantum physics. He also passed the Massachusetts engineering exam and was a board member of the National Science Foundation.

Holy shit.

He had given up his lifestyle to move into solitude because he couldn't stand society anymore. Made his living writing books and giving online written lectures.

This guy must have terrified all the uber-nerds in the United States. Can you imagine disagreeing with him on the fundamentals of particle acceleration? I mean one sideways glance and the geeks would crumble and assent to whatever Ship said. I mean wrote down in his notebook. I chuckled at the thought of Ship being king of the nerds and he looked at me quizzically.

I let him know what I was thinking and he smiled too. I began to talk and he began to listen. I was in the process of telling him about being bitten, when he became rigid and looked nowhere special. He stood stock still and put a finger to his lips. His massive frame moved past me and he extinguished the lantern we had been using. He parted the dark curtains, and looked outside, then motioned me to do the same.

In the pre-evening gloom, I could make out shapes moving in the woods not too far away from the tree house. Directly below us was something I would never forget. Standing in the snow, not the least bit bothered by the cold, was a man in a bloody cop uniform with an arrow protruding from his chest. He stared up at me staring down at him. His mouth was impossibly wide open and he let out that mournful moan that was like a dinner bell for his buddies. They came as quickly as their dead legs would carry them.

Ship and I both kind of backed away from the window. We looked at each other and he shrugged and beckoned me to follow him. We sat near his laptop and he powered it up. It was plugged into the wall. I asked him how he had power and he told me that the solar panels were functional, and he had two windmills for additional power an eighth of a mile into the woods in a clearing. Fifty-six yacht batteries stored the power for use and the whole house and two small sheds were rigged for off-grid power. Genius.

He jotted something down on his notebook and passed it to me. *Plenty of food and drink. If they go away we're good, if not we will go take them out in the morning. Power is out across the country, but some nuke plants and solar/wind arrays are still functioning.* Ship pointed to the screen, which held a map of the U.S. with different colored dots all over it. *Red or blank means no power. Yellow means fluctuations, green is powered up.*

Most of the country was blank. Just a black screen. Scattered lights of the three colors dotted the map. Surprisingly, one in southeastern Massachusetts was a bright green. I pointed to it, "Pilgrim?"

He nodded his enormous nut, (nut also means cranium, get your head out of the gutter); it was the Pilgrim Nuclear Power Plant in Plymouth, Mass. Still supplying juice to some I guessed. I knew that quite a bit of those facilities were automated, but somebody must be alive down there to pull switches and push buttons.

My brow furrowed and I asked him how it was possible that he could get on the internet.

As long as the servers and nodes have power, the clients will work fine, certain sites will start to drop off soon as their batteries deplete. Other critical sites have indefinite power and will remain online, but as the nodes fail we won't be able to access them.

"Nodes?"

He rolled his eyes and shook his head at the same time. He grabbed the notebook and passed it back almost immediately. One word glared at me from the lined paper:

Noob.

That was mean.

Ship checked several other sites, including a Pentagon site that was still functional and being monitored. They were none too happy about the intrusion and they let him know it. I was actually watching somebody hack a government website. I was in the presence of another criminal. Suddenly his computer just shut off. He tried to turn it back on but it wouldn't. *SOBs bombed me.* Was all he wrote.

We conversed for a while until the sun went down. Ship didn't want to turn on any lights, so he showed me to the most uncomfortable couch in the world and gave me a sleeping bag and a pillow. He pointed to his crotch and then to a door that was apparently a bathroom. I nodded in understanding and we went to bed.

What's the most unpleasant sound in the world? Fingernails on a chalk board? Your mom yelling at you? Baby crying? Nope. How about the sound of your cell door closing for the first time? Now that's bad. Terrifying. Even the cell door can't compare to the sounds of the undead though. The noise they make is...wrong. It's just wrong. You can sit there as you read this and moan, and try to make it as spooky and weird as you want, but it won't be the same. There's no way you can be alive right now and not have heard them, so you get it. Their cries can't be imitated. They're just *off* somehow.

It's maddening. I could hear Ship's light snores in the other room, but those damn wails were about fifteen feet below me and they seemed to come from everywhere at once. I didn't want to plug my ears in case one of them somehow got up here with us, but in the end I got so tired I jammed a .38 round in each ear. It worked. I fell asleep.

I woke up to the unmistakable sound of a pump shotgun being charged. Another terrifying sound. My eyes flew open and I stared cross-eyed down the unbelievably huge barrel of said shotgun. I had to pee and my morning missile shriveled away instantly.

Not taking his hand off the gun, an infuriated Ship pointed to my leg, which was hanging off the birch wood couch. The bite mark was glaring. It was still red and purple, but it looked much better than it had even yesterday before I took the bandage off for good.

"I'm immune."

Ship shook his massive cranium in the negative and I told him I had been bitten over a week ago. I had been with him for more than twelve hours and I wasn't sick. "Nobody bitten could last that long without being sick," I pleaded as I raised my hands, "so you know I'm not going to turn."

He seemed to ponder this for a moment as his gaze focused elsewhere, then he lowered the shotgun and sat next to me. He scribbled something in his book and passed it to me.

Explain.

I told him everything as quietly as I could because I could hear shuffling in the snow below us, although the moans had ceased. I showed him the wound on my leg and the other one just below my collar bone. That one did show signs of infection, but not by the plague. Ship took notice and he cleaned it out for me. To my everlasting shame, I screeched like a baby when he put that stingy shit on me, and then the moans started again. *Baby*, he mouthed.

That was mean too.

He put away the antiseptic and threw another log on the fire. I bandaged my shoulder boo boo and he began writing in his book. Actually, he wrote so long I thought he might be writing another book. When he finished, he passed the pages to me and I began to read. Lots of question marks at the right side of the pages.

Weapons fire from outside interrupted my reading.

THE CRIMSON COLLARS

There were a lot of *Woo-hoo's* and *Yee-ha's* accompanying the gunshots. Some of the fire was automatic too. It was over in about a minute, and then Ship and I heard voices.

"Now this here's a fine idea. We'd be off the ground and…"

"Jed! Clem's been bit!"

Wonderful. Yee ha? Jed? Clem? I looked at Ship and he was already looking at me. My large friend's laconic nature was emphasized by one mouthed word: *Rednecks.*

I was equally as terse this time: *Shit.*

"How many times I gotta tell you boy, don't interrupt me when I'm talkin'!"

"But Clem's been bit!"

A single shot echoed through the trees, followed by sporadic laughter, "And now he won't bite nobody else. Didn't like him none anyway, smelled like possum."

Possum? Smelled like possum? No doubt in my mind anymore. I had held out brief hope, what with the fall of humanity and all, that these good old boys would be friendly. That hope evaporated with the mention of possum, and the quick decision to end someone because they smelled like said critter. These assholes were going to shoot us.

I peeked down and saw their weapons. Military stuff. M-somethings, all black and wicked looking.

Jed called up to us and asked us if *we was in here*. I looked at Ship and he nodded no, while he fished for something. He brought out a little green thing rolled up in a black wire, which he began unspooling. He was almost done before the first bullet tore through the bottom of his house. We ducked and I hit the table, jarring it and knocking my beerymid to the floor. (A beerymid is when you take some beer cans and stack them in pyramid fashion.) The scowl from Ship was worse than when my dad caught me smoking at age thirteen. I just shrugged.

"You boys comin' out?"

Ship had already passed his notebook to me. It read: *Them or us,* and Ship held up the little green clicker thing. The wire snaked into the wall near the floor by the computer. He flicked a little silver toggle and a single tear dropped from his left eye.

Ten or fifteen bullets ripped through the floor and walls of the A frame, fired from an automatic. I could smell the cordite and I was inside. I looked at Ship, thinking that we were in it deep, but he was on his back. There was blood on his head and he wasn't moving. They had gotten my new buddy. I told him I was sorry and grabbed the green thing with the wire.

Oh yeah, and the place was on fire. The bullets must have hit something flammable, because flames were licking up the far wall and had spilled across the floor.

Then I yelled down to the bad guys: "Hey Jed! Why don't you eat a big bag of dicks you sheep-shagging redneck!" I clicked the handle together expecting something monumental. Nothing happened.

I heard Jed outside, "Did that sumbitch just call me a homo-sex-shal?"

I clicked the thing again and nothing happened a second time, so I double clicked it in a panic, and something outside went boom. It shook the A frame, and it was loud. I was inside and my ears were ringing. Screams of pain and terror were carried to me on the air, each one a nail in my soul, and I dared a peek outside. I probably shouldn't have. Those that were still alive wouldn't be for long, and pieces of them were scattered about on the reddening snow. One was trying to keep his insides inside with his one arm, and another was making a feeble attempt to crawl away with half a leg, leaving bits of himself behind in a red trail as he moved through the white world. He didn't get far and the screaming turned to whimpering in about a minute.

I had now killed living men, dead women, and a Runner, however you classify him. Infected? I was thinking that I had been in prison for a year, but I had never killed anything other than bugs and a particularly unlucky chipmunk in my life until the past week, when I heard movement behind me.

Ship was sitting up. He was more than half my height sitting down he was so huge. Dealing with a gigantic zombie in a small room which, incidentally, was aflame, was going to be tricky. Not to mention his hundred pound leg was directly across the trapdoor. The big guy was starting to stand, so I darted for the shotgun leaning against the table. I was fast and I grabbed it, jacking a round into the chamber. What I actually did was jack the only shell that was in the weapon out onto the floor, where it rolled away and under the torture device Ship had called a couch. Shockingly, the weapon wouldn't fire. Ninja like, I flipped the shotty around, brandishing it by the barrel, and with a war cry that would have put Conan to shame, I swung my bludgeon at his noodle in an arc designed to take it off at the neck.

The creature's left hand shot out like a striking mamba and halted my wayward attempt at decapitation mid swing. It then grabbed me by the neck with its free hand and lifted me off the floor. My vision started to blur, and I have no doubts my face went from peach to cherry to plum with little pause between. Dead bastard was going to eat me standing up.

Then he put me down gently and shook his head in disbelief. He passed me back the shotgun and put a hand to his head, drawing it back in a moment. He looked at his hand and swooned, sitting on the couch with a creak. Apparently, my Ship had not sunk.

I stood there in shock until he opened the bullet-ridden fridge and grabbed a beer. It also had been murdered, so he tossed it, grabbed a survivor and put it to his head. I was still in shock when he whipped around and saw the fire behind him. He stood quickly blinking hard, obviously woozy. Grabbing a fire extinguisher, he pulled the pin, pointed it at the fire, and pulled the trigger. Momentary confusion set in for both of us as nothing happened, then he held up the extinguisher, and noticed that it too had been killed in the redneck attack.

The whole A frame shook when he hit the floor. The slaughter of his house, his fridge, his fire extinguisher, and most importantly his beers must have been too much for him, and he had passed right the hell out. I opened the trap door and tried to move him to it. Nope. I'm a strong guy, six four, two forty, little bit of flab, but I worked out in the joint. I couldn't budge him. I slapped him twice. His eyes fluttered, but only for a moment.

I ran through his burning home to the kitchen and grabbed a pitcher, filling it with water. I dumped it on his head and that woke him up. We climbed down the ladder, almost falling because I forgot to release the bottom half, and he sat in the snow about fifty feet away against a pine tree. I was struck by an epiphany and raced back up the ladder. The place was really burning now and I reached for the shotgun, but it was too hot to pick up. My revolver was nowhere in sight, the last time I remember having it was when I was on the couch, which was now merrily ablaze. I was able to find the two items I originally went back for though, and as an afterthought, I dumped the fridge over and grabbed the last four beers with no holes in them.

I scurried back down the ladder and made my way to my buddy, whom I had known less than twenty four hours. He was on his back, and his head was bleeding profusely, a small red puddle in the snow next to him. I popped the tab on one of Ship's beers and drank the whole thing down. Sloshing behind me made me turn around quickly.

The rednecks were coming, although considerably less alive. There had been eight of them, two of them down for good, two beginning to stir, and four headed our way. All I had was my lighter and three beers for defense, and Ship was down for the count. I did the only thing I could think of, I ran right at them. I pushed down the only one standing and searched the snow. A hand wrapped around my ankle and I screamed an extremely unmanly scream. I found what I was looking for and picked up the cold metal. It looked like one of the guns from the movie Platoon, so I guessed it was an M16. First to go was ankle biter, who was dragging both me to his mouth and his mouth to me at the same time. I aimed and fired at his head, turning it to goo, but also having the gun buck and shake as I spit out about fifteen rounds. The shots went everywhere when I spun the weapon out of control.

I used more control when I took out the others who were coming for me. One headed for Ship, but he was the one with no legs, and I was out of ammo. I picked up another of the same type of gun, but this one had a cool scope on it instead of that handle thing on the top. I peered through the scope and a little red dot was in the middle. I put the red dot on Quarterlegs' head and ended his misery before he could snack on Ship.

The big guy's pulse was strong when I checked, so I gathered all the weapons and ammo from the twice dead hillbillies and stacked them near us, then built a fire. It was easy, as the A frame was now fully ablaze and I was able to get some burning stuff and drag it to where we were. I had also been able to slide Ship's massive frame across the snow, although it was difficult, and we were now outside his locked shed. This was no ordinary shed or lock either. The shed was steel and the lock was a combination lock built into the door.

I washed out Ship's wound with snow. So happens it was just a graze, but he's huge, and it was a scalp wound so it bled a lot. He woke briefly and was able to stand. He input the code into the door and fell through. I pulled his legs in, turned on the light and shut the door. There were a bunch of guns and backpacks and survival stuff in this particular shed. It also held another stove with some small pieces of wood and stacks of white bags of anthracite, which I thought could only be coal on a pallet in the corner. It sure burned well.

He came to again some hours later, after I had bandaged his noggin with some stuff I found in the shed. I got him on a cot, and passing him the two items I went back into a burning tree house for, I asked him what went boom. He used the items to write one word: *Claymores*, and he promptly passed out again, pen in hand.

Oh, and the chipmunk? Poor guy had had the misfortune of running out underneath my bicycle tires when I was about eight. I cried for a week.

RETREAT

I kept an eye on my new friend for some time. I also tied his foot to the cot with a length of heavy duty orange extension cord just in case. His bandage soaked through in an hour or so and he stirred when I changed it. I took a look around the shed, which was about a hundred degrees in a half hour after I got the coal burning. I had used a piece of Ship's house to help get it started.

The shed had everything a budding survivalist would need: workbench, computer station, rack of rifles, gas masks, canned and packaged food and drink, and a bookshelf of "How To" books. The weapons from the dead rednecks were arrayed on the workbench for us to fight over when my pal woke up. Three M16s, two black shotguns, and a black rifle with a huge scope. There were also nine pistols of different types and a bunch of knives and machetes. I didn't want to take the dead guys' clothing as it was covered in gore, but I did search through their crap, finding lots of ammunition, watches, walkie-talkie looking radios, and other sundries. I had appropriated a small black automatic pistol with two clips (I would later learn from Ship that they are called magazines, and the pistol was a Glock 23) and a chrome .357 magnum with two speed loaders. The Glock was in a shoulder holster and the .357 was on my right hip. *Now* I was a badass. I just needed to learn to hit something with my freakin' bullets.

I also got a chance to read what Ship had written in his notebook when he found out about my immunity. There were many questions. The easy questions were things like when/where was I bitten and did I get sick. The difficult questions were longer, but they all asked me if I had taken any combination of odd drugs, a lot of antibiotics, or if I had taken part in any medical studies. Ship had no idea that two weeks ago, I was in a six-by-eight concrete box with bars for a door.

The big guy woke up while I was cooking rice and beans on the stove and reading *Sign Language Made Simple,* a book I had borrowed from his shelf. He sat up and looked quizzically at the cord around his ankle and then at me. I just shrugged, and he smiled and nodded. I made the sign for head and he made a sign back. I searched the book for what he had done with his hand, but I couldn't find it, and I told him so. He leaned over to remove my clever orange restraint, then thought better of it and sat up straight. I brought him the notebook and pen, and he shockingly wrote just one word: *Hurts.*

I told him it wasn't bad, just a graze, and he wrote that it felt like somebody hit him with a sledge hammer.

So I did what anyone would do in that situation. I called him a baby, and untied the cord.

He asked me about the tree house, and I told him that it had kept us warm for a while, and in fact some of it was burning merrily in the stove right now, but I hadn't been outside since the redneck zombie slaughter. He stood, and once again I marveled at his gigantic frame. He moved to the work bench and flipped on the computer monitor. I was amazed there was still power, but his solar panels and mini wind farm must still have been doing the trick. When the monitor came to life, it was divided into quarters, each portion showing a different area outside the shed. Captain Survival had struck again, with little surveillance monitors strategically hidden throughout his small plot of land. This guy had been *prepared.*

One of the monitors showed the smoldering ruin of his house, and he nodded in acceptance. He took the loss way better than I had, and I had only been there overnight. Immediately, he pulled out a black military-looking backpack and began shoving choice items in it. The pack was huge, and I was thankful that he would be the one humping it should we have to leave. When he finished packing it, he passed it to me with one hand. I accepted it with one hand and it crashed to the floor. It had to weigh eighty pounds. He pointed to a shelf and I placed this pack next to another pack that had already been prepared.

Ship took stock of the weapons and gear I had procured from the bad guys, and he turned at me and winked, holding up one of the walkie talkies. He switched it on, something I had not even thought to do, and we were subjected to redneck radio. The news was on, and it wasn't good.

"…elve hours. Repeat, Jed still ain't checked in, and it's goin' on twelve hours." A woman's voice.

"Him and his crew o' idjits is prolly chow by now, but I'll take my guys and run a sweep of the area up north o' Wilson's Farm." This guy had his mouth full of something while he was talking. It was kind of gross, and difficult to decipher, but the woman who had originally spoken seemed to have no trouble with it.

"Roger that. I'll let Hugh know, but I can tell you he's gonna want you to check in every fifteen minutes now that Jed ain't been heard from."

The guy with the other guys didn't like that too much. He didn't want to keep talking into the radio because it gave away their position, and he didn't know who else might be listening. The woman said she didn't make the rules and the guy had some choice words for her.

I had been staring down at the work bench listening, and when I looked up Ship was holding the notebook toward me. *We leave in twenty minutes.*

I was going to ask him if he was, in fact, nuts, because of his head wound, the heavy packs, the cold, and the zombies, but he beat me to the punch. He flipped the page, and I continued reading.

We're directly north of Wilson's farm. They'll see the smoke and come right here, where they'll find their dead friends. It won't take long for them to see the shed, then they'll kill us. I don't have the tools to take them all.

Shit.

He grabbed two of the radios with earbuds and we each tested one. I spoke to him and he gave a thumbs up. He used the squelch button, which, previous to that moment I could never figure out what that was for, and I heard him fine.

We gathered some more gear and it was time to go. I kept the weapons I had taken as spoils of war, and asked Ship if he would pass me one of the M16s from the bench before we left. He held up four fingers, and I told him there were only three M16s. He shook his head no, and wrote a single letter and number in the notebook: *M4.* Then he pointed to my gun. I got it and asked him what the difference between an M4 and an M16 was. *12* was all he wrote, and I swear I never got that until right now.

He left the door unlocked, but he also left some nasty surprises for the hillbillies. The explosive kind. I asked him what if a kid found his way in here before the rednecks, and Ship wrote that blowing up was better than being eaten or subjected to whatever the bad guys would do. I had to agree.

We exited the shed and moved to another. I helped him clear some snow from in front of the other shed's door and inside was a two-seater snowmobile. Later, Ship would tell me that he had a horse, but it had been at the vet when the plague cropped up. He had been on his way back from the vet's when he stumbled upon me and my dead pals chasing me. I guess the horse had been a meal for a bunch of those things, including the undead vet.

After we had maneuvered the snowmobile out of the shed, Ship set another trap. He started the machine and I almost shit myself it was so loud. We both mounted it, and without a backward glance, we split that scene.

We travelled west for a long time. I don't know how long but it had gotten dark, my face was frozen, and we were *flying* across the snow when I saw something weird in front of me. The snow was lit up in spots for just a moment at a time. I squinted, but kept seeing it. Realizing that the spots were moving with us, I couldn't comprehend what it could be. It made no sense until I looked back over my shoulder. Three lights were screaming through the frigid darkness behind us. Snowmobiles most likely and they were about a half a mile back.

I leaned forward and yelled to Ship that we had grown a triplet of tails, and he stiffened. You know, his body, I was hugging him. In the most manly and extremely hetero way possible, I was *holding on* to him as we zipped over the frozen ground.

The big guy altered our course and he headed north. The lights behind must have been following us (shocker) because they did the same and bore down on us.

Let's say, for the sake of argument, that you've just killed a bunch of inbred bumpkins that were intent on stealing your stuff and then murdering you to death during a zombie apocalypse in a frozen setting. Let that sink in. Now imagine the buddies of said bumpkins are aware of the purge and you see lights behind you in the dark as you flee. What would you think? I'll tell you. You would think that the bad guys were on their way to finish the job their friends had started. Nevertheless, you still hold on to a ridiculous pipe dream that the lights behind you belong to a gaggle of bikini clad supermodel nymphomaniacs carrying beer and Buffalo wings in the saddlebags of their snowmobiles.

Well that's just fucking dumb.

Damned if I wasn't thinking about beer and wings when the first bullet hit me. It actually hit the metal stock of the rifle that was slung across my back. I wasn't sure it was gunfire, as we were travelling at high speed away from the shots and I couldn't hear shit over the engine we were straddled over, but it hurt, and I didn't think it was a bee sting. It came to me quickly what was happening, when I heard auto weapons fire. Of the fifty or so bullets that these dickweeds had fired at us, one had actually struck us, but they didn't know that.

We flew (we actually flew) over an embankment, and suddenly we were on a snow-covered road. The only reason I knew this was a road was because I saw a frost-blasted SPEED LIMT 35 sign. Screaming down the road, someone stumbled into our way, and Ship skirted around him. He was quite dead, and followed us with arms outstretched in that classic zombie pose. I saw a house go by on the left, and then another, and then a bunch of them on both sides, with parked and abandoned vehicles in the street, and I realized we were in a small town.

The noise from the flying engine we were on was exceptionally loud in the relative quiet of the dead place. It didn't take long for dead people to show up looking for a late dinner, and soon they started coming out of the woodwork. Zipping down the frozen streets of this shit stain little burg was one of the most terrifying things I had ever taken part in, as the dead people seemed to materialize out of the darkness in ever increasing numbers, reaching for us with infected claws. One of the things actually managed to latch on to the right handlebar, and we jerked violently to the right. Ship grabbed the thing's hand and lifted it away from us as if it were a child's appendage. I swear I saw a couple of its frozen fingers break off. He just let it go and it fell behind us, but the damage was done.

We sideswiped a Toyota Camry, which was ridiculous in its own right. I mean what self- respecting hillbilly would own a non-truck, let alone a *foreign* non-truck? Regardless, our right tread was damaged in the collision and started to make that noise. You know that noise, the one that every vehicle you've ever owned makes at some point. The one that screams *This isn't right*, and you get all nervous about a five-hundred-dollar mechanic bill for a water pump or brake rotors.

Our trusty steed was faltering. We made it another eighth of a mile before the tread broke off and almost took Ship's leg with it. We spun chaotically out of control and wound nose first into the brick façade of a barbershop. Now, I'm no insurance adjustor, but I could tell you that this extremely expensive snow toy was all kinds of totaled, and there was no protection check inbound. Remember a couple of paragraphs ago when I told you that I was scared when riding through the streets? Yeah, well that was paltry compared to when I heard that first throaty, gargling moan from someplace very close.

We grabbed our stuff and Ship used his size twenties to persuade the barber shop door open. The shop was blissfully devoid of all things alive or dead except us, which was good because the damn pack (an ALICE pack for you enthusiasts) weighed in at ten million pounds and I was already tired after six feet. Ship wrenched the barber's table off the wall and braced it against the door just as the first slap of a dead hand smacked against it. I looked at the shop front and the zombies that were showing up looked right back at me through an entire wall of plate glass.

This simply would not do, and I turned to tell the big guy, but he was already moving toward the back of the shop. The front window imploded and I jumped a little. The zombies hadn't even started pounding yet and I was confused, until the mirrors on the far wall exploded and I heard gunfire.

Damned if I didn't hear *woo hoos* and *yee hahs* again.

I hightailed it through the shop following Ship, who threw the lock on the back door, and we stepped out into a long, skinny alley.

OK, so I've told you about how scared I've been a couple of times already, with the cannibal heifers, and the Superfly runner, and evil rednecks, and zombies and more zombies, and moaning and crashing snowmobiles into walls, and most importantly, being bitten. Well, when we opened that back door and I stepped out into that alley, and we saw how many dead people were there milling about, I was even more scared. They all turned like a flock of birds, and every single dead eye in the bunch focused on me. I don't even know if they saw Ship, even though he's almost seven feet tall and four bills. I'm telling you, every one of those predators saw me as the sick gazelle, and every one of them wanted to eat me. They leaned left and right to look around my colossal friend. When the closest one turned and took a step, and it crunched in the frost, *that sound* is what scared me the most. Not holy crap I just got a two thousand dollar tax bill scared; not my God, where's my kid in the department store scared; this was pants-shitting, total panic, fuck all, my agonizing death is most ricky-tick imminent terrified.

Now multiply that sound times one hundred as the fifty dead bastards in that back alley streamed toward us en-mass.

DOMESTIC TROUBLES

I heard the tell-tale crunching of shoes on glass in the dark barbershop behind us, but as there was no place else to go, I ran back inside with Ship hot on my heels. He slammed the door extra hard, so it was extra loud. I couldn't see any dead yet, as they hadn't made it to the small corridor from the main room to the back room. I raised my rifle to deal with the first of the mini-horde that would be approaching from the shop, but I heard a door open behind me and the strong fingers of death on my shoulder.

It was Ship, he had found another door with a set of stairs going up. He dragged me through the door and I shut it quickly. It was a flimsy interior door that a cat could scratch through given the time. A cheap knock off of a Home Depot fifty dollar special. Some draped Charmin would have slowed our antagonists better, and I could have used some right then anyway if you catch my meaning. Pounding had already begun on the back door, and it was only a matter of time before every pus sack in the area found our little sanctuary.

I thundered up the stairs after Ship, who hadn't made a sound, to another door, this one open and beckoned us into its shadowy maw. Ship stopped dead...poor choice of words...at the top landing, and let me tell you, in a three-foot-wide stairwell, there was no getting past this man. An octagonal window let moonlight in to illuminate my friend's enormous frame. He cocked his head almost imperceptibly, then pulled his machete. I thought my machete was all tough and mean looking, but his looked like the wing from a Boeing as he cleaved the air in front of him. Turns out it wasn't air, but a dead woman looking for an evening nibble. She dropped like a hot rock, her head split in two down to her trachea, and Ship yanked his weapon out of her noggin.

What seemed like a steel cage melee was going on below us; I can only imagine that the inside horde had missed our side door as I initially had and opened the back door to confront the pounding of the outsiders. I had a brief moment of levity when I considered that the two groups could pound on either side of the door for eternity with only bloody stumps remaining before they realized they were hunting spoiled game.

Ship stepped farther inside the room, which turned out to be a kitchen, and I came in after him. He shut the door, and to my relief, it was somewhat sturdier than the one below, but still not made of three inch Chobham with offensive lasers on the outside. I stood watch on yet two more doors that led out of the kitchen, while Ship pushed the fridge up against the door. It was on wheels, so he tipped it over in its side and gently lowered it to the ground. As an afterthought, he opened it, reaching in and grabbing two cool bottles of water. I remember thinking it was absolutely freezing in that kitchen above a barbershop, so why wasn't the water, which was in the fridge, cold too? We put our packs on the floor.

Movement in the shadows from the left side door made me ready and I dropped my water. I nudged Ship with my boot and he nodded and pointed to the other door. He shone the light on his gun into the darkness, and I once again thought how stupid I was for not remembering I had one too. I fumbled with my light for a second before it popped on, and I had one second to pan it into the doorway before the horror that was in there crawled out.

It was a kid. A little boy that had never done anything but watch SpongeBob while eating Captain Crunch on a Saturday morning. People had loved this boy, and he had loved too, but this virus or whatever the fuck was happening had turned this precious child into a *thing*. I sobbed as I saw this mockery of life drag itself toward me, scrabbling with one arm, the other missing. He was wearing bloody Spiderman pajamas that used to be blue. Fat, salty tears fell to the floor as this pathetic creature mewled and scratched. I wiped my eyes and moved forward to end his misery with the butt of my rifle.

When it was done, I sat down on the bed and cried. The moonlight shone through the curtainless window and glinted off a series of photos hanging on the wall. One had fallen off and smashed on the floor, probably during whatever struggle had ensued when whoever had been infected up here turned. I picked it up and shook out the glass slivers. Holding up the picture to the moonlight only made me sadder. The boy had been so God damned cute in life. Blonde hair and blue eyes, sitting on his little red bicycle, his good-looking mom on the left and his strapping dad on the right. His mom looked like any loving mom and wife prior to all this. She was looking at her son with nothing less than adoration in the picture. The kid's dad was… His dad…

His dad!

I whipped my head up when I heard the slapping of feet running down the wooden slats of the hall. This was not the stumble of a zombie, and Ship, big as he was, never made a damn sound when he moved. I dropped the photo and raised my rifle at the same time. The tactical light illuminated yet another revulsion, as what used to be Dad tore into the room. This former father threw his hands up in front of his face when the tac light hit him in the eyes, momentarily blinding him. I would like to say that I used that moment to pull off some crafty tactic, or Houdini my ass out of there, but honestly I was just trying to keep my shit on the interior so I wouldn't need to change my drawers on the run. The dad-thing recovered exceptionally quickly and he threw himself at me, hissing.

I yanked the trigger on my M4 and not a damn thing happened. I was still pulling the trigger when Dad tackled me and we both toppled off the bed, me on my ass and him on top of me. He threw his head back to scream that scream that they scream before he turned me into fillets, and I did the stupidest thing in the history of mankind. I reached up with both hands and grabbed his head. I drew it to me using all the strength I had, and I sunk my teeth into his neck. I ripped out a chunk of meat that would have made a great white shark proud, gagged, and spit it back at him. Dad's left hand was on the wound, as if it could stem the flow of his life's blood, and I looked into his eyes and saw the only other emotion other than hatred that these things can display. Surprise. He looked right back at me, and if he could have spoken, doubtless he would have said: *Are you fucking shitting me?*

The sentiment turned from surprise to rage in the time it would take a fat kid to snatch a doughnut. He was going to kill me before he bled out. Well fuck him. No. I punched that infected prick right in his Adam's apple. Bastard wasn't gonna yell and alert his buddies either. Now both of his hands were fastened on his own neck, and he was making a sound like *Gah!* but it was weak and quiet like he was choking. He tried to stand, but I was having none of that, and I grabbed his filthy flannel shirt and rolled on top of him. I pulled my knife and drove it through his left eye and his struggles ceased immediately, his hands dropping to his sides.

His son's body was right next to us.

Ship appeared out of nowhere, looked at the bodies, and dragged me to my feet. I was spitting blood and my sweatshirt was covered in gore. He shone his light on me and searched for a bite mark, but I was still pissed and I pushed him away. Well, I pushed him and fell on my ass because it was like trying to push a continental plate. He helped me up and held his flashlight to his face. *Where did he bite you?* he mouthed slowly.

"He didn't. I fucking bit him," I said, spitting for emphasis. "Now let's get out of here before the hundred zombies that are in this building figure out where we are."

For the second time in thirty seconds, I got the *are you shitting me* look. It was just as frustrating from the uninfected.

We moved to the kitchen from the bedroom and into the little boy's bedroom. The kid had an Iron Man poster on the wall and one of those Wal-Mart plastic container thingies full of Legos on the floor. I just remember the Iron Man and Legos is all, they stuck. We both searched for another way out, but there was no other exit. The first thud hit the door to the kitchen at about that time and it sent tendrils of ice down my back, and my nuts shriveled even further up.

We were on the second floor, but it was still a good fifteen foot drop if we decided on it. I would most likely just turn an ankle, but if Ship hit the ground from that height, there would undoubtedly be a geological event. We searched the living room and even the pantry. I had an idea of an attic trapdoor, but like the beer-toting hotties, that was another birthday candle wish that wasn't happening.

The door was taking a serious beating and the frame was starting to crack when I looked in the kitchen. The fridge had moved away from the door an inch or two as well. We frantically looked for anything to help us, but there wasn't even anything larger than an end table to hide behind, and all the interior doors were reminiscent of the door that led upstairs. Under the bed or in a closet would end with us as bowel movements if these things took dumps, so that was out too.

I was searching the kid's room for a lightsaber or time displacement equipment when I had an epiphany and threw open his window. Attached to the side of the building was a fire ladder, bolted to the brick with big ass masonry bolts. Our secret was most assuredly out, so I yelled to Ship to get his ass in here, it was time to flee.

He made it into the room with both packs, as I climbed out on the ladder and the kitchen door gave way. I heard the refrigerator slide across the shitty linoleum and figured the jig was up. Ship tossed the packs out the window and they landed hard in the snow.

Now picture a four hundred pound guy trying to squeeze through a window and grab a ladder. Keep in mind this guy was recently shot in the dome, so he's not all there anyway. The dead were coming, and poor old Shipster got his giant ass as stuck as a roach in a motel. They check in, but they don't check the F out. He looked at me, and I honestly thought I saw fear for a moment. It was the first and only time I would ever see that on his face, although he would tell me later that he was scared shitless on many occasions.

Yes, you figured it out, our gallant and valiant hero ain't gonna buy it right here.

Ship put his hands on the bottom of the top window and pushed. The thing snapped into glass-laden kindling and the big guy was free. Lacerated but free. Blood rained down on me from his wounds, and I saw him kicking his right leg as one of the zombies, a dentist or doctor by the look of him, had latched on. Of course as Ship kicked, the damn ladder became unstable because as I may have mentioned on one or two occasions, the man is big.

The zombie was unceremoniously dragged through the window, and a wad of pant leg must not have been enough to support it because it fell the aforementioned fifteen feet to the frozen ground. Its pals were already climbing through the gaping hole in zombie family's house, and they too fell like lemmings.

In true superhero fashion, I clenched my sphincter, and unclenched my hands from the rungs and slid that last eight feet or so down the ladder while holding on to the frame. Ship copied my unfathomable awesomeness and did the same, his thud infinitely more resounding than my own, landing like the guy in the poster on the zombie kid's wall.

Of course now we were on the ground with a couple hundred dead cannibals on the way, some even raining from above. Oh, and well-armed rednecks, don't forget the rednecks.

And I know what you're thinking. I know it, and you know I know it. The answer to your unasked question, the one you've been holding on to, is yes, dude tasted exactly like chicken.

RUN!

Have you ever been shot at? It's not fun. Wondering if that next sound is the bullet that will hit you is a terrible thing. I understand that the shot gets there before the sound does depending on the range, but still, it's the noise that scares you the most. That *Pap! Pap!* sound and then brick shatters next to you, or a window blows out, or a zombie jerks a little and shit flies out of it. The anticipation of the pain, not knowing how much it will hurt. If the round will hit you in the knee, or the throat, or God forbid, in the testicles. If you're a lady and you're reading this, you can't understand what that means. Hell, not having been shot there, I can't fully get it, and I've got nuts. Big ones.

Regardless, there were zombies to the left of us, rednecks to the right, and there I was, stuck in the middle again. A thud behind me reminded me that it was also raining dead people. I tried to fire my rifle again, but nothing happened. I was in such a panic and so pissed off that I couldn't figure out what was wrong and I yelled to Ship to tell him so.

He took one five-foot step and turned my gun on its side. He flipped a switch and pointed at the gaggle of zombies off to the left, the look of reproach and disgust on his face was worse than those of my seventh grade soccer pals when I scored a goal against my own team. *That* sucked, let me tell you.

I pulled the trigger and a round fired. I had had the safety engaged. Hey, I told you, I wasn't the gun-toting type of criminal.

Ship was busy firing at the yokels who had ducked behind some abandoned vehicles and the dead folks on the right. I had chosen the forehead of a dead man in overalls with no shirt on as my first target. I gently pulled the trigger and was rewarded with my first long-distance rifle kill. It was about a hundred feet away, and it was yet another fat woman from New Hampshire. I totally missed the guy I was aiming for.

Hey, it was dark, people were shooting at us, zombies trying to eat us, and I was a rifle virgin. I squeezed off a few more shots, and to my delight dropped two more creatures, including Mr. Overalls. By this time, the clodhoppers had their own problems, as a moderate-sized horde was flanking them from the right.

Ship decapitated one of the dead folks that had come from zombie kid's room with a backhand swing, and it was time to go. The big man grabbed both packs, and handing me one, we escaped through the thinned herd that Ship had blasted. They were grab-assing as we moved through them, but the only one that actually succeeded in grabbing me was a teenage girl, and my buddy cut her hand off with his machete before she could take advantage. None of them got close to Ship. Guy was a monster, but also damn fleet of foot.

We made it to a boarded up house, a failed last stand so it would seem, and we moved in quickly. I heard screams from outside, and I could only guess that one of the bad guys hadn't been fast enough and had gotten caught. Good. F him.

I thought we would hole up in the house for a bit, but Ship plowed right through and we went out the back slider. A six-foot stockade fence surrounded the large back yard, and Ship barely slowed down as he crashed through it. He made a sharp left, and we moved quickly through the back yards of several houses and into a church parking lot. I was having trouble keeping up with him, and he noticed and stopped briefly. Heaving, I whispered my desire to know what the plan was, and he motioned me to follow. He ran up the back steps of the church, and down the street we heard the snowmobiles fire up again. The hicks were getting the Duck out of Fodge. Apparently, they had either written us off as dead or escaped, or they were getting swarmed.

Ship looked under a planter and came out with a key, which he used to open the back door. We hurried through, and he closed and locked it. He put his hand on my shoulder, and when I tried to move he stopped me. It was pitch black, so I couldn't see what he was trying to tell me if he was trying to communicate at all. I just stood still, trying to catch my breath. I could hear him trying to listen. I swear I could hear him trying to focus over my intake of breath. He took a step and grabbed my hand. It scared the shit out of me, but I figured out quickly enough that he wanted me to follow him. Ship pulled me forward, and as I said, I couldn't see diddly.

We moved into the room a little farther and he deemed it OK to switch on his tac light, letting go of my hand when it came on. There was a short set of wooden steps up to huge ornate door, and the moment Ship put his gigantic foot on the first stair, it let out a creak that told everyone in North America where we were.

The door flew open, and we were looking down the four barrels of two exceptionally large double-barreled shotguns behind which was a room bathed in light.

"Ship!" One of the shotty wielders whisper-yelled, "Damn son, what the hell are you doing out here?"

"For Christ's sake, Ernie, let him in and close the damn door!"

Both weapons were lowered and we moved up the steps. Ernie closed the door behind us, the other man clasping Ship's enormous paw. "We just heard a ruckus outside, big fella, was that you?"

Ship nodded and pulled me forward. "What's your name, son? Mine's Dick."

Dick? Has anyone been called Dick since the fifties?

I told them my name, shook both their hands, and we all sat down in front of a small fireplace in an antechamber of the church.

They looked at all the blood on me, and the bandage on Ship's head, and gave each other a sideways glance. I told them that even though the big man's noggin looked busted, and I was absolutely drenched in gore, neither of us was infected and that seemed to placate them. We then traded stories, me leaving out being bitten, and of course biting.

Ernie and Dick had been working on the grounds when the shit hit, volunteers and whatnot. People were being bitten, with zombies and Runners everywhere. The two had some shotguns in Ernie's truck, as they were going to do a little illegal deer hunting after they had winterized the church. The reverend had called them inside to tend to a young woman with a bite on her neck. The men helped as best they could, and with no family in the area for either of them, they decided to hold up in the church and began to reinforce the front doors. When finished, they returned to the pews, where they had left the reverend and the girl, only to find that the girl had eaten the reverend while he was probably giving the last rites. Trying to reason with either of the infected proved fruitless, so they put them down with the shotguns.

They had been here ever since. Plenty of food and water were in the pantry, and the only exterior doors into the chapel were the gigantic front doors, and two fire doors that had been secured. The antechamber door was the only other exterior door and it was locked and extremely solid. All the windows into the church were stained glass with iron frames and inserts and above chest level on the outside. They even had a sniper/look-out spot in the bell tower.

They'd had zero contact with the outside world though and hadn't seen anyone, other than the odd truckload of hillbillies, but that was getting rare.

"You boys is the first livin' souls we've seen in about a week. When's the army gonna get here and clean up all these crazy folks?"

Ship and I looked at each other and then back at Ernie. "Oh shit. How bad is it out there?" he demanded.

"Bad. I don't think there's a lot left. No cops or social services of any kind. I haven't heard of any Army guys anywhere since I left Boston, and they were pulling out."

"Pullin' outta what?"

"They were leaving Boston because they were getting their asses kicked. Calling it a day. Quitting. The zombies were killing everyone and making more zombies. And it wasn't just Boston. Every major city, and most of the smaller ones, had outbreaks."

Ernie looked at Dick, then back at me. "So there ain't no Army no more?"

"I don't know. Like I said, it's bad."

They both just nodded and seemed resigned to the fate of the country. At this point, none of us knew the extent of this plague. We didn't know that the entire planet was screwed.

"Well, at least we're safe in here," Dick sighed.

Ship and I once again glanced in each other's direction. "Uh, I don't think you're safe in here Dick."

He raised his eyebrows. "Didja see them doors, son?" He pointed to where the large front doors would be in the chapel proper. "Or the one we let you through? Them doors is damn strong, *and* we done reinforced 'em. They'll hold out a hunnert o' them sick folks."

Ship began writing in his book, but I beat him to the punch. "What about a thousand? What about ten thousand? Would those doors hold back ten thousand people trying to get in? OK, forget them getting in, what about you getting out? Let's say they don't even try to get in here, which is unlikely by the way. What happens in a month, when you're chewing on your last piece of spam and drinking your own piss? You won't make it twenty feet before they get you. Then there's the rednecks, who might just kill you 'cause it's fun."

"This is New Hampshire boy, we's all rednecks."

"Sorry, *evil* rednecks."

"Son, I'm tellin' you—"

"No Dick, I'm sorry, but I'm telling you. You can't stay here. Not in a town full of—"

"Sickies?" interrupted Ernie.

"They're not *sick*, guys. They're *dead*."

It was their turn for sideways glances. Ernie folded his hands, put his elbows on his knees and looked at me. "Now I know we just met and all, but are you touched, boy?"

Dick did the opposite of Ernie and leaned back in his chair, folding his arms. He shook his head. "Dead folks don't get up and walk around."

I stood. "They do now. I've seen them crawling around with half of them missing. No insides. No heart or lungs. You getting the picture? There's no way they could be alive. Well, not all of them. The ones that run, they're alive, but the moment you shoot one, it dies and gets back up. Oh, and they all want to eat us for some reason."

"Explains the bites I guess, but I ain't buyin' they's dead." Ernie looked at my large companion. "What do you say, Ship?"

He spun his book around so they could read it:

Ship folded his arms, finished.

"This is too much voodoo fer me," said Dick, "so what do we do?"

"We leave," I said. "We pack some shit and literally head for the hills."

"Boy, I'm sixty eight years old. Ernie is a might older." Ernie brandished a middle finger. "We can't be runnin' around at all, let alone in winter. And we's already in the hills."

"So you're going to stay here?"

"Yup. You boys is welcome to stay too."

Ship looked sad when he passed me the book: *Dick is right. They won't make it out there, and they'll slow us down.*

Well, he was right about that. We'd probably be a lunch buffet if we tried to assist these guys outside the church. At least here they would have food and water and relative safety for a while. Every point I made as to why they shouldn't stay reverberated through my skull for a second, but the bottom line was that these poor guys were better off staying here.

Ship and I left the following night. We said our goodbyes, and the boys tried to give us some food to take but we told them to keep it.

Ship left the key to the back door with Ernie, and the moment the door clicked closed, I was reminded of my first night in prison, except this time my sentence was in Hell.

Fifteen seconds after we left the church, we were passing by a chain link fence, and one of the pus bags saw us. It rattled the fence and caterwauled for all it was worth, alerting every damn thing in the vicinity to our location.

And they came.

So we ran.

The friggin ALICE pack weighed a ton, but I kept up with the big guy as best as I could. We evaded instead of engaged, and we got all the way to the end of the street before it all went to shit.

I felt a tug in my shoulder and heard a loud noise close by, and then I spun around and fell. The pain guy turned the volume way the hell up, and my vision went all green for a moment. A roaring in my ears commenced, and I was barely able to hear Ship's rifle as he fired in full auto off to the left. He smoked two pus bags that got close, then helped me to my feet. The roaring was getting louder and I must have been a little off because Ship slapped me. I blinked and told him my shoulder hurt. He nodded and held up his hand; it was covered in blood.

Somebody shot me.

The big guy practically dragged me off to cover, but the zombies, all of them I think, were on the way. We couldn't stay where we were, so we moved off toward the woods, cutting through backyards. I made it another two hundred yards or so and then the dizziness set in hard. The world was moving away from me down green tunnel, and all of a sudden everything felt totally fine.

KAT GOT YOUR TONGUE

I remember snippets. Slung over Ship's shoulder like a very light sack of potatoes. The dead reaching for us as he ran with me draped over said shoulder. Pain going for the Mike Tyson knock-out on *my* shoulder. I was in and out, but the thing I most remember thinking was that we were leaving a blood trail on the snow that even a blind zombie in a wheelchair could follow. Also, that blood was coming from me.

When I woke up, I was on a cot in the darkness, and I was freezing. I knew it was cold outside, but there was a fire in a stove next to me. It didn't compute. I was shirtless, my wound bandaged and my arm in a crude but effective tape-sling. I tried to sit up, but my pain receptors gave me an exceptionally impolite F-U, and I had to lie back down. I was immediately nauseated and thought I was going to barf, but pain punched out the nausea and showed his title belt to the crowd. I was very thirsty as well.

I glanced through the darkness as my eyes adjusted and I noticed I was alone. Terrified, I called quietly to Ship. My voice sounded like it was crashing through broken glass, and I swallowed and tried again. No dice. There was a canteen and an oblong object on the table next to me. I was able to move my damaged shoulder enough to take a drink and turn on the flashlight that my buddy had left. A note stuck in the canteen chain said: *Back soon. Lost a lot of blood. Stay near the fire.*

It was time to man up, so I sat up. It was tough, but I did it. I drank half of the canteen and stood, panning the beam from the light around. My weapons were near, on a bench. I seemed to be in some type of metal structure. A shed or hangar, as the sides sloped down from the roof in a half circle. Draping the blanket around me, I was able to get my gun belt on, and checked my weapons to make sure they were loaded. The pistol was loaded, but the rifle mag was empty. Two loaded spares were on the dresser.

I explored my little world and found out that I was at an airport. There were airplane parts and manuals all over and some old flight plans that I looked at. Even some tires sat in a corner. On a desk was a phone, and I just had to know, so I picked it up. Like most people, it was dead. There wasn't much else to do, so I waited, probing my boo-boo for pain spots. There were plenty.

I think the closest I came to death that night was when the door to the small hanger flew open and a hybrid sasquatch-Santa Claus ducked its head and stepped over the threshold. The humongous Saint Nick plopped his blue toy sack, which was actually a sleeping bag, on the floor with great care. The door closed, and Ship stepped forward, giving the prone form a nudge with his boot. It struggled weakly out of its tubular prison as Ship folded his massive arms. When its head popped out, it looked up and I was shocked to see a teenage girl staring at me with wide and terrified eyes.

I was still smiling at Ship, and realized what I must have looked like to the girl. I probably looked hungry, with a bloody bandage and no shirt on. I immediately stood, and that was a terrible idea because I got woozy, and the kid probably thought I was drunk too. Sitting back down, I offered her my canteen. She just looked at me with those scared eyes.

I took a drink. "We won't hurt you."

Ship stood there with his arms folded, giving me the stinkeye. "What?" I demanded. The look continued.

"Relax partner, I didn't go line dancing, I just checked the perimeter. You got shot in the damn head if I remember, and you were driving a snowmobile with my ever-so-sexy ass on the back the same night, so shut it." I lowered my glance toward the kid. "Where did you find her?"

He pointed at her, made a gun figure with his thumb and index finger, and then pointed at me.

"No shit?" He nodded his giant melon. "She shot me?" I looked at her. "You shot me?"

She started to cry. What a dick I was. Kid had probably lost her whole family, they might have even tried to eat her. She had been holed up who knows where in that crappy hick town, hungry, terrified, with redneck rapists and dead cannibals everywhere. Yup, a giant, heartless dick.

I was horrified. "No, no it's OK, we aren't going to hurt you, I swear. He brought you here because you were dead if you stayed in town. Eventually it would have gotten bad for you."

She looked at me with those teary doe eyes, and for one second I thought she was going to bolt for sure. It wouldn't have done her any good, because short of an Olympic sprinter, or unless she had an Abrams tank handy, she wasn't getting by Ship.

"Look, did he scare you?" I pointed at you know who. "I know he's big and scary, but he's super cool, I swear to God. I'm cool too, right buddy?" I looked at him and he stuck his hand out palm down and wiggled it. *Mezza mezza.* I flipped him off and it hurt like hell. "He can't talk, he was born that way."

She looked at him and sniffled, then looked back at me. I stood and took a step toward her. She stiffened visibly and I held the blanket out to her. "Take this and sit by the fire, you look freezing. I'm going to get dressed." She took the blanket but didn't move.

I most assuredly had special needs when it came to putting on a shirt. The hole in my shoulder screamed at me to knock it off, but the kid was scared and I had had enough of the pain. Ship tossed me something that rattled, and it hit me in the forehead and fell on the cot. It was a pill bottle, but there was no label.

"Pain pills?"

Ship shook his head in the negative.

"Antibiotics?"

More stinkeye from the Shipster. Try as I might, I couldn't open the damn bottle either. I couldn't move my arm correctly and it was very weak. The only people that can open those child-proof bottles are children anyway, and as it would happen, we had one. She tentatively held her hand out and I passed the bottle to her with my good arm.

She opened it in three seconds, passing the bottle back and then the cap, "I'm sorry I shot you," she said staring at the floor. "I thought you were with those other…people. They killed my dad."

"We are *not* with those assholes. They've been trying to kill us too," I shook my head in disgust. "You would think what with the end of the world, and humanity on the brink, we would be better to each other."

A small gasp, and a tiny voice: "End of the world? You mean it's not just here?"

Stinkeye, complete with follow-up eye roll. Guy could make me feel terrible on a whim. How was I supposed to know she didn't know the extent of whatever was happening. Hell, I didn't know either at that time, I was just making assumptions.

"No kiddo, it looks like it's all over. I came from Boston, and it was all kinds of awful there…what's your name?"

"Katrina. But everybody calls me Kat."

I sat down and rubbed my shoulder; it ached. "Well Kat, here's the plan…actually, I have no idea what we're going to do, but I'm sure Ship does."

She perked up. "There's a ship? Is it safe?"

"No, no," I said, pointing at my large friend. "He's Ship."

She looked confused, but perked up immediately when the first fist smacked against the side of the hanger. It was followed by many more. If

I thought she had been scared before, she showed all new prowess in the scared-look area when the moans began. We had a crowd outside, and with the wind howling it was impossible to tell how many.

I pulled my pistol, as there was no way I was going to be able to use my rifle. As an afterthought, I passed the rifle to Kat. She grabbed it, but I didn't let go straightaway. "I'll be wanting that back when this is over."

She nodded, wide-eyed, and I let go, "If you would kindly not shoot me again, I would be grateful."

I turned to look at the big guy, and he gave me the worst look yet. He really didn't like the fact that I gave this girl a weapon. "What? She needs a gun if she's going to help." I shifted my gaze to the terrified girl. "You do want to live, right?"

She nodded quickly.

"Then shoot any that get past us."

Ship shook his head no, then pointed at himself, then to the door. He pointed at me and then to the cot.

"Nope. Not letting you do it by yourself." I jacked the slide on my Glock, and spears of agony lanced through my shoulder and into my neck. I tried my best not to show it, but it was tough. Ship scribbled something in his book and passed it to me. I used the flashlight to read it: *You're a liability out there. Watch her.*

He was right, and I knew he was right. The worst part of it was he knew I knew it. He stood there waiting, like a smug Sasquatch that had just won a bet. I walked past the girl and whispered in his ear, "The rifle I gave her isn't loaded." He nodded, slung his rifle and pulled his machete. He shushed us. He actually shushed us with his finger in front of his lips, then strode to the door and ran into the storm. I holstered my pistol, slamming the flimsy door.

There were windows, more like skylights, in the top sides of the metal structure, and I stood on a desk and peeked outside. I couldn't see anything, not even the falling snow.

The pounding and moaning continued, echoing back and forth through that metal tomb. One of them had found the door and had begun to whack at it. Kat racked the bolt on the M4 and then looked at me funny. "I'm from New Hampshire. I know when the gun is empty." The little square window in the door gave way, and a lacerated arm clad in flannel poked through.

My machete was brandished in my good hand and I pointed to a full magazine on the desk. She dropped the old mag, grabbed the fresh one, popped it in, and charged a round. I walked to the door and waited with the machete. Ship didn't want any unnecessary shots fired, as they would draw more dead to our little sanctuary. The reaching arm was pissing me off, so I hacked at it a couple times and it fell to the floor. The thing that the arm belonged to stuck its face in the window and growled. I was horrified and overcome with sadness at the same time. The dead thing was Ernie. I spun, thinking that this was no time to be sad, and saw the kid with the rifle. The weapon was pointed at me, center mass.

I lifted my machete bearing appendage toward the sky. The other arm was tied to me with the sling. The gun looked damn big when I was on this side of it.

"I could shoot you now. Just let me go," she said between Ernie's growls.

"Kid, you can leave at any time, but you're better off with us, and I'll make you shoot me before I let you leave me without my gun. Again. I mean shoot me again, you already shot me once."

She brought the rifle to her shoulder and looked down the sight. I lowered my machete, putting one hand on my hip. I could hear Ernie and a couple of his new buddies scratching at the door. One of them had grabbed the window frame and was either pushing or pulling, I couldn't tell.

"They're in here with us in thirty seconds, if you're going to shoot me, get on with it." I turned around, waiting for the shot that would kill me, or further incapacitate me so that the dead could kill me. When it didn't come, I hacked at whatever was sticking through the window. Digits and pieces of arm fell on both sides of the weakening door. I heard steps behind me, and all of a sudden she was there with a spade shovel. She used it well, pushing one of them back from the door, using the tool like a spear.

I knew they were going to get in, so I used a poking motion and went for the eyes of the one closest to the door, apparently Ernie had been shoved aside. I got one eye before one of them grabbed the machete with both hands. A normal human would have let go when the brush-clearer bit into their palms, but this thing didn't care, and it had two arms to my one. I had to let go of the machete, or I would have been dragged through the window.

Kat stabbed the one-eyed critter in the other eye, the orb going with a squish, and we had ourselves our first blind zombie. I drew the Glock and took a step back. "Can you shoot?"

She looked at me dumbfounded. "New *Hamp*shire!"

"Then back up and get the rifle, this door is done."

She dropped the shovel and ran for the rifle. Ernie was back, his face a mess, and he was reaching for me with his remaining arm. I don't think he was inviting me to tea. The door was almost down, and I cocked the hammer on the Glock and pointed at his nose, but suddenly there was something sticking out of it. It was a machete blade, and it was withdrawn as quickly as I had seen it. Ernie collapsed, lifeless. Well, more lifeless, and another dead guy went down with a split cranium. The crowd at the door turned around to see what was going on, and they were cut down one by one.

The door fell to the ground and Ship stood there, covered in gore. He was surprised to see Kat pointing an assault rifle at him, but remembered it was unloaded, and the surprise was replaced with a mild disgust directed at me.

Ship's surprise was reignited when Kat raised the rifle and fired.

A zombie woman fell to the floor next to Ship, half her head missing. Ship looked at the kid, who shrugged. "I reloaded."

ESCAPE

Ship and Kat fixed the door while I got some noodles cooking on the stove. I was still freezing, and Ship told me via notebook that I was cold because I had lost so much blood. Kat apologized again when she heard that she had almost killed me. I was already feeling better, and the big guy told me I had been out for over a day. I had thought it was the same night that we escaped from the town that the zombies had found us at the hanger, but it had been the following night. Ship also told me that I would stop feeling cold in a couple of hours.

Ship's jacket was covered in zombie goo, so it had to go. We couldn't risk him or Kat getting infected because of a jacket. Unfortunately, there was nothing else big enough for him to wear. The big guy and the girl sat down to some noodles, and when they were done, Kat asked for a knife. I gave her one of the knives I took from the dead rednecks, and she started cutting up the sleeping bag Ship used to transport her. She found some wire, and soon enough my giant buddy had a functional poncho. He smiled at her and she smiled back.

We got some shut-eye, Ship taking the only watch, and had crappy coffee and some kind of chicken MRE for breakfast. Kat announced that she had to pee, and we were shit out of bathrooms, no pun intended. I still wasn't up to doing much, so Ship took the kid outside, both of them armed to the teeth, while I checked our packs and started making a list of what we had and what we would need.

We were OK with food for a while, and there was plenty of snow to melt for water. Ammo was good too, with a total of six hundred sixty rounds for the Glocks, twenty six rounds for my .357, and two hundred and eight rounds for the rifles. Ship had been carrying most of the ammo, and it was damn heavy. I distributed some into my tactical vest ammo pouches, but Ship would still have to carry more than I would. I would carry the MREs and other sundries, but I wasn't ready to travel yet, and just performing these mundane tasks exhausted me. Every now and then the pain regulator dude would let me know he was still in control and amped up my substance p. Pity there's no more Google, or you could look up what substance p is. Guess you're shit out of luck.

I hit my rack pretty quick, keeping my weapons near. When the makeshift door opened and Ship and Kat strolled in, the bright outside light hit me hard in the face. They had been gone longer than it takes to take a piss, so I asked what was up. This was when the Sasquatch clued me in to his little strategy.

Apparently we were flying out of here, and Kat wanted to come. She had decided that if we meant her harm, we had had plenty of time to do said harm and hadn't. We were the lesser of three evils, zombies and rednecks being the primary two. Ship had a plane, which is why we had come through Psycho Town, and were now holed up in a hangar. His plane was in another hangar across the tarmac. Problem was, there was a foot of snow on the runway, and the plows weren't running. Solution was that Ship had found an airport plow, and it was gassed and ready. It was already at the end of the airfield.

So the plan was to pack our shit into the plane, which was fully fueled, tow it through the snow with the plow to the end of the northern runway, run the plow down the runway a couple of times, and take the F off. All the while we needed no zombies to come looking at what the plow noise was, or rednecks to shoot holes in our plane when we were airborne. Great plan.

We were all dead if we stayed here. Even though the area was less populated than a big city, there were too many people, and everybody wanted to kill us. If we went north, there would be less people, but the infrastructure would be as collapsed as it was here, so we weren't sure if we could land the plane in the snow that would undoubtedly cover any runway we would use. It would truly suck if we survived zombies and evil hillbillies to die in a plane crash because somebody left a toolbox on a runway. On the other hand, if we were to pursue a southern course, there would be plenty of places to go, but all of them had the potential to be infested with dead folks.

Ship told me that the aircraft had a one thousand mile range. I found that hard to believe, at which point he told me it was a Beechcraft J50 Twin Bonanza. I had no idea what that meant other than it probably had two engines. The look of smug superiority on his face when he told me that the plane was already full of ammo and rations was priceless. He also told me he had two more aircraft at other fields in a twenty mile radius, all equipped with limited weapons, ammo, and food. This one had been the closest and it was in a private hanger.

The reason we were holed up in this hangar was that it had the stove. Ship helped me off of the cot and we looked at a chart of the area. There were several small towns, lots of lakes and mountains, and dozens of small roads. The interstate zipped north to south off to our east, and I could see just about where my prison pals had left me to die, not that I blame them. The irony. They were all dead, or undead, and I wasn't.

In the end, we decided to go south. We made good arguments for north, but there was just no way to safely land the plane, assuming we could even find the runways under a carpet of white. Ship knew of a runway in a town in Tennessee. Tenne-fucking-ssee. It was right at the outside of our operational fuel range, and as far as I was concerned, it was hillbilly heaven. Can you come from Tennessee and not be a redneck? *Exceptionally rural* was what Ship wrote in his book. The good side was that the entire populace; every single person, had multiple weapons, and were trained in how best to use them since they were sperm. This might mean less of the dead folks. It could also mean that those folks were worse than the fuckers that lived in this area, no offense to Ship or Kat. At that point, all we had was hope.

We loaded our stuff into the plane, which was quite spacious, even if it had been built right alongside that Airstream trailer I almost died in. The plane was manufactured in nineteen sixty one. Not ninety one, *sixty one*. You read it correctly the first time. The aircraft was more than fifty years old. I hope I look as good when I'm fifty though. It looked brand new. Shiny.

I was still scared shitless to ride in it though. Kat and I watched as Ship, clad in his sleeping bag poncho, trudged through the snow toward the plow. He got in, and as instructed, we closed the hangar door.

The sound of a diesel vehicle engine starting up when everybody else is dead, and there's no other sound at all, is indescribable. I mean, it was so quiet we could hear the snow falling. I shit you not. Whatever a bejesus is, it was scared right the hell out of me, because I knew what was coming next. Zombies, lots of them.

The length of the runway was about a mile, and Ship plowed it like a pro. He had to make four passes. Before he was done, there was a white coating back on the tarmac from the falling snow, but it was well under an inch. All of our stuff was on the plane, and the big guy backed the truck up to the hanger and we hooked the plane to the rear sander with a length of chain. Kat and I got in the plane and waited. Ship had to be careful pulling the aircraft so as not to damage the front strut, which is where the chain was attached.

When we were taxied up to the northern end of the runway, Ship got out of the truck, removed the chain, pointed down the end of the runway, and got back in the truck and started her up. The dead folks had arrived in force and were coming from every direction. They were already on the far south end of the runway, finding it easier to trek through the plowed areas. As it turns out, although intended for snow, plows are also adept at removing the living dead from runways.

Ship took care of all the dead people from the southern end of the runway, and the ones near the plane. There were more coming, but from angles that wouldn't affect us if we got going soon. The big guy parked the plow off to the side of the plane, but was doing something inside the vehicle that we couldn't see. A guy in jeans and a red t-shirt was high-stepping through the unplowed snow from around one of the hangars. He was moving at top speed toward the plow. Even from a couple hundred feet away, I could tell he was infected. Something about the way they carry themselves and the way they move just isn't...human.

It was then that I found out planes don't have horns, or if they did I had no effing idea where it was in the copiousness of dials and switches. I wanted to beep a warning, but I couldn't. I struggled with the door to the plane, and Kat demanded to know what the hell I was doing. I informed her that our pilot was about to get jumped by a Runner, at which point she demanded to know what a Runner is. I pointed to the infected guy and told her they looked like him. I got the door open and stood on the stairs with my .357. There was no way I could hit the target from here. I started yelling, and popped off a round at the truck, which missed wildly and threw my shoulder into total rebellion.

Ship got the message when he heard the gunfire and got out of the truck wary with rifle raised. He couldn't see the infected from his vantage, and I began gesturing wildly with the magnum in the direction of his impending doom. Standing on the snow-dusted tarmac now, I took aim again and heard the gun fire before I pulled the trigger. It had been from above and behind me. The guy in the red T-shirt spun and fell to the ground. I looked back up at the plane, and sure enough, Kat was scanning the area with my M4. She had put down the bad guy with one round.

Ship made it to the plane and we all got back in. He made it to the cockpit and took the left side chair, strapping himself in and indicating I should do the same. Kat was behind us in another chair, holding on to my M4 like it was a new born baby. Ship looked like an elephant on a stool sitting there checking things and flipping switches. The plane started, and so did I when a thump came from outside followed by another. The dead had reached us.

The plane lurched forward a couple of times, then got into a rhythm, and moved down the tarmac gradually picking up speed. I didn't want to think of what would happen if we hit one of the zombies while screwing down the runway at a hundred miles per hour. As luck would have it we didn't, and I felt the wheels leave the ground in just a few moments, leaving those pus sacks behind. I felt euphoric at being away from a zombie plague, at least for a while. We could finally relax.

Of course had we known what we were flying into, we would have headed north instead of south, but hey, hindsight is twenty-twenty.

16

I'm not crazy about flying. I thought it was a control thing, you know, you're not in control of the plane so somebody else has your life in their hands? That's bullshit. Ship taught me the ins and outs of flying that thing in ten minutes. Now, I'm not saying I could fly by myself, but I had the basics about what does what and why, and I got used to making small corrections quickly.

I was still scared. Something about being up so high and looking down on the world was unnerving. Especially when the world had totally gone to Hell. We were only about five hundred feet up, but I could see that entire towns were on fire or just gone. There were traffic jams as far as I could see on the big roads, all the vehicles abandoned. Several bridges blown up and streets destroyed. A downed airliner, which seemed to have caused a raging fire, chasing infected out of the woods, all of them reaching up to grab us as we sped off overhead.

Town after town moved by underneath us, and the only thing they had in common was infected. They were everywhere, and it got worse as we got farther south. Eventually, we passed over a small city. Ship pointed to a chart and it was Albany New York. It was pure Hell. We saw carnage and destruction all over, and the infected were still hunting. They were spread out over the city, moving in crowds. The plane was going fast, but I could see living people. They were on a roof, and at first I thought they were infected because they all reached for us, but the way they moved told me they were human.

They were doomed. The building they were in was surrounded by the dead, and smoke was billowing out of one side. I was really scared, but not for them. We were travelling over the city, and if anything happened to the plane, there was no way we were getting out alive even if Ship landed it like a pro. I heard sobbing from the passenger compartment, and turned to see Kat very upset.

She looked at me with wide, sad eyes. "It's everywhere. All those people…"

I moved back and sat next to her, and she wiped her tears away, beginning to get mad. "They killed my mom and dad. They killed everyone I know. I'll take as many down as I can before they get me."

I took her hand in mine. "I believe you."

I sat with her for an hour or so in silence before Ship gave a hard whack to the cockpit bulkhead. I looked up and he motioned me in. Big guy had to pee. He pointed to the controls and I understood. He wanted me to fly the damn plane. Me. Terrific. He passed me his notebook and I didn't know whether to be proud or insulted. *Don't touch anything unless you have to.*

He moved his giant ass past me into the cabin and toward the back. The plane didn't have a bathroom, and I remember thinking he might just open a door and piss out into the sky. When he came strolling back, I pointed off to the right side. A river was on fire. It was weird.

My shoulder hurt. I started thinking that I would probably never eat another slice of pizza, even though the pizza in the joint was atrocious. Then I got to thinking about Legos, and Iron Man posters, and I almost started to cry. I wondered how many kids were eaten by the very people who were supposed to protect them. Or vice versa. Could you shoot your kid if you had to?

It was mid-afternoon when the plane began to descend. I had moved into the passenger area and fallen asleep after taking some antibiotics with water. I woke with a start as the sound of the aircraft changed. Kat was nowhere to be found, and I suffered a moment of panic and shouted up front. She stuck her head around the bulkhead and smiled at me. She gave me a thumbs up and told me we were landing. She looked cute with the airplane headphones on. I looked out the window and was wondering how we were going to land in the middle of a forest, when I heard the radio come to life. Ship had set it to blare out over the intercom, as he can't speak back.

"Unidentified aircraft, this is Arlo tower..."

Then the radio went dead. The voice had sounded panicked.

We flew over a single dead woman standing on the white 6 designating runway 16. She immediately started after us. The tarmac was one mile long, and she was on the extreme far end of it. I was guessing the dead stumble at about three miles per hour. Using my phenomenal mathematical skills, I deduced she would reach us in twenty minutes. This didn't account for the rest of the country, most of whom were dead, and all of whom looked at us like the coyote looked at the road runner.

We landed with a squeak of tires and a jerk of the plane and taxied to the end of the runway. We grabbed our stuff, Ship sticking a ton more MRE's and ammo from the plane into our ALICE packs and pouches.

Kat was carrying some kind of rifle with a wooden stock and a scope and had a little black pistol in a holster on her hip now. I had my M4 and other weapons. Ship was Ship, and probably had a nuclear device on him someplace.

The Sasquatch opened the door and the sun hit us in the face. I raised my hand to cover my eyes from the sun, but I used the wrong hand and pain lanced through me. When I was done bitching, we took the four steps down the fold out stairs and were heels down on the tarmac. It was warmer in Tennessee, but it wouldn't have been comfortable very long without a jacket. Maybe high forties. The dead broad had halved the distance and I didn't want to waste ammo, so I tugged on Ship's sleeping bag poncho and pointed. He grabbed my hand like a big-foot-ninja and I thought he was going to break my arm.

He let go immediately and mouthed a sorry. My wrist hurt like hell too, and I couldn't even rub it properly. The big bully wrote one word in his book and showed it to me: *Listen*. I didn't hear shit. I mean it too. Other than the sound of the birds, there was nothing. Then Kat said she heard something too, and I finally heard what sounded like an engine.

It ended up being three engines. One a Jeep full of (wait for it) rednecks, all armed and all in flannel. Picture a blue Jeep with rifles sticking out every which way, cigarette smoke pouring out the top and sides, and lots and lots of beards and baseball caps and you're right on the money. The others were military Humvees, and these were full of soldiers and the Hummers had the biggest guns I had ever seen on the roof. They got out of their vehicles and the army guys approached us while the hillbillies checked the perimeter. One of the army guys moved past us and went into the plane. All of them stared briefly at Mr. Enormous because he was, like, enormous.

An army guy with a gray buzz cut stepped forward and introduced himself as Captain Simmons. We told him our names and that Ship didn't speak. The man asked us where we were from and if any of us were bitten. He looked right at me. We replied that we were from New England and no, the bandages were from a gunshot wound. He frowned. "Why were you being shot at?"

I nodded toward Kat, "Ask her."

Simmons and his soldiers looked at Kat, who looked terrified. Yup, I was a dick again. Cut me some slack, a month ago I was in prison.

"It was an accident," I said, rubbing my wrist where Ship had grabbed it against my shirt. "She thought we were evil rednecks."

He looked back at her. "And are they?"

Kat looked right in the captain's eyes, and to her credit, showed no more fear. "No, sir. They saved me."

A shot sounded, and the dead woman was face down on the runway. Simmons told us that we would have to come with him and get checked out by a doctor if we wanted to stay.

Kat perked up. "Stay where?"

"At the compound," replied the captain. "Isn't that why you landed here?"

"Don't know what you're talking about, Captain, we landed here because we were out of fuel, and my large friend here knew about this landing strip."

The soldier came out of the plane and called for three other men to help him offload the crates of MREs and ammo that Ship had on the plane prior to departure.

"So then you're gonna steal our stuff," demanded Kat.

"No Miss, we are appropriating what you couldn't carry. What you have on your persons you will keep if you leave. If you stay with us, you will divvy up your rations among the residents of the complex, as they did when they arrived." Another shot rang out, then another, and soon the shots got somewhat steady. "I believe we have worn out our welcome. The sound of your aircraft and the shots fired will have this place crawling with Rotters in minutes. I should tell you that you may have to surrender your weapons when we reach the compound."

Ship stiffened, and I told the Captain that there would be a blood bath if he tried to take our guns. Best leave us here.

He smiled. "Son, you wouldn't last an hour. There's about ten thousand dead in these woods."

"Gonna be a few more if you try to take our guns. *Sir*."

He beamed, as did his soldiers. "We might find a use for you yet." He spoke into his radio and told his crew to saddle up. The hillbillies must have been in radio contact because they all came running too.

And so did the zombies. Staggering, lurching, stumbling, shuffling, and in some cases sprinting. The sprinters were dealt with first, and we were all in the vehicles with the plane buttoned up before anything reached us. We peeled out and headed down an access road toward this compound place.

The compound place was a walled community with several buildings and a massive wrought iron gate. A school bus with plate steel welded to the side was blocking the gate from the inside, and it moved for us when the Captain radioed our arrival. Maybe fifteen houses comprised the meat of the buildings, but several other structures were present, including some type of clubhouse.

We came to a stop and Simmons was whisked away by a flock of corporals the moment he stepped out of the Hummer. I stepped out after him and noticed that there were several towers of plywood and four-by-fours erected near the wall, each manned with an army guy or a redneck. The two biggest houses had sniper teams on the roof, and a tank and two other tank-like vehicles were parked near the clubhouse. I remember thinking this compound might just be a great place to stay.

A guy showed up with a couple of well-armed soldiers as we were pulling our packs out of the Hummer. He gave Ship the obligatory shock glance, but moved on quickly to Kat and then me. He came over, looked at my sling, and in all seriousness he said, "Nice job," while nodding his head. He shook my hand and then Ship's, then introduced himself as Dr. Smith (no shit). He asked us to follow him, and we took our stuff and did. We ended up at the clubhouse, which was apparently the command center and hospital. We had to check in, giving our full names, and where we were when the shit hit, and what our former professions were. Ship and Kat both listed Student, and I told them I worked in a garage, which was partly the truth. I had worked on some of the prison vehicles and knew my way around an engine.

The doctor told us he would have to examine us for bites, and I got a little antsy. The one on my collar bone looked like a scrape, but the one on my leg looked exactly like what it was, even if it had healed. I had an injury, so I went first. One of the guards stepped into a little room with the doc and me, and I was instructed to remove my clothing starting with my boots. Up until then, the guard had had his finger on the trigger guard of his rifle. He rested his index finger on the trigger, but I played it off like I didn't notice.

Let me tell you, it was a bitch to undress, so the doc helped me. We opted for the sling first instead of the shoes, and it hurt. Pretty soon I was standing there without my shirt on, and he was checking the stitches that Ship had stuck me with. I hadn't even known they were there. The doc looked impressed. "Who treated this?"

"The sasquatch I came in with."

He smiled and pulled the bandage off of the back of my shoulder. "Hmm. Little chip of the scapula, do you have any pain here?"

"OW! Fuck! Yeah that hurts!"

"Yes, a small chip. I could go in and cut it out, but I don't think you'd like it as I couldn't spare any pain meds."

"Can I live with it?"

"Oh yes, but it might get sore if it floats."

I harrumphed. "Then screw that noise, leave it."

"Your friend did an excellent job with the stitches and bandaging, but I'm unclear on how you remained without infection."

I told him to check the pill bottle in my pack. He pulled it out, and even though it wasn't labeled, he immediately said, "Ciprofloxacin. Excellent." There were six pills left, and I didn't fail to notice that he pocketed the bottle.

He helped me untie my boots, and then it was on to the fun stuff, "Drop your drawers, my friend."

I got scared, and he picked up on it immediately. Worse, his soldier buddy did too, and he frowned and the barrel of his gun came up almost imperceptibly. I didn't hesitate and dropped my pants as best I could. The semi-circle bite mark screamed "HEY LOOK AT ME!" to all three of us, and the gun was now pointed directly at my face. The doctor hissed, "Wait!" The army kid didn't know what to do, but he kept the gun on me and I started to sweat.

The doctor pressed the wound hard; it was mostly healed and probably wouldn't even scar. "When did you get this?" he said that as he breathed out. For some reason, that scared me more than the gun, but I didn't know why at the time.

"About a week ago."

"A week ago." Guy was a fucking parrot now. "That…that's not possible."

"Does it look healed, Doc?"

"Yes but—"

"Do I look like I want to eat you? Do I look like I'm rotting?"

"No. No you don't." He furrowed his brow and folded his arms. He glanced over his shoulder and almost shit. "For Christ's sake, lower your weapon," he almost screamed at the poor army kid, who complied instantly. The poor kid had no idea what to do, and kept looking back and forth at me and the doc. "Go get Regan. Go! Now!"

The kid split the room like his ass was on fire, and the other soldier burst in the room with wild eyes. He saw me standing there in my skivvies, and pointed the rifle at me. "NO," screamed the doc and he grabbed the barrel.

"Oh shit," I said, and a single shot rang out. I felt my head snap back, and suddenly I was falling down a dark hole.

COMPOUND FRACTURE

And I had called Ship a baby. Let me tell you, if you get shot in the head and it doesn't kill you, it effing hurts. I was in and out of consciousness for a while.

Why did everybody want to shoot me? I may have been in prison, but I wasn't a bad guy, I just had some bad luck. Those that didn't want to shoot me wanted to eat me, or just plain tear me to pieces. I know I've mentioned this before, and quite recently to boot, but I'm really, truly, a wonderful individual. Stop shooting me. Stop it. I will make you a peanut butter and jelly sandwich.

Voices woke me. My shoulder hurt, but it was playing second fiddle to my noggin, which was telling me that under no circumstances should I even consider motion of any kind. I opened my eyes and that was my first mistake. It was bright, so I blinked a couple of times. This was more movement, and my head had been quite clear on not performing *any* type of motion. My cranium told me I was fired and I promptly passed out again.

I was lying down on a bed, my back propped up with pillows. Voices again, and for a moment I thought the pain in my head was actually speaking to me. The door opened and I looked at the doc and another army guy. The army guy was in command; I could tell that from the moment he stepped through the door. He was also younger than I would have thought.

The doc was all smiles. "You're awake."

I don't know how he made his voice so loud, or why it reverberated around my skull like a drum-beating hippy, but I informed the doc of my displeasure.

"It was just a graze, sir," said army dude. Poetic effing justice I'm thinking Ship would say.

I raised my hand to my temple. "Let me borrow your pistol, I'll shoot you in the head, and then we can compare pain levels."

"Fair enough. My name is Major Regan." He extended his hand.

Guy had a firm handshake. I immediately knew that even though this guy looked younger than me, and we were in the midst of probably two hundred million dead cannibals, this man had absolutely no intentions of being fucked with.

"Sir, I wanted to speak to you about your injuries. It seems that—"

"Where are my friends?" The not-being-fucked-with dynamic notwithstanding, I needed to know, and I was still uncomfortable with authority, although nothing like now.

"I assure you, sir, they are quite safe."

I assure you, sir? Seriously? "If they're safe, let me see them."

The major stepped into the hall briefly, and stepped right back, "They are on the way. In the meantime, I would like to discuss your bite mark."

I tried to sit up, but both my head and the doc were having none of that, and both of them said they would feel better if I remained mostly horizontal.

"I got bitten by one of those things when I was trying to fix a car for some people." It just came out. I didn't mean to say it. It just leapt from my lips. What an asshole.

The doc and the major looked at each other for a long second before the major piped up. "I've seen hundreds of people bitten. Good men and bad. Women. Children. All of them, absolutely every one died and turned inside of a day. How are you still alive?"

"No clue." My head hurt.

"You're telling me you have no idea how you survived a fluid transfer from one of the creatures?"

"Um…" dramatic pause while I inwardly snickered at his inadvertent comedic transgression, maybe a second or two too long, "no, do you?"

This earned sideways glances from the major to the doc and vice versa. Smith was flabbergasted. "Do you have any idea what this means?"

"Uh…"

"It means we could fabricate something from your blood! An antivirus! A vaccine! We could inoculate thousands so that if they were bitten, or even if they died of natural causes, they wouldn't turn."

"So you'll need my blood? But I need that…don't I?"

The doctor smiled. "We only need a few vials." He lost himself in thought. "Of course, I don't have the equipment here to process an antivirus. We will have to figure out how to appropriate the things we will need. Setting up a clean room should be easy, but…"

Ship and Kat arrived with a wiry guy as the doctor kept talking to himself. Kat smiled and came over to take my hand. Ship looked like the

Hulk and just stared at me reproachfully. Kat looked at the major with venom. "Who's the dickhead that shot him?"

"Whoa, Kat. That list is getting long. I'm not dead, and everybody is tired and scared. I don't blame these folks, and you shouldn't either." Kat blushed and nodded, probably remembering that she had also put a bullet through me. The Major seemed taken aback, but only for an instant. I didn't know then nor do I know now if it was because of what Kat said or what I said.

Ship passed me his notebook: *Next time, duck.*

"Love you too big guy, kisses." I blew him one, and he actually smiled.

The wiry guy smiled too and introduced himself as Lynch.

The major, the doctor, and the wiry guy left us after some more interrogation, and Ship and Kat left me soon after so I could get some much needed rest. As if anybody could ever really sleep again.

The next couple of days went without incident, although there were constant gunshots from the wall. Ship told me that the military men at this walled eleven acre complex were a mix of Army, Marines, and National Guard that had banded together when things had gone to shit in the small city of Athens to the south. They fled north through the wooded areas, dangerously low on fuel and manpower, although they had a truckload of ammo. The dead were relentless and hounded them the whole way. Ship had asked the major what kind of loss the United States was looking at, and his simple reply had been: *Total.*

Also, another tidbit of info that you need to know is that I had grown a tail since I had shown up, bitten but not dead. No, dumbass, not a fuzzy new appendage on my ass; Lynch. Guy was shadowing me everywhere I went. I didn't always see him, but I knew he was there.

I asked Ship for the skinny on him, and apparently the guy had worked for the government in some capacity, and was on the road with Major Regan's combined military forces when they had found this compound and sealed themselves inside. They had been making forays into the surrounding towns, picking up supplies and any survivors that wanted to come with them. This Lynch guy had been invaluable. He found stuff and people too.

In my ignorance, I thought he was looking out for me because I was valuable, or at least my blood was. Turns out, I was right.

We got some food together on the second day, and we sat with some other survivors and chatted. It was all the same, and after a while it became monotonous. My husband, wife, mom, dad, brother, sister, second cousin on my dog's side, was eaten and I ran and ended up here. Everybody's story was the same. We were the only folks to arrive in a plane though, and that seemed to get everyone's attention. Until we told them it was out of gas.

After lunch, most everybody dispersed, but we managed to latch on to a couple who had been eating with us. The guy, Bob, was maybe fifty, and the lady he was with was considerably younger. Her name was Carla. Between the gunshots outside, Bob began to tell us that the compound wasn't all roses and unicorns.

Bob worked the wall sometimes with the army guys or other rednecks (yeah, Bob was a self- professed hillbilly) and apparently ammo was getting low. There were periodic attacks on the wall by relatively sizable forces of undead. Up to now, it had been easy to dispatch them, as ammo had been plentiful, but the last time he had stood in one of those towers, the private that had been up there with him told him not to shoot unless something was crawling over the wall.

About fifty of the things had built up in one area and they were piling up on each other. When the first hand reached over the brick and cinderblock, the private used his rifle, and had called on the radio. A team showed up with wooden spears in a few minutes to try to cull the horde. It had worked, but Bob had seen the fear in the eyes of the soldiers.

Bob also told us that teams of soldiers had been going out to kill the things that got too close, or to try to find more supplies, or to rescue some civilians that had radioed in from an attic or a basement or a water tower in a nearby town. The returning teams were always down a man or two, and the only supplies and ammo they had brought in in the past couple of days came from Ship's plane, although they had brought in a couple of survivors.

In addition, some of the guardsmen were getting bossy, thinking that they were better than the civilians. These guys were barbers, burger flippers, and hardware store owners that had been called up as weekend warriors to help the regular army.

"And have you seen our rear defenses?"

I had to admit, I hadn't gone to the back of the compound.

"The front wall is tough, built out of reinforced concrete and brick, I checked. It's pretty and it's strong, but it's only there because it's visible from the street. A façade. The former owners of the houses in this complex, all of whom were dead when we got here by the way, either didn't want to spend the money on a wall all the way around the complex, or didn't think it was necessary."

I frowned, "Wait…what?"

"The entire rear of the compound, the part that's closest to the woods, is all chain link fence. Doesn't even have barbed wire at the top." He had pronounced it *bobwire*, which I would have thought was funny if I didn't get a bad feeling in the pit of my stomach.

Our spam and coffee was digesting nicely when Bob took us to the ass end of our new home. And by the way, I had never had a cup of coffee in my life pre-plague. I needed morning caffeine just like anybody else, but I drank Mountain Dew. And that could be a bitch to acquire when incarcerated. Yup I hate coffee, and F-U and your judgments if you're a militant coffee consumer. Bob pointed to the last two houses in the area, and lo and behold a seven-foot chain link fence separated us from lots of teeth and death. The fence was maybe sixty feet behind the houses, through an overgrown backyard that once had been perfectly manicured. I thought all rednecks lived in trailers? There was a fuel tanker back here as well. Must be how they could supply all their vehicles.

In the front of the compound, the zombies that attacked the wall or gates were brought back here when they were re-killed. There were piles of burned corpses outside the fence, many still smoldering a greasy black smoke. A crew was out there now, tending to one of the piles like farmers under careful sniper scrutiny. Rifle fire here and there put down any stray dead person who approached the crew.

I may have actually shit myself when a man stepped out from behind one of those plastic tool sheds and said, "It may look flimsy, but it's held out the infected so far." It was Lynch. SOB was like a bad rash.

Bob was quick to say good bye, and he took off with his tail between his legs. Lynch leaned against the siding of the house we were standing next to and looked off into the woods. "We have snipers on the roof, and extra towers there," he pointed, "and there. We're as safe as we can be, and there hasn't been anything even close to a breach yet."

"Mr. Lynch…"

"It's just Lynch."

"Fine, Lynch, what's the story with the rest of the country?"

"President and the Joint Chiefs are dead as far as we know. Every major city is gone. In fact, every city with a population of over fifty thousand is dead. At least that's the intel I got before the intel stopped coming."

"That's not good news."

"It gets better: It isn't just here. Every country in the world has had outbreaks, and every major city is lost. We estimate more than six billion people dead. It was fast. Ridiculously fast. Probably because nobody believed what was happening. In a month, the entire planet was dead. It only hit here two weeks ago, and in just a few days, our military and civilian armies were gone. Everybody's dead." He looked at me. "Except you."

I felt dirty. I felt scared. I felt pissed off.

He continued, "Why is it that you, a simple inmate from Cedar Junction in Walpole Massachusetts, didn't die when everyone else has?"

Boom. Ship and Kat both looked at me. Ship had an eyebrow raised, but Kat looked at me like it was no big deal. If this asshole had made an attempt at making my friends view me different, it didn't work. I had saved both of their asses, and vice versa. I hadn't known either of them for very long, but they were my family.

"Interesting," I said.

"And what's that, sir?"

"That you could come by this information when nothing works."

"Who said nothing works?" He walked around the house and was gone from view.

"Look guys, I…"

"Forget it," Kat said. "My dad did two years and he was the best man I know. Don't worry, you two are still in the top three." She punched Ship in the arm.

"What about you, Sasquatch? What do you think?"

Stinkeye. He wrote in his book for a long moment and passed it to me, staring off into the woods. *I doubt that man even remembers his own name. He's dangerous. We should leave, if he lets us. I have friends in the area.*

Ship was right. Lynch's moral compass was such a mess, I wondered how he was able to find me so effectively all the time.

While we had been talking, the sporadic gunfire from the towers had gotten more steady. A few soldiers had arrived in a Hummer to assist, and I heard one of them say *Holy shit.* I peered off into the woods, and I had to agree with the soldier's assessment. Holy shit.

An exceptionally large group of dead people were streaming out of the woods toward us. Captain Simmons showed up with another group of soldiers and rednecks, and they poured out of their vehicles and started loading up.

Simmons looked at us. "You might not want to be here."

Yeah, like we had appointments. Where were we going to toddle off to exactly?

Ship grabbed Kat and we moved quickly back to the house we had gotten assigned to. The gunfire was heavy at that time, and I heard the big gun on top of the Hummer come to life as well. It was loud. We got our packs and made sure our weapons were good, but again, where were we going to go? Besides, I wasn't going to be running anywhere. I had a head and a shoulder wound.

People must have figured something was up, because the whole compound was a flurry of activity. Not panic yet, but the adrenaline was definitely amped. We ran into Bob and he had his and Carla's stuff packed too. He was carrying weapons as well, and I wondered how many people actually surrendered their guns to Simmons when he had demanded them.

Bob told us he had access to a truck. He had been on one of the crews that worked outside the gate and he still had the keys. Another Hummer and two pickups full of gun-toting locals roared past us toward the rear of the compound. Bob went to get Carla

It was slow going up the stairs in the gorgeous house we were in and my head hurt. We were on the third floor; six other families and a bunch of military types were housed in this house. I got to the third floor landing and looked out the window. I hadn't noticed before, because who looks out those little windows anyway, but I could tell that if we went up to the roof we might be able to get a decent view of the chain-link fence and the tanker truck.

Ship thought that might be a good idea, so we made our way to the attic. There were beds up here too, and people were hurriedly packing things. They let us in, and we moved to a small balcony thing with beautiful French doors (So? I like French doors. That doesn't make me gay or anything) and we moved outside. We had an excellent view of the rear side of the complex. An excellent view of the sea of dead people that were already pushing on portions of the fence. There were hundreds, and the woods kept expelling more. Some of the army guys and locals were spearing some through the chain link, and the men with rifles were shooting any they could sight in on. Over the gunfire we could hear people screaming for more ammo. Some folks were running up ammunition crates to the men and women on the line, but they would need a lot of rounds to deal with this particular event.

Inevitably, the fence began to buckle as the dead pushed against their brothers to get to the meat inside the compound. One man in a red flannel jacket and jeans, with a black cap, clicked empty and screamed for more ammo, but nobody came. He looked up and down the line, slung his rifle and ran. Others saw this and did the same, some dropping their weapons, and soon half the defending force was high-tailing it out of the danger zone. This was all the impetus the zombies needed, and the fence came down in a long section as Simmons first screamed at the retreating men to return to their posts, and then screamed a general retreat himself. Many of the living men were caught by the dead ones and went down in a flood of gouging fingers and snapping teeth.

The dead still streamed out of the woods directly at the compound. Ship moved quickly, and we gathered what gear we could carry and I ran down the stairs with my friends, my noggin letting me know that this headache discussion was not over. When we reached the front yard, we could see the compound was in total pandemonium. Everyone was running in every direction. The tank and the other two heavy vehicles, (I had found out that one was a Bradley, and the other was a Stryker, but I didn't know which was which at the time) were moving toward the chaos at the rear of the compound.

A gray truck pulled up to us and Bob was driving with a passenger. I had expected the passenger to be Carla, but it was Lynch. Lynch had a gun on Bob. "You," he said, pointing at me, "get in."

"There isn't room for everybody."

"Everybody isn't going. You, me, and Bob."

I folded my arms, "No."

"No?"

"No. You won't shoot me. So, no."

"Wow, you're a smart one," he said, rolling his eyes, then pointed the gun at Ship. "How about now?"

"You shoot him and I'm not coming."

"Yes, you will." He shot Ship high in the chest and Ship flew backward landing on his back. Lynch pointed the gun at Kat. "Get in the truck or she's next."

I was kneeling over Ship's prone form when Lynch sighed and got out of the truck. "Get in the truck now, or I swear to Christ I will shoot that girl in the face." I listened for one more second but I couldn't hear a heartbeat from my friend. Lynch had killed my new best buddy. This asshole was toast, maybe not now but soon.

"You bastard," Kat screamed and launched herself at him. He caught her wrist and did some flip thing as nonchalantly as you would yawn. Then he yawned. "We don't have time for this." He raised his pistol and blew away a zombie that had snuck up on us from between the houses. He shot it in the head from a hundred and fifty feet away, barely taking his eyes off me for a moment. Kat was on the ground and he put the pistol to her head. "I can do this all day."

"She comes too."

"Fine, but in the back." We both helped Kat into the bed of the truck, and then Lynch pointed the gun at Bob, "Out."

Bob got out immediately and Lynch told me to drive. "Bob, get in the back, I need you too."

"I need to get Carla."

"If she's not here now she's dead, look," he said, pointing back to where the tanker was. Dozens of dead were streaming from between the buildings. I watched in horror as a runner took down a woman and began to tear into her. The runner had been wearing military fatigues. People were screaming and running in all directions now, and the gunfire was pretty much the same.

Bob got in the back of the truck, his face in his hands. Kat put her arm around him and Lynch and I got in the truck. It was already running, and I put my hand on the gearshift to put it in drive when a hand smashed through the passenger side window, latched on to Lynch and dragged him out of the vehicle. The giant form literally threw the prick across the yard. To Lynch's credit, he went into a roll and came up with his weapon drawn. He fired two shots at his attacker, then had to grapple with a zombie that had grabbed him from the side.

The big thing that had pitched Lynch opened the passenger side door and sat in the seat. The whole vehicle took on a starboard list when he plunked his ass down. Yup, it was Ship. I looked at him and he was pissed. He jutted his chin forward and I threw the truck in gear. Zombies were beginning to notice us, so I drove away. I saw Lynch fighting off three of the things as we drove toward the gate. F him. I wish I had some steak sauce to give to the zombies before we took off.

"Thanks for not being dead, although I have no idea how you hid your heart beat."

The big guy pulled his sleeping bag poncho up to reveal body armor. Mr. Smarty Pants strikes again.

I raised my eyebrows. "Kevlar. Huh. Where the F is mine?"

MILES TO GO

I was doing my best to drive like hell, while at the same time not bouncing Bob and Kat out of the bed of the truck and ignoring the colossal, tequila-hang-over quality headache I had. The compound was total bedlam, with people and zombies everywhere. I heard the roar of the tank firing its main gun, but I couldn't see what that was going to do. I saw a young woman go down under a mob of those things. The dead were pouring out from between the buildings and entering the houses themselves. The clubhouse was on fire. How the hell did it go to shit so fast? Ten minutes ago, we were looking out at the fence from the balcony.

I saw Simmons. He tackled a guy in a white lab coat. Simmons was fighting hand to hand with Dr. Smith. One of them must have been infected, but I couldn't tell who, as they were both covered in blood. I was betting Simmons as he was the tackler. I guess the doc had better things to worry about than stealing my blood now.

We headed for the gate, the carnage around us starting to get closer. The school bus was in the process of moving, some people had the same idea we had. We had to slow down as other vehicles were lined up to get out. The bus moved and the vehicles tore out of the little cul-de-sac street headed for who knows where in several directions. I hope they all made it.

It was our turn. I started to roll the truck forward when Kat began to bang on the window. She pointed behind us, and I could see that Bob was frantic. Carla was sprinting toward the truck, hands waving and screaming. She had a host of infected on her heels, but they were all of the slow variety, so she outdistanced them quickly. I slowed the vehicle down, but if I stopped then the infected to our flanks would reach us. Carla ran for the truck, and leapt on to the back of the tailgate. Bob threw his hands out to help her in and Kat screamed. Carla climbed into the bed like a spider as Bob pulled on her, and she wasted no time ripping into him with claws and teeth. He fought her off and they were both screaming, but she tore him up pretty good before Kat was able to pull her pistol and shoot Carla twice in the side. Poor infected Carla tumbled out of the back of the truck as we sped away.

Kat told me later what transpired behind me as we drove: Bob sat up, looking at the deep red furrows on his forearms that were just now beginning to fill with blood. His face and neck were covered with scratches as well, and a small bite mark had drawn blood on the outside of his left elbow. He sat there and nodded, then rapped on the window. He asked me to slow down, and I asked him if he was effing nuts. We were moving at about forty miles per hour, and I wanted to put as much distance between us and that doomed compound as possible. Ship put his massive paw gently on my arm, and he also asked me to stop. I did. We were a good half mile from hell right then and there wasn't a zombie in sight. Bob and Kat hopped out of the truck and Bob moved to the window. He showed me his elbow and I knew he was screwed.

"I might just hang out here for a while."

I got out, a little woozy from my bullet head butt. "Jesus Bob, come with us. We'll take care of you. If you stay here, they'll catch up and tear you to pieces."

"Nah. Don't want to take the chance. I could turn quick, or just get my blood on you. You seem like nice folks and I couldn't do that."

"I'm so sorry about Carla," Kat said and began to well up.

"I liked her, but I just met her a few days ago. We promised to take care of each other." Bob looked at his shoes. "Couldn't even do that."

Ship came around to our side of the truck. He handed Bob a bottle of water, then shook his hand. Bob shook my hand, then Kat's. He said good luck, then turned and walked into the woods. He was lost from sight before I could try to change his mind.

I started to get back in the truck, but Ship stopped me. He pointed to the passenger's seat and then got in to drive. Big bastard didn't trust me. Probably better what with my throbbing noggin. Kat rode in the middle and we drove on down the road.

We travelled a peaceful half mile before we began to see signs of the apocalypse. An abandoned car, doors open with bloody, smashed driver's side windows. What was left of a body on the side of the road, mercifully facing the woods. We crested a rise and stopped, looking down on the carcass of what had been a quaint little town. I looked at Ship, but he had thrown the truck into park and was in the process of busting out a map. He was quite annoyingly not paying attention to me. As he unfolded the tremendously huge map of what must undoubtedly be the galaxy, I noticed movement in the town ahead of us. A Humvee and a white pickup were zooming through town down the infected main street. The armored Hummer swerved a few times to avoid the infected that got in the way, but on more than one occasion, it ran one over, the thing spewing out the back like a rag doll from a dryer; all floppy and shit. The front of the white truck was a dirty brown.

Ship was staring intently at the map when I nudged Kat and pointed. She saw the trucks headed for us too and nudged the big guy. He spared her the reproachful look and directed it (shockingly) at yours truly. That just wasn't fair. I pointed toward the oncoming vehicles, which must have seen us by now, and were on the way regardless. Ship lowered his map, took a long three second gaze, and I could see the wheels turning. He was thinking hard. He sighed and opened the door. He folded his arms, expecting us to get out and do the same. I looked at Kat and we both shrugged and got out of the truck.

After a second of standing there with our arms folded, I had to ask, "Well Robin, what's the plan, asked the Caped Crusader."

Ship stiffened and turned to face me slowly. I got the biggest stinkeye yet, and did I detect a hint of rage? He fumbled for his notebook and wrote furiously for a few moments. *They've seen us. Probably a patrol. We have one of their trucks, and they probably don't know us. There's a fifty cal on the roof of the Hummer, we can't outrun that, and if anyone is Batman, it's me!*

Pretentious prick.

They were pulling up next to us by the time I had finished thinking the Shipster was a dick.

True to form, the Hummer contained soldiers, and the truck was full of rednecks. This was becoming common place. The driver rolled down his window and asked us where we were coming from. The big gun swiveled in our direction, but didn't point at us. Every weapon in the hillbilly Chevy was trained on us however, and some of those toothless bastards were smiling and looking at us like we were the cheese in a grilled cheese sandwich. Roughly translated: they wanted to shoot us. Not that I wasn't used to it.

People just suck.

I stepped forward, hillbilly guns sticking out a little bit further, and told them what happened at the compound. The driver of the Hummer just shook his head and said, "We're all fucked then."

One of the rednecks shouted at me, calling me a liar, but the others looked scared. They probably had family back there. The truck peeled out and left the Hummer parked where it was. The look on the young guy with the black cap and the beard was full of malice and hatred as the truck drove off. What the F did he hate me for? I didn't start a worldwide zombie epidemic.

The driver got out. He was wearing woodland camo and a boonies hat. "Alvarez?"

"On it, Sarge." The guy swiveled in his turret and looked in all directions. A guy got out of the passenger side and another from the rear passenger side. They took up positions to the front and rear of the vehicle scanning the tree lines and the town behind us.

"You're the folks from the plane, right? What happened back at base?"

I looked at Ship. "They do know us." I told the Sergeant what had transpired, leaving the part about my blood out of it. He seemed to sadden as I progressed. Nodding and asking pertinent questions.

"Did you see Regan at all?" demanded the Sarge.

"The major? No. I didn't see him at all. Simmons was infected though, and I saw him attack the doc."

"Damn it. For all of Regan's ineptitude, Simmons countered by being a good man. He and I told Major Asshole that the rear of the compound wasn't fortified nearly enough, but Regan wanted us to forage instead of shore up our defenses. We were there damn near two weeks, and the only thing between us and the enemy was a fence." He shook his head and rolled his eyes. "Idiot."

"Sarge, we've got maybe ten minutes," said the soldier at the back of the truck. He pointed back toward town, and we could see the zombies in the distance moving toward us. Dozens of them.

"Less," the sarge said. He drew his knife and walked past me. A zombie stumbled out of the woods and came at us up the embankment, its arms forward in that classic zombie pose you used to see in the movies. Kat started to cry. It was Bob. The Sergeant moved to the zombie and juked when the Bob-thing did that super-fast lunge that they do. He kicked poor Bob in the side of the knee and we all heard the crack. The zombie stumbled and Sarge jammed his weapon under its chin and yanked it out in what looked like one motion. Zombie Bob collapsed.

"Sorry Bob," was all the sergeant had to say.

"His girlfriend was infected and she bit him." I furrowed my brow. "But that was only about twenty minutes ago. He shouldn't have turned yet."

The soldier on the front side of the Hummer looked at us. "I saw a guy turn as one of those pus sacks was gnawing on his neck. They were still standing up. Couldn't have been more than thirty seconds after he was bit."

Pissa, I thought. *Wicked pissa.* If you're not from Massachusetts, you probably won't understand pissa. Again, no Google, sorry.

The radio blared to life and the guy in front went to answer it. He leaned through into the driver's side of the hummer, "Sarge, Lynch for you."

I almost shit myself. Guy was like the plague. We were already in the midst of a plague. We didn't need another.

Sarge grabbed the handset as he hopped back in the car. "Reynolds. Yes, sir. No, sir. Yes, I heard. Actually he's right here." The sarge pivoted his head to look directly at me. "We're north of the town of Bethlehem's Gate on Route Eight. Roger that, sir, devoid of hostiles, at least for the time bein. Your ETA? We'll be waiting, Reynolds out."

Ship had moved his gigantic paw toward his sidearm during the conversation, as had I. I looked toward the Sasquatch to see when he would make his move. He must have had poop for breakfast because he had the biggest shit-eating grin I had ever seen on his disapproving face.

Have you ever had one of those moments of absolute total confusion? One where you wake up and you're not where you thought you were, or somebody says something and it's not even close to what you heard? That's how I felt when Ship extended his aforementioned massive mitt toward the Sarge. The GI got out of the car and shook with Ship, the big guy swallowing the soldier's hand in his.

"Never did like that spook son of a bitch. Saddle up, we're moving back through town." The sergeant and two of his four man fire team got back in the Hummer. "One of you can fly a plane right?" Ship nodded. "Good, because I happen to have one, but I came up shit-short on a pilot." He looked at Ship. "Follow us. You're the half-back, I'll block."

I looked at the Sergeant. "What the fuck just happened?"

"I just cut my own throat. We're not north of Bethlehem's Gate, we're south of Pinkton, which we now have to go back through to get to Arlo. Ten miles in the other direction."

I was as lost then as you are right now.

He saw that and elaborated. "Lynch wants you. Don't know why, don't care. He probably wants to kill you for something, and I've seen enough death, especially concerning that bastard. We're going to get in that plane and get the fuck outta Dodge, comprende?"

I nodded.

We got in the truck, and true to his word, the soldier's vehicle spun around and headed toward the undead on the road behind us. They were now much closer. Ship followed closely behind as we made our way toward the infected town.

The first bloody jumble of parts that came tumbling out from under the Hummer and struck our front bumper scared the ever-loving shit out of me. I still wasn't feeling well, and when I noticed the bloody, hairy thing moving across the corner of the windshield, I initially thought it was some great spider skittering in to attack me. It was some undead guy's scalp, or part of it. I swear I saw an eyebrow. He had dark hair.

The things were all around us as we moved forward, but we were traveling at speeds upwards of twenty five miles per hour, and we were right up the military vehicle's ass, so it was hard for those rotten pus sacks to get to us.

We got through the first, largest wave, and Ship had turned on the wipers and squirted some fluid to clean off the goo. The scalp-spider flew up and over the windshield, and I almost puked as I saw the inside of it. *Almost* might be a tad disingenuous, but it's my effing story. If you tell me that after all this time that you haven't tossed a cookie here and there after witnessing some of the things this new world has to offer, I righteously call bullshit.

The second wave of them wasn't nearly as bad, although the stink had mounted. Have we discussed stink yet? I'm pretty sure we have, but just in case you need a reminder; the undead stink. They smell bad. Their aroma, or bouquet, or odor, scent, fragrance is something that you simply can't get rid of.

I heard someplace that the only sense you can't forget is a smell. I agree. Zombies are scary to look at; rotten and bloody with bits of them missing and filthy clothes. The sounds they make are absolutely terrifying. Mewling, screaming, moaning, growling. Ugh. The really rotten ones are squishy to the touch, and that's just nasty. I'm thinking I'm the only living human to have actually tasted one of the things and lived, even though my infected dude was still alive. I can't speculate on the taste of a rotten one. (I actually had to swallow a gag as I wrote that.) But the end-all-be-all of the zombie is the smell. None of the other senses can compare to the smell of them. If you've never smelled them, and I can't see how that's possible, then you have no idea. A five days dead raccoon, on a ninety degree day in coastal Florida, covered in maggots isn't even close. The smell of a zombie, even a relatively fresh one, is just...*more*. It somehow smells worse, an all-out assault on your olfactory tract. And it stays. It won't go away even after you wash whatever was touched by the offending stench. At least for a while.

I can't imagine the terrified soldiers in the cities who had set up defensive perimeters, only to have that stench attack them prior to the claws and teeth. I wonder how many men and women died because they couldn't stand the smell, doubled over retching, and were caught and eaten, unable to even fire their weapons. Yuck.

I think we're on the same page now about the smell. It was awful. This had only been the second town I had been in since the start of the plague, and the town in New Hampshire had been frozen. Huh. I wonder why the zombies didn't freeze? Anyway, this stink was beyond anything I had yet encountered. It must have been pretty bad for Kat too, because she climbed over me to get to the window and spew. She didn't make it, as the windows were up. Hey, it was cold and there were dead things reaching for us. A pane of safety glass was better than nothing against both of those adversaries so don't go getting all high and mighty.

Did she fight off the urge to vomit? Nope. Do you think she puked on Ship? Nope. I sat forward in that truck, arms held out, palms up, dripping someone else's mostly digested breakfast, feeling that wetness seep in, and all I could think was that the smell had gotten better.

Kat wiped her mouth with her jacket. "Sorry."

What could I say?

Ship coughed too, and he wiped his poncho across his mouth and looked at it. He didn't get to pull it away before I saw a smear of red. My buddy was hurt, and I was immediately flooded with concern.

We blew through the town quickly, and continued down the road for about fifteen minutes before the Hummer pulled over. I got out and wiped myself off as best I could. My jeans were soaked with vomit and there were some errant chunks to get rid of. One of the soldier kids in the Hummer was standing there looking at me, his rifle slung, and barely able to contain his mirth. He chuckled and I pointed to Kat. She raised her eyebrows, looking at the kid, then folded her arms, her eyebrows arching slightly higher. He stopped laughing instantly and suddenly found something he needed to stare at intently in the area of his left boot.

The sergeant stared at me for a sec, then busted out a laminated map on a ring with other maps, like I was, in fact, not covered in vomit. "We're here," he said touching the map. "Arlo is a little town north-north west of here. It has a small airfield and a tower, which until recently was manned. There's a fuel truck here," he said, pointing to a spot on the map near a hangar. "I'm not going to screw around with gas cans, we're taking the truck and we're going to drive it to your plane." He produced another laminated map from the attached ring, and put it on the hood of the car. He put his finger on a spot on a totally different runway, twenty miles in between. "Here."

The sarge pocketed his maps and looked at me. "Any questions?"

"Do you have any spare BDU's in there, Sarge? I stink." I indicated the vomit on myself.

"Sorry son, no."

I had a spare pair of jeans, but my jacket was just gross, and we would have to live with it. A shot from the front of the jeep had us all looking north. A wayward shambler had crept up on us through the woods, and the guy up front had done his job in eliminating it. It was scary, but not nearly as terrifying as the wicked loud sound that came next.

Two jets screamed over us just above the trees. The sound and subsequent concussion blast from the jets throwing my injured noggin into fresh spasms of agony. I had my hands over my ears as I asked the sarge where they could have come from, but he just shook his head like he didn't know. A series of distant explosions reverberated through the trees, and though we didn't see them, we could all feel the air change around us. They had been big booms.

"Hades?" asked one of the soldiers nervously.

"No, too small. Definitely came from the direction of the compound though."

I took my hands off of my ears. "Guess those guys in the truck should have stayed with us, huh?" I may have said that a little loud.

"Fuck em," said the sarge, "they would have killed us and stolen our shit the moment they realized their protection was gone. I'm more concerned with the spook. Saddle up, we're moving out now."

We did. We followed the Hummer for a few miles until the Now Entering Arlo sign was behind us. The bottom of the sign had said: Best Little Town in Tennessee! Pop 655.

They may have nailed the population part, but the first portion of that little notification was a fucking lie. I still have the scars to prove it.

OUTSIDE ARLO

The sarge looked through his binoculars at the town we had to pass through before we could get to the airfield. "Holy shit," was all he said.

There was one road. One. How can you call a pathetic, one avenue rural center a town? Looked like a friggin spaghetti western. I mean, what's the definition of a town? I don't have a dictionary with me right now.

Maybe fifteen buildings, mostly businesses lined the single street. There was a stoplight, but there was no other road! WTF is that about? Who has a stoplight without a reason to stop? I wonder if the city taxes in this shitty place went from eight bucks to nine per year when they installed the damn thing. Technology had reared its ugly head.

The most important thing to us right now was that directly under that ridiculous stoplight were an absolute shitload of people, all of them dead. Well, kind of dead. They moved around, bumping into each other like filthy bumper cars. I sat in a bumper car at a fair once, and it had a dead seagull in it. It was gross. How the hell did a dead seagull get in my fucking bumper car? Yes, I drove the shit out of it anyway. Hurt my buddy's neck, dead bird and all, when I ploughed into him doing at least seven miles per hour. I didn't see the dump-duck until I tried to get out of the ride and crunched down on it with my boot. Bumper cars and avian flu notwithstanding, there were a ton of dead people to deal with in the here and now. Actually, that was almost a year ago, so it was the *there and then*, but if the sign just outside of town (I scoff) was correct, then all six hundred and fifty five people were down there, every single one of them. It didn't make sense that over six hundred people lived in that little pissant place. Something didn't sit right.

Sarge and one of his guys were looking at the laminated maps, flipping through them and talking in low voices. "No, remember that pile up? We couldn't get through there, then there's the fuel truck. That's the mission now."

The kid swallowed hard. "There's no other way?"

"I'm open to options." Sarge put his maps away and looked at us. I didn't need binoculars to see the dead milling about, crammed in like sardines between the buildings on the main street, which was undoubtedly called Main Street.

"No," I said to him.

He raised his eyebrows and I continued, "I choose life." I pointed at the mini-swarm. "That's all kinds of the opposite of life. If we were in a tank, maybe, but not in these." I indicated our vehicles. "I don't want to be canned spam."

"Son, we're not going through that town, we've got to go around, but there aren't any roads but this one. We have to go through the woods unless you have any better suggestions?" He honestly looked like he wanted them. I don't think he thought travelling through Arlo was the best plan, but I had nothing.

I felt a tap on my shoulder, it was Ship's notebook. It had one new word written and underlined: *STEALTH.*

I showed it to the sergeant.

"Gonna need more than one word, son."

My nothing turned into something as I thought on the Sasquatch's suggestion. I used hand motions that followed my words. "We sneak around town on foot. Get to this fuel truck, create a diversion to bring the dead running, and drive through when the town empties of pus sacks." I looked at Ship expecting monumental stinkeye, but he looked…pleased? Proud? Satisfied? I don't know, but I felt better.

"Um yeah. That's what we just said. Almost word for word. The only issue is what kind of diversion?"

***

What are the cardinal rules that keep you alive in a horror movie? What do you never, ever, EVER do?

1. Go off alone to check something.
2. Run upstairs instead of outside.
3. Put your weapon down.
4. Have sex.
5. Split up.

There was nothing to check, we were already outside, and my weapon was attached to me via sling, possibly forever. I had recently been released from prison, albeit somewhat shy of the time I was court ordered to put in, so when I tell you that the wildlife in the woods of Tennessee may have looked good in booty shorts or a miniskirt and heels, you can understand that I was constantly thinking about sex. I'm a guy, we do that. Nonetheless, I wasn't having any, and with my injuries it may have been difficult anyway. But that last one? Good old number five? Yup, we did it. We split right the F up.

Three of the soldiers were to create the diversion outside of town to the east, and the sarge and my peeps were to go west, then north to get the truck. We would all meet back where we first looked down on the infested town. Grade A plan. Top notch.

The soldiers did their hooah's, shook mitts, and we walked off in different directions leaving the vehicles where they were. The truck team (the one with me in it) worked our way around the town (again, scoff, not a town) to the west as planned. This was where the plan went to shit. It seems that the six hundred or so dead folks that lived in the area didn't all live in the town, or if they did, they had relatives that liked to play hide and seek in the woods. Oodles of them.

This particular forest was fairly thick with trees, which blocked a lot of the light that otherwise might reach the ground, but that having been said, it was in the area of two o'clock in the afternoon, so we had good visuals. The shadows thrown by the trees and the almost leafless canopy were spooky, and now and then Sarge, who was leading, would throw up his fist and we would all stop. Usually he would point, and we would see a lone zombie standing a few dozen yards away, admiring the foliage. Sometimes they were in twos or threes.

We got maybe a mile into our trek when we heard stirrings around us. Sarge did the hand thing and we all stopped again. A dead woman, all torn and gooey stepped out from behind a tree not three feet from us. She had her back to us, which I took as a kindness. We were all frozen solid, even the zombie. She turned her head a little to the left, but still didn't see us. Sarge could have reached out and touched her, I shit you not.

Ultimately, we were undone by a squirrel. I had liked squirrels until that moment. They were cute little critters that sat on their cute little asses and ate cute little acorns with their cute little paws. Now squirrels can suck it. Difference between a squirrel and a rat? No, not the tail. Existentialism.

That little shit might have been sitting there terrified in that bush next to zombie lady for hours without making a sound. We stand next to him, and the little fucker bolts through the winter leaves, making a racket that sounded like a busted chainsaw in the woodland quiet. Prick ran up a tree, perfectly safe too. All four of us living people looked up that tree and that fucking squirrel looked right back at us. I think he shrugged before he dashed into his nest in the tree.

Dead lady looked at him too. Then she turned in super slow motion and looked right at us.

Bitch drooled. No lie. It was black and nasty, and her equally black tongue darted out and caressed her upper lip. Her lower lip was missing. All five of us, living and dead, were frozen for a second, and I honestly thought the sarge was going to K-Bar her into true death when that fucking squirrel tittered and it was on.

Without any ado whatsoever, dead broad snapped her rotten paws out like a striking mamba and latched on to the soldier, with a…well…a death grip. She leaned in but before she could fasten her jaws around anything soft, a crashing blow from Ship's massive right hand hit her in the forehead and sent her sprawling. It must have stunned her because she did something zombies simply do not do. She let go. She skittered to a stop about four feet away in a crumpled heap. Several of the shadows moved when this happened, they seemed to want to investigate the sound.

We all thought dead bitch was truly dead or had a zombie concussion, but she looked back up at us and gave that mournful wail. Then all those shadows really came to life, or un-life, and suddenly the woods we were currently traversing absolutely filled with pus sacks, and it was really on.

I stood there for a nanosecond looking at the dead people coming from every possible direction and I thought of the compound and how quickly that had fallen. That nanosecond was all it took for Ship and the sarge to vault into action. Ship raised his rifle, and the sarge hissed: "No guns!" The big dude nodded his exceptionally large cranium and we ran. More to the point, they ran, I hobbled awkwardly, close to passing out. My head HURT. I was instantly nauseated, and I had a cramp in my right arm. Yeah, I don't know why the cramp was in my arm, it just was. That hurt too, and suddenly the area was awash with the permeating stench of zombie. I stumbled on a root, and went down, skinning my knee on pretty much nothing. Kat came to my rescue, and suddenly she was grappling with a teenage boy she probably would have thought was cute six months ago. Another punch from the Sasquatch felled the zombie, but this one held on. Both Kat and dead high-schooler were on the ground and before the thing could bite our friend, Ship brought one of his size twenties down on its melon, which burst like its namesake.

Sarge had outdistanced us, probably as intent on the mission as remaining uneaten, but I think all the deaders in the area had focused on the three of us. Their cries were terrifying and the stink was debilitating. Fear and tension were mounting as more and more of them came into view. A runner sprinted in from in front of us, fighting its cousins to get at the good stuff, and that sealed the deal. Kat raised her rifle and put a round through its chest. Now we were in it. The shot echoed through the trees, and the wails of the dead picked up exponentially. They were inbound to our position as fast as they could shamble.

The guy in charge of adrenaline opened all valves, and I yanked Kat to her feet. "Run!" Renewed vigor had all of us sprinting and dodging grasping fingers and snapping mouths. Zombies poured from the forest, behind every tree and bush. Both Ship and I had pulled our machetes, and keeping Kat between us, we hacked anything that got close. A huge specimen with half a beard (and half a face), naked below the waist grabbed Ship from the side. I brought my machete down hard on its wrist and Ship was free almost before he knew he had been caught. The zombie looked pissed and growled at me. I don't know if it was because its hand was still attached to my buddy, or because I had denied it its prize.

Inhuman screaming from behind us alerted us of another Runner. Ship bent quickly, picked up a rock the size of a cantaloupe, and side-armed it into the nuts of the speedy son of a bitch before he could grab me. I heard crunching and my left hand involuntarily moved protectively to my balls. Ew. Ship had reminded me of Roger Clemens snapping up a weak hit and chucking it to first like it was an early inning. On target and ninety miles per hour. The runner was down with a broken something, but he still crawled after us. Even his dead buddies were faster than him now, and they staggered past.

Somewhere off to our right, a gigantic explosion shook everything. Even the dead that were chasing us paused to look in that direction. Some even moved off that way, but most were just intrigued until they remembered (if they remember) that food was in the immediate vicinity. Then they looked right back at us all hungry and motivated and shit. What a pisser. Again, for you non-New Englanders, there are exceptionally vast connotational differences between pisser and pissa. Granted when someone from my neck of the woods says either one, they sound the same, as our hard R pronunciation goes out the window prior to us leaving the womb.

Pisser = bad. Pissa = good. You kind of have to be from New England to get the nuance. And wherever you're from, our pizza was better than yours. Don't judge, just keep reading.

Most of the pus sacks in the area decided that the food in front of them was better than the food that might be near the explosion. Us live folk were hoping that the explosion was the diversion. Unfortunately, our first-rate strategy didn't include the woodland zombie clan following us to our mission objective, and from the way the dead people kept materializing out of the forest, there may have been more in the woods than in the town.

We weren't exactly surrounded, but they were converging from most directions. The sergeant's rifle fired once, then again. Apparently, he had bagged his noise discipline as our secret was most definitely out. I caught sight of him on a little hillock, shooting back toward us. Several of the dead that were getting close fell, their craniums sufficiently ventilated. Sarge screamed at us, "Come on!"

We almost made it to him. We got so close. Ship and Kat were at the hill, but I was a good forty feet back, and I wasn't going to make it. The zombies had encircled me other than directly to the left, where a small copse of bushes blocked my only salvation; a relatively clear path. I did the only thing I could, I crashed through the shrubs.

"Through," is probably a misnomer here, as I got stuck fast halfway in. It was some kind of torturous thorn bush with thorns the size of brand new number two pencils. Whoever invented this type of bush (or mosquitoes, taxes, and people who talk at the theater) can blow me. They're assholes. This bush had me mired, and I could only go back into the waiting arms of the dead. There were three that were almost on me, and Ship took out one, but the sarge missed his target and the slimy bitch grabbed me. She lost nearly the entire top half of her head to my machete, but I lost my machete in the deal as it stuck in her melon. The third thing had grabbed me too, and the fucker bit me on the back of the shoulder before I could escape. It pulled its head back, but only ripped my jacket. Oh, he got me, but it was only the jacket that tore. He chewed twice as we grappled, then spit out the offending tidbit. Must have tasted poorly.

"He's done for," yelled the soldier, "let's go!" Ship and Kat didn't move when the sarge turned to leave.

The damn critter was holding me fast, and his buddies were coming hard. He didn't like his grip on my jacket so he was trying to adjust when I brought my forearm down on his wrists. The jacket zipper popped, and I shrugged out of my warmth, giving it to the zombie. Ship shot the dead dude that had me and I was able to make my way to my friends when it collapsed.

Sarge looked sad. "You're bitten, son, we'll sort that out when we get to the truck."

I grabbed the shoulder of my shirt. "How bad is it?"

"There's only one kind of bite, sorry."

"We'll talk about *that* when we get to the truck too," I told him.

The four of us moved through the woods with a shitload of dead people chasing us, but the mass of them seemed to be behind now. A speedy one sprinted toward Ship, and the big guy went into a crouch and threw the infected bastard against a tree before it could do anything. Its bones were at all angles after the impact, and I heard it gurgle as we moved past. I would imagine it turned into a walker shortly after we left it.

I saw the corner of one of the town's buildings when we booked it out of the trees, across a street and into a small field. I could hear the creatures, but I could no longer see them, although I had no illusions they had given up the chase. We swung north, running for all we were worth. The other three were a good ten yards in front of me and I was running out of steam. My vision began to blur and my head was pounding. I tried to call out but I got as far as SH…before that tunnel vision hit me again, and the ground rushed up to meet me.

SHIP'S LOG

While I don't share my friend's penchant for hilarity, or his prolific use of profanity, I have read his journal and it is true and accurate to the best of his pathetic ability to pen his thoughts. Although some of his references to me personally are insensitive and full of crass nicknames, I believe his recordings have merit and should continue.

My name is Ship. My friend is unconscious, and I don't know if he will survive. Personally, I know what a head wound is like, and his former ramblings about the pain involved are, for the most part, factual. Moreover, a state of confusion and general nausea exists when subjected to said injuries.

I will continue his journal should he succumb to the harm that was done him. I will also attempt to further tell his tale here, while he either recovers or expires. He is, as I write this, on the far right side of the fuel truck bench seat, hands zip-tied behind his back, with a bit made of an elm stick firmly tied to his mouth. The sergeant would not allow him to come with us unless he was bound so, even though both Kat and I repeatedly elucidated that my friend is immune to whatever has affected the rest of the population.

I am unable to form a hypothesis as to what will transpire should my friend perish. The fact that he appears to be insusceptible to contracting the syndrome does not necessarily denote that reanimation will not occur. We had to take steps to ensure our safety should he attempt to attack us upon rousing. It will pain me greatly to have to euthanize my comrade should the need occur.

I must admit, I am becoming unnerved by the amount of creatures in this area. I believe "zombie" is a ridiculous, Hollywood term that only serves to confuse. The true Haitian zombie, if there is such a thing, is nothing more than a human being that has been either chemically or mentally subdued to the will of another. They are not the living dead, and they do not consume the flesh of the living. To equate said individual with the creatures that are now probably the dominant species on this planet, is both irrational and nothing short of folly. This having been said, zombie is a term that the masses will understand, although I refuse to use it.

Having stated my intentions, and the current disposition of the original author of this journal, I feel it imperative to catalogue what transpired after his poorly timed loss of consciousness.

Kat noticed him stumble and faint. I was able to pick up and carry him, granted his weight is not substantial. Dainty is a word that comes to mind. I threw him over my shoulder, Kat, Sergeant Reynolds, and I running from the crowd that had come out of the woods on the west side of the road. We moved quickly, and the lack of the faster of variety of creature was a boon to us as we made our way to the truck that Sergeant Reynolds assured us was waiting for us. A lone creature stood up in the high grass immediately next to me as we rushed through the field. I swung my shoulders using my friend's legs as a makeshift truncheon to propel the creature away from us. Other than that, the run from the field to the truck was uneventful, with no signs of the dead other than those pursuing us, and we had far outdistanced them. Once at the truck, however, things got somewhat more tense. Several dead were in the vicinity, and needed to be cleared prior to us engaging the engine on the vehicle. We destroyed four of the rotten things efficiently and quietly, using hand to hand weapons. I placed my friend on the ground next to the truck, to cover Sergeant Reynolds as he attempted to start the vehicle.

The sergeant opened the driver's side door, a blackened hand snaking out and grabbing him by his fatigue jacket. In his haste, Reynolds hadn't checked to see if the cab was empty and it almost led to his demise. As he already had his combat knife in his hand, he was able to dispatch the creature quickly, although his shout of surprise did not go unnoticed, and other creatures began to show from shadows and heretofore unseen corners and niches. They quite literally came out of the woodwork, and in moments we had a crowd of sixteen of them en route to our position.

Reynolds discarded the body and climbed into the vehicle. There was a moment of overwrought confusion when the keys that had previously been left by the Sergeant's team behind the driver's visor were not where they should have been. The creature must have crawled in the truck while alive, and succumbed to a bite or scratch only to reanimate and knock the keys to the floor. Reynolds jammed the key into the ignition, at which point the truck refused to start. It did not sound like a dead battery to me, but more as if the ignition coil was cold, so I remained as calm as I could until the vehicle started on the third attempt.

Kat and I were forced to fire on the numerous dead that rounded both sides of the truck at once, compromising our stealth. I picked up the lifeless frame of my friend and attempted to pass him to Reynolds, who outright refused to let him in the cab. Kat's fire was becoming sustained as she screamed for us to hurry, and still the soldier rejected us. He passed me two white zip ties and told me to bind my friend or we could all stay here. I complied, but Reynolds slammed his door and pointed to the other side. I moved quickly to the other side of the truck, and was again intimidated by the sheer numbers of creatures that were headed for us from across the field and significantly closer. There were dozens, perhaps a hundred or more.

Several corpses were strewn about thanks to Kat's handiwork with her rifle, but this same action was what was drawing the creatures to us. Kat climbed into the vehicle and I unceremoniously tossed the dead weight in after her, then clambered in myself. None too soon either, as a slap on the side of the fuel truck announced the arrival of the vanguard of the dead.

We began to move forward, and the sergeant passed me a stick, demanding that I tie it in our unconscious friend's mouth to ensure he couldn't bite us should he reanimate. When we drove a quarter of mile back towards town, I switched positions with my friend in order to have him closest to the door for quick ejection should the worst come to pass. It was cramped in the cab, as the bench seat was made to accommodate three, and there were four of us, and as my comrade constantly states, I am not small.

No, I would not depart with my friend infected; I would get out and destroy the creature he would become.

The truck moved quickly, moving us back toward the small town of Arlo. Several dead remained in the street, but for the most part they had moved on, the distraction provided by Reynolds' team proving adequate. As we drove through the town, signs of devastation were ever present; smashed store fronts, broken glass, bloodstains, skeletal remains.

One of the creatures lurching toward the fuel truck wore bloodstained and shredded ACUs. Reynolds slowed the vehicle as the thing came at us from the side. It slapped its hands against the door panel and Reynolds sighed, "Foster." This had been one of the men sent to create our diversion. The sergeant nodded, and we drove forward another fifty meters before the truck stopped. "One second," Reynolds said over his shoulder as he jumped to the street. One report was heard, and he was back in the truck forthwith.

"What were you doing?" Kat demanded somewhat harshly.

The soldier's reply was equally as severe, "Don't worry about it."

I scribbled in my book, telling Kat that Reynolds had undoubtedly destroyed his former squad mate, unwilling to leave him as a wandering infected. She nodded appreciatively, respecting the man's decision.

Returning to our original position, the other two soldiers had failed to make the rendezvous. Our new companion looked nervous as he scanned the area with his binoculars. Several undead were making their way from the town up the street toward us. They would reach us within a half hour or so.

"We'll give 'em ten minutes. No more. I want to get to the plane and fuel it before dark."

We waited the ten minutes, several undead coming from our western flank as well as from the town. We destroyed them as they came. I needed to make a tactical decision as to our vehicles. We had three vehicles, the Humvee, the fuel truck, and the pickup that we liberated from the compound. We would abandon the pickup. With Reynolds driving the Humvee, I would drive the fuel truck with Kat, who could minister to our cataleptic comrade. Truth be told, I wanted her to watch him closely, as his breathing had become labored, and when I checked his pulse it seemed weak. She could eliminate him should he turn, or at least keep him restrained while I pulled over to euthanize him.

I would not leave him to infect anyone else, and I would not leave him in that state.

These preparations were all for naught, as I heard muffled noises from our zip-tied, seat belted partner. Human noises. The bit in his mouth must have been causing him extreme discomfort as well as it being exceptionally humiliating. I smiled in spite of myself.

Kat pointed her pistol at his forehead and asked him her name. We both heard only one syllable, but it sounded like *Gah*. A familiar sound indeed. She asked him a series of questions anyway, to which he could nod. Finally, she undid his bit, and he immediately began to rant about his treatment. The last thing he said before he huffed and fell silent was: "Why did you ask me so many stupid questions before you pulled that damn stick out of my mouth?!?"

"Oh I knew you were human the second you opened your eyes," Kat told him. "I was just playin.'"

REPERCUSSIONS AND LOSS

Son of a BITCH! I am NOT dainty! I do not faint, I pass the F out! I am a large, muscular individual. I was in PRISON for Christ's sake. Dainty people don't spend time in prison, and no, I was nobody's bitch.

That big, arrogant, goat cheese-gobbling, shitbird should keep his Andre the Giant-sized mouth shut! I know he didn't actually say anything (HE FUCKING CAN'T), he wrote it, but the sentiment is still the same.

He has stones calling me dainty. I mean, Jesus, the guy would look down on Shaq. He's bigger than a God damn great white shark. EVERYBODY is smaller than him. He has balls calling me insensitive too, after what HE wrote in MY book! If it wasn't important, I would cross that shit out. What is it called? Redacted? Yeah, as soon as I get around to it, I'm gonna redact the shit out of his totally unnecessary comments. Fucks up the flow.

He thinks he's got a stinkeye? Just wait. Prick can't talk, so all he has is his stupid looks. No, wait, that came out wrong. I don't think he's pretty, he has all those awful looks he gives me. Reproach, disappointment, anger. You get it. He's not my dad, I'm older than he is.

I'm still thinking of a way to exact revenge. Maybe I'll steal his precious notebook so he can just shut the F up all the time. Let's also not forget that I ran into a burning building to *get* the notebook.

Maybe I'll just keep mentioning how wonderful his voice is. Ha!
Dick.

So they kept me zip tied until we got to the airfield. I thought that was unfair. Kat was all smiles and she and Ship had a big old guffaw. Except his was silent. It was ridiculous seeing him shake. That's how he laughs. Fucker doesn't make a sound, he just shakes. HEAR THAT SHIP YOU BIG BASTID?? YOU LOOK STUPID WHEN YOU LAUGH!

Teach him to read my shit. Zombie fucking apocalypse and the one and only time the prick laughs is at me when I'm tied up on the bench seat of a fuel truck.

So when they were done laughing, the army guy pulls a gun and points it at me. "He's bitten," is all the prick says. Not my best day. Kat steps between us and folds her arms so now the gun is pointed directly at her, now I'm a little antsy.

"Whoa, whoa, whoa, calm down, Sarge, I'm immune."

"Nobody's immune. I've seen a thousand people killed by bites or scratches. They all died. Every one." His weapon was still pointed at Kat, and I could see Ship inching the nose of his rifle up.

"I'm going to pull my pant leg up, then I'm going to pull my shirt down. You'll see the bites that I got before today have healed."

He kept his gun on us and I gently nudged Kat to the side. I showed him the one on my collar bone, and he didn't seem impressed. The one on my leg though, there was no denying it was a bite.

"That's not possible," he said in whisper, then his head whipped up. "The spook! That's why Lynch wants you!"

I let my pant leg fall and looked smug. "And they say you're just a grunt."

I was starting not to feel so good. If the past was any indication of what was to come, I was in for a rough night. When I had been bitten before, I got very sick. Hopefully neither Ship, nor the sarge would *euthanize* me (Sasquatch prick!) after I passed out. As I vehemently stated above, I do *not* faint.

"Let me see the wound," demanded Reynolds.

I unbuttoned the top two buttons on my shirt and he had a look. "It isn't bad. Semi-circle bite pattern with broken skin and some blood. On anyone else this would mean death."

"The last time I was bitten, it was twice in a two hour span. I got real sick, but I felt better when I woke up."

"Woke up?"

"Yeah," I said, looking directly at Ship. "I PASSED OUT, and when I woke up, I felt like a million bucks. At least I didn't want to eat anybody. Well, maybe that chick from Hooters."

Ship was looking at me quizzically, and Reynolds was pulling out a bandage when we all heard an engine approaching. The sarge and Ship pointed their weapons at a white pickup headed in our direction.

"Looks like your truck."

"It was Bob's truck," Kat told him.

"I liked Bob."

Both rifles were trained on the pickup as it stopped. A soldier got out of each side; they looked like babies. "Thanks for waitin', Sarge."

"Never did like you much, Alvarez. Tried to leave you behind." The men walked up to each other and clasped hands. "I see you brought Richards along with you. One more mouth to feed."

Alvarez looked at his boots and Richards held up a bandaged forearm. "F-U Sarge, you cook like shit anyway."

"Sorry, Richards," Reynolds sighed. The kid nodded. "We lost Foster too. We got separated."

"He's dead."

"What kind of dead?" demanded Richards.

"I took care of it."

Richards looked at his arm and laughed. "Doesn't even hurt. Well, let's get this show on the road. None of you assholes could probably fuel the plane anyway." He moved to the fuel truck and unrolled a hose from a wheel. He was fueling the truck in two minutes.

"Sorry about your friends," Kat said quietly to Alvarez. She was seventeen. This kid was probably ten seconds older than she was, and not bad looking. I could see where this was headed, and I smiled despite myself.

The plane was fueled in about fifteen minutes and Richards was beginning to look like I felt. He came from under the wing of the plane and stood near us. "Ok, now it hurts."

We could smell the death on him from five feet away. "Want me to take care of you, son?"

"Nah. I'll do it, Sarge. Thanks though. You'd better split, you've got company." He pointed behind us and we turned to see a dead person walking toward us from the field behind the runway.

"I don't want to leave you."

Richards smiled. "I'm already dead, Sarge. Don't sweat it. You didn't leave shit. Get on the plane."

We all shook his hand, then got on the plane.

Ship got in the pilot's seat, and I moved to sit with Kat and the soldiers, but Ship motioned me forward and I sat up front with him. He pointed off to the left. A large contingent of pus sacks was coming, but they were far off.

"Never a dull moment, buddy."

He shook his head, tapped me and pointed to his eyes. He started the plane and we taxied around, the length of the runway now in front of us. He wrote something in his book and passed it to me: *Put your hands on your yoke, just touch it to get a feel of how much I'm manipulating it.* He pointed to the plane's steering wheel thingie.

We took off, me getting a feel for how that was done, and in seconds we were in the air. We did a slow circle to check for Richards, but the truck was gone. Reynolds came forward when we leveled out. "There's a base in Gulfport, Mississippi," he said. "Keesler Air Force Base. Last we heard it wasn't over run yet."

We headed southwest.

KEESLER; TOTALLY ZOMBIE FREE

"Keesler AFB, this is Nairobi 308 Lima Victor bearing forty degrees, come in, over."

Nothing.

"Keesler, this is Nairobi 308 Lima Victor requesting permission to land, over."

Sarge, who had moved up front and sat with everybody's favorite yeti, looked back at us, "Keesler, do you read, over."

"If they don't *read*, and we can't land, it's going to get messy in here," Kat said, her legs crossed.

"Think about your grandmother naked being spanked by Mickey Mouse."

She looked down for a long three seconds, then looked at me all weird, "*What?*" she demanded with her palms up.

"Did you think about what I said?"

"The grandma thing? I really kind of couldn't think about anything else for a moment."

"Do you still have to pee?"

"Uhh. No."

"Boom." I folded my hands together behind my head and leaned back victorious.

I looked back to Reynolds, who didn't appear happy. He was pointing out the starboard side of the plane. Alvarez was asleep, buckled in the back. He had fallen asleep within thirty seconds of the wheels leaving the tarmac.

Kat and I moved to the right and looked out the window. The entire area was crawling with infected. Fires raged. Things wearing the skins of people shuffled about in groups, hunting.

Same old. I yawned. We were screwed.

I yelled up forward, "Sarge, any luck?"

Apparently, I was either not worthy of a reply, he didn't hear me, or he was too busy, because he didn't say shit to me.

But he did say; "Roger that, Keesler. Negative, five on board, none bitten. Reynolds, Sergeant First Class and PFC Alvarez, over. Negative Keesler, all civvies, over. Copy, runway zero three, out."

I looked out the window as we banked right. We were going to land here? Are you shitting me? The whole city was screwed. Half of it was on fire, and the other half absolutely crawled with *them*.

"Reynolds," I yelled. "Sarge!"

He turned and looked at me from the cockpit.

"We can't land here, it's toast!"

"The base is secure son, and every other place we might want to land will look just the same." He turned right the F back around; this conversation was over.

I looked at Kat and she seemed nervous. Can't imagine why. We came in low over the smoking city and approached runway zero three. The chain-link fence surrounding the base seemed to be up, but there were dead hands pulling on it or milling on the other side in countless places. It looked all too familiar.

As we landed, we saw several Hummers whip past us. I thought they were coming to greet us, but they kept going. When we taxied off the runway, one of those armored things, not a tank, was waiting for us, the barrel of its gigantic gun pointed forward and mercifully away from us. A deuce and a half truck full of gun-toting military types was also waiting, and they had their guns on us the moment we stepped off the plane. There were different types of clothing on the troops, but they were all some type of that military camo shit.

Reynolds opened the hatch and let down the stairs, we all followed. A little guy stepped forward and shined some weird light in each of our eyes, then yelled "CLEAR," and the guns lowered. The kid looked twelve.

A guy who looked exactly like Captain Simmons walked up to Sergeant Reynolds, who immediately saluted. The guy returned it, and began to speak. "My name is Captain Gregg, US Army. I'm to escort you to the brass for debrief and reassignment. The civilians will have to surrender their weapons and all of you will be inspected for bites immediately."

This shit again, he wasn't getting my guns. Nope, not happening.

An average-sized guy moved to Ship and tried to take the big guy's rifle. Ship wouldn't give it up. "Sir, I have to take your guns, I'm sorry."

Gregg stepped up; the top of his head came to Ship's midsection. "Sir, you and your friends will need to give up your weapons."

"I'll vouch for them, sir," Reynolds added quickly.

The Captain shook his head, "Doesn't matter, Sergeant, this is still a United States military base. Civilians will not run around armed."

"Sir." Reynolds looked at us apologetically. "Gotta give 'em up. Sorry guys, he's right."

I could see there would be no arguing with this asshole, and they had way more guns than we did, plus that armored thing with the friggin cannon. Oh man did this feel familiar, and last time we got to keep our guns, not that it did any good. What was I going to do, go all Josey Wales on their asses and get us all killed? They had us, and all my toughness fled. I reluctantly handed over my stuff, even my pack, and they took it. Ship and Kat did the same. Now we had nothing but my sharp wit to fend off a continent full of zombies.

A wiry little doctor type, complete with stethoscope jumped from the back of the deuce. Where the other kid looked like…a kid, both Gregg and this doctor looked haggard. This was getting to be a theme. Ten of the soldiers surrounded us and we had to strip down. I had to take the bandage off my head, and the doc looked at all of my bullet wounds, the bites that didn't look like bites, and the bite that there was no mistaking was a bite. And he glossed right the hell over it and moved on to Kat. "If you would step over here young lady. I'm sorry but you will have to remove your clothing as well." Alvarez stiffened noticeably, (his shoulders, perv.) but he acquiesced. They moved off behind the deuce, and were back in short order. Thank all that is holy the newest bite on my back shoulder didn't look like a bite.

After we were all checked out by either soldiers or the doc, the doc said we were clear and we got dressed. As if it were the most natural thing in the world, the doc casually asked me when I was bitten. Every single barrel of every single gun that didn't belong to my friends was now pointing at me. Even Gregg had his pistol out. "Weapons down, this man was obviously bitten by a living person, the bite on his leg is weeks old and healed."

The rifles relaxed, but the eyes didn't.

"I got in a bar fight before the plague," I said. "Bastard bit me on the leg. I had to get shots."

This seemed to placate the men, and Gregg holstered his weapon.

"And the scratch on your back?"

"No idea. But nothing's gotten close to me if that's what you're asking."

The doc didn't even look up from his clipboard. "No, no. With your hours-long plane ride, you would have been seriously ill already, I was just curious."

Reynolds and Alvarez looked all fidgety.

My next question was for the soldier. "Captain, how is it you've kept the infected outside the base?"

The captain used his hand to indicate we were to get in a Humvee. "Let's get you debriefed."

I couldn't help but notice a few of the soldiers boarding our plane as we got in the vehicle.

Photographs of a little girl and a little boy playing with a spotted dog sat on the Colonel's desk immediately next to a commemorative Super Bowl XLVI Giants statue. Terrific. An effing Giants fan. I got zombies, Runners, redneck dickweeds, ancient planes, a three-letter-organization spook douche, and now the guy in charge is a Giants fan. I HATE the damn Giants. Tom effing Coughlin can suck it, and the only thing worse than a Giant, is a Giants fan.

Ship, Kat, and I were sitting in a semi-circle around the aforementioned desk, Kat having just taken five solid minutes to pee. Alvarez and Reynolds were curiously absent.

Colonel Jessup, commander of this base, wasn't even Air Force. He was regular Army. He told us that the base had accepted any elements of the military and had promoted him to officer in charge immediately upon his arrival. The Air Force Major General in charge of Keesler, along with his entire leadership staff, were dead. One of the general's staff had been bitten early on, had turned, and infected the others. When Jessup had pulled in at the head of a big convoy, the base gates had opened and he had all new worries. Now he was in charge of over three thousand troops and just as many civilian refugees from the surrounding area.

Although well-armed now, this base was only a training base, and as such had been full of trainees when the plague started. Now every single one of those Air Force trainees was a battle-hardened, ground-pounding veteran. Or they were dead.

The Colonel had given up plenty of information, but still hadn't asked a question when he noticed I was looking at his Giants knick-knack. "I was at that game. Twenty-one to seventeen, good guys." He smiled and leaned back in his chair.

I couldn't help myself, I just couldn't. Smug New York assholes had been rubbing this in us New Englanders faces since it happened. The look of smugness on this guy's face was irrefutable, and I don't give a rat's flea bitten ass what he was commander of, he wasn't getting away with it. "That game proved that it's possible to win but be second best."

Immediate evaporation of smirk. "A New England fan." Not a question.

He did smile after a second, but it was all business after that. Where did we come from, how did we get away, what gear did we have, what kind of horrible was it up north? Then the kicker: had we seen anything weird or different.

I guess I had had enough of the same old God damned questions, "Weird or different? Yeah, Colonel, there are dead people walking around trying to eat us."

He smiled again, but it never touched his eyes and was as fake as the tits on a porn star. "I can see you're tired. Perhaps we can take this up again after you've had some rest."

He stood, we didn't.

"Actually, Colonel, we have some questions."

Jessup sat back down and steepled his fingers. "Shoot."

"We can't, you took our damn guns, which is the first question; when do we get our gear back?"

"Sir, you can understand why I can't have you armed inside a military base. It's protocol."

Ship harrumphed. Big bastard actually harrumphed, and the babies who looked like guards in the room shifted nervously. "With all due respect, Colonel, (I can't even fucking begin to tell you how cool that sounds when you say it to an actual Colonel), your protocol is ridiculous. It's obvious to you by now that we are capable. For Christ's sake, we're *alive*. That should be reason enough to let us keep our guns."

He leaned forward, which I would have thought was impossible given his initial position. "And how do I know you're not a group of terrorists? How do I know you aren't going to take your weapons and blow a hole in my fence, or kill some of my men?"

Shit. I didn't think of that, and although it REALLY pains me to write it here, the man gained a small measure of respect when he said that. Still a dick though: Giants fan.

I nodded. "Fair enough. OK, so how have you managed to keep the infected out? Everywhere else I've seen or been to or heard about has fallen, military bases included."

"Quite frankly, we haven't kept them out. There have been repeated attacks on the fences, and dozens of my men have been killed both inside and outside the fence. Every now and then some infected get in regardless of how much we patrol. Your real question is why haven't they overrun us? The answer to that is that they aren't done with the city yet. As soon as they are, we estimate they will be on the way in force."

"And then what?" demanded Kat.

"Then you get your guns back, and we fight them off or die. I have fifteen hundred acres of base, encircled by chain-link fence. It's not even electrified. Before the plague, there were almost thirty thousand people on this base, but only about five thousand active military." He leaned back, "Jesus, most of them were Air Force retirees and family members. Some contractors and civilian staff, but few real fighters. Now there are about six thousand people here, and of those probably only twelve hundred battle-ready men and women." He looked up. "That includes me. And you if you're not terrorists, or undead sympathizers."

"So basically you're lined up to be a smorgasbord? Why don't you get the F... uh, the hell out of Dodge?"

"So I'm supposed to evacuate six thousand people? To where? Where are we going to go? There's no place left to retreat to, it's all gone. No. No, we fortify and remain here or we die."

I just realized how tired Jessup looked and I felt like a total dick. Don't get me wrong, he's still a Giants fan, but I could have been a little more empathetic to what he was dealing with.

I stood, and so did he. Bastard actually came around the desk and extended his hand to Kat, who shook it, and so did Ship and I. Did I like this guy? Shit.

"If you have any other questions, please ask one of my staff, and if you absolutely need to speak to me, I will do my best to comply, but please understand it might be a couple of days."

"One more question, Colonel?" He looked at me expectantly. "Where are Reynolds and Alvarez?"

He had no clue who I meant and looked to one of the guard-kids. "Regular Army that came in with them, sir, a First Sergeant and a PFC."

"Ah. They will have been re-assigned by now. Captain Gregg would have put you three in the civilian barracks, but the First Sergeant and the Private will hot-bunk with whomever they can. I will see to it that you get a copy of their schedules so you can visit them off hours. Also, everyone here contributes, so you will be given duties as well and can volunteer for certain things should you like."

We said our thanks and left with one of the escorts. Actually, I could really use an escort right about now... Brunette, five-foot six, one-fifteen, sweet rack. You get the picture, but I digress.

It would be almost ten days at Keesler before bad things happened. Ten days of relative peace, with no running. The constant reminder of our adversary as it clawed at the fences was unnerving, but it was the first long stretch of time where I wasn't absolutely terrified.

When the shit hit, it wasn't the dead that started it, but they sure as shit finished it.

TEXAS HOLD 'EM

Ship got sent to help the engineers. Kat got sent to the kitchens. I got sent to the southern Wall. The Wall was actually a wicked long, eight foot chain-link fence that encircled the entire facility. I'm sure you can see where this is going, and I was more than adamant that the colonel hear my gripes that this very type of barrier is the reason a whole bunch of people were converted to the enemy back in Tennessee.

They laughed at me. Fuckers laughed. They said everybody was aware that this was just a fence, but what could they do? I was all, "Hey, why don't you reinforce it with something?" And they were like, "Dude, with what?" Sorry about the teen-speak right there, but I've been spending a lot of time with Kat lately. She's a good kid, and more like my baby sister than my daughter if that makes any sense.

So my patrol on the southern Wall (that's the last time I capitalize wall, it was in my written orders like that). My patrol was nothing short of excruciating. Me and five other guys walking for twelve hours and looking at marshland through the holes of a chain fence. Three soldiers and two civvies. Alvarez was one of the soldiers, and when we broke for lunch, we played cards. We would rotate a guy in and out every few hands and always keep an eye out for pus bags, of which there were few. We had to radio check in every twenty minutes.

Sometimes our lunches lasted a tad more than an hour, but hardly anybody came to check up on us ever. The stray Hummer would drive by and ask how we were doing and maybe drop off a case of water, and did we see anything, did we need an MRE or ammo.

Oh yeah, they gave me my guns back, but only while I was on patrol. That was cool of the colonel. (Still a Giants fan.)

You know I never considered myself a card player. I knew how to play, but believe it or not cards are frowned upon in the joint. You take a guy for ten cigarettes, or worse, lose and don't have them, and you get shanked. I didn't want to get killed for cigarettes, even if they are just like cash inside. I don't even smoke. Anyway, I may not have been the best card player, but these guys I was with absolutely sucked. I'm talking bad. Initially we had nothing to play for, so we just played for fun. Then it was little pebbles and bottle caps. One of the Hummers drove by one day and a corporal got out and handed us a bag. There was almost three hundred thousand in cash in the bag. They had rescued some folks from a bank, and the cash was just sitting there. It was just paper now. I won that entire three hundred grand in less than two hours of play time.

A little aside: no matter how rich anybody ever got, I guarantee nobody ever really wiped their ass with hundreds more than once. Guaran-damn-tee. If you're ever desperate, and trapped in bank or something, I'm telling you, don't. Just don't.

The bets graduated to bunk time, or best bunk, or who would have to stand watch while the other guys played. Cigarettes, booze, and other contraband. Then it turned to food. Desserts out of the MRE. Coffee out of the MRE. The whole MRE. You get the idea. Problem is, you can't win everybody's food for three weeks. It doesn't work that way.

So I mentioned before that there were two civilians. Me and this guy North. Initially I liked the guy, I really did, but he began to get kind of pricky. You know, a real prick. He would say stupid shit, like calling Alvarez a job-stealing wetback, or telling me my M4 was slung wrong, and proceeding to put his hands on me to correct it. I'm not crazy about being touched.

Anyway, we're playing cards while one of the soldiers, Cartier (not Carter, it was pronounced Car-tee-ay, like the jewelers, but no relation.), is watching for rotters. Alvarez and I are getting smoked by North, who usually sucks as bad as Alvarez. North already has all the desserts for three days and four whole MRE's, and the other soldiers, Westbrook and Eastham, (no shit) are getting restless. I could see it going down, this arrogant prick was going to get lynched by his own group, but he was clueless. You just don't fuck with a man's life, and food was life. He didn't see it or didn't care. Being me, I decided that enough was enough, and went all in with my three hundred grand to shut this little fucker (actually he was fat as shit) up.

"Nope," he says to me.

"Nope?"

"Nope. That shit is worthless, I wouldn't even use it for toilet paper." Stinger right there. Little did he know, I had already tried the hundred dollar TP thing, and I wholeheartedly agreed with his assessment.

"Fine then, what do you want?"

He looks me dead in the eyes and says, "Cat."

I honestly had no idea what he meant, but Alvarez flipped the safety off of his weapon and it got real. I stood up looking for rotters, still unaware of what was transpiring less than two feet away. When I saw nothing of interest, my attention focused back on North. "What the hell are you talking about? What Cat?"

Alvarez stood too, his rifle pointed toward the ground. "He means Kat."

I know this doesn't make any sense, but when Alvarez said her name I knew immediately what this fat asshole was saying.

"Yeah," he began, "that hot little number you've been banging. You got no right keeping that all to yourself. I want a taste, and all you have to do is win this bet and I'll go to bed alone."

The other two directions, East and West, stood as well. The only one sitting was North, and he could fucking stay there.

"Firstly, douche, Kat is my friend. That's it you sick fuck, she's like my kid sister." He harrumphed and I continued, "That having been said, if you ever even look at her, shit if you even mention her name again, Christ himself won't be able to keep me from ripping off your head and shitting down your neck."

He stood and folded his arms. Then he got all snide and superior. "Well how about I tell Jessup about our little card—"

He didn't get to finish because I kicked him in the balls. He doubled over and put a hand on the ground gasping.

"Tell him whatever you want, you fucking pedophile, what I said still stands. Go anywhere near her and I will fucking kill you. I'll sleep great after too, you fat fuck." I pushed him on his ass, kicked the bets and cards all over the place, and spun around to join Cartier on watch. Alvarez walked away with me.

"What the fuck was that abou..." began Cartier, and his eyes grew wide.

Aww shit.

I tried to spin around to face North, and I got all the way around before I heard two shots. One was North shooting at me, and the other was West, shooting him at point blank range with his Beretta. North's bullet sailed right past my head, it sounded like a bee. West's bullet hit North in the side, right below his armpit, and in less than one minute of choking and gurgling, we were down to two directions.

West kicked the .38 revolver away from North's corpse, then shot the dead man between the eyes. "Sick bastard was gonna kill you dude."

"Thanks."

"All good." West ejected the magazine and jacked the slide on his Beretta, ejecting a single bullet, which he caught in mid-air. He passed the weapon and his M4 over to East.

None of us knew what to do.

"Call it in," said West and he sat down.

Three Hummers showed up in five minutes. Twelve soldiers, Jessup included, leapt from the vehicles and approached us. The colonel, his sidearm in his hand, looked at Alvarez. "Report!"

Alvarez showed no signs of fear when he told the colonel exactly what happened. Afterward, the colonel turned around, removed his cover, and ran his fingers through the stubble on his head. "Fuck!"

West stood. "Sir, I take full responsibility, I shot…"

"Save it, Corporal," Jessup told him. "Tell it to the court martial. Round them all up and bring them to the stockade."

They took my guns again and I was going to the stockade.

Prison. Armageddon was here and I was going to prison. At least something was going to be familiar.

FIVE STAR ACCOMMODATIONS

So they separated us. They wanted to corroborate our stories, and didn't want us in contact with each other until the trial was over. I was grilled for about six hours at different times, maybe two hours at most at once. Just like Boston PD, they kept trying me to get to change my story, but you can't change the truth. Well, I guess that's bullshit, all you gotta do is lie, but I didn't. I wouldn't, because as the age old adage tells us: The Truth Will Set You Free.

Yeah, that's a load of bullshit too.

My exceptionally un-free ass was lounging on a cot in a cell when Kat and Ship showed up. The MPs and a county sheriff wouldn't let them in my cell, but they brought my buddies chairs to sit on so we could talk through the bars. The cops watched Kat and Ship like hawks though. No files in birthday cakes.

"We heard what happened," Kat told me and looked at her shoes. "I'm sorry?"

"You're sorry? Why are you sorry?"

"Cuz it was my fault."

"So a fat, sick bastard wants to have his way with my kid sister but it's her fault. Huh. Didn't take you for a dumbass, Kat."

She smiled and cried at the same time, "Kid sister, huh?" She wiped her eyes.

"Yeah, never had one before. I kinda like it."

Ship passed a note to one of my jailors, who read it before giving it back to Ship to give to me.

So now you make little girls cry. Well done.

I got pissed and looked at him, but Shrek had a grin on his face like he had had shit for breakfast. He was joking. A new thing for both of us, and that was worth the prison time.

"Yeah," I said, "kids and would-be rapists."

Kat looked up confused. "Alvarez said you didn't shoot him."

"I didn't. I just thought that his balls needed a little adjustment, and my foot acted of its own accord." I shrugged. "It happens. I stood to walk away and the bastard drew and fired on me, trying to shoot me in the back. Westbrook shot him. I'm both happy and sad, because I wish I was the one who blasted that prick, but at the same time I'm glad his fat fingers jerked the trigger and the shot went wide."

One of the MPs snorted. "I wish I could have shot him too."

"Me too," said the sheriff from out in the hall.

Everybody knew what was going on, and if that was the case, what the hell was I doing on this side of the bars?

"Wait... *Alvarez* said? You went to see him before me?" I was a little hurt. Still manly as all Hell, but hurt.

"No, he came to find us. He told us what happened."

"Wait... What? Alvarez is out?"

Kat looked at me weird. "Out of what?"

"Jail! Prison! He was set free? What the Hell am I doing in here then?"

Before she could answer, or Ship could write something disapproving, a little soldier showed up and passed a piece of paper to the big guard, who looked at it and produced a key, "Looks like you're out too." Kat and the Sasquatch moved over so the guard could let me out, and out he let me.

I stood tall as a free man, and Kat did the strangest thing, she jumped into my arms and hugged the shit out of me. Ship put his massive mitt on my shoulder and nodded in what looked like relief. That was weird too.

"We heard they might execute you guys," Kat said, "we were scared."

"You were, huh? Both of you?" I craned my neck to look up at the Yeti. Stinkeye, but it was half-hearted, and I shook it off.

I felt great.

So of course that was when the base alarms began to sound.

NIGHT OF THE LIVING DEAD

The group of us in the stockade all looked at each other. The sound was interior and low, as Jessup didn't want the sound of giant, building mounted alarm klaxons screaming our location to all the damn zombies in Mississippi. As it turns out, the entire dead population of Biloxi was en route to our position with or without super loud WAH-WAH-WAH sounds.

Apparently, every person that could hold a weapon and didn't have other orders was ordered to report to the walls, which as we all remember were fences anyway. My guns were handed back to me, and I raced with Ship, Kat, and the sheriff to our bunks. We found Alvarez and Cartier getting in a Hummer, and told him to wait for us while we got our shit. We were about a half mile from the nearest fence.

We got our stuff and the Hummer was still waiting, so we jumped in, the sheriff running off to find someone. We raced to the eastern wall, which was close to the main gate, and joined a whole bunch of other scared people. Some guy I had never seen before was quietly dishing out orders and told us to pick a spot and wait. He tried to send Kat back to be an ammo runner and I told him that not only was she a better shot than anybody else out here, but if he tried to make her move an inch from us Ship would eat him. He took one look at my towering buddy, nodded, and made a hasty escape to dish out more orders.

Then we waited.

Word got around that some satellite imagery had shown a sizeable force of infected on the way to our position, and that had been confirmed via helicopter. The pus bags were en route.

Quiet settled in and everybody hunkered down behind sandbag emplacements that had been put up for just such an occasion. There was one of those LAVs about fifty or so feet from us, and two of the Army Bradleys which I thought were tanks, but EVERYBODY told me they were fighting vehicles, *not* tanks. Hey, if it looks like a tank, and acts like a tank, it's a fucking tank.

The vehicles weren't running, but each had a bunch of people surrounding them and tending to stuff, and the LAV had an open hatch with a guy sticking out of it. The front gate, which had a bunch of trucks jamming the opening, was about a hundred yards to the left.

Two helicopters flew over us, and moved to the east. Maybe fifteen seconds later, they unleashed hell on the ground. Big explosions lifted into the air maybe a mile out in mushroom fire clouds, and those tracer bullet thingies spit from the sky into what I can only assume was a crowd of dead folks. Watching it was sublime. We couldn't see the helicopters, but we could see the rockets and bullets and shit they were shooting. It looked like the ordnance was just materializing and heading down. Had the approaching force been alive, it wouldn't have been for long.

The choppers flew back past us toward the base, probably out of ammo. A plane of some kind zoomed low over us, and a bunch of people pointed and said *warthog*, or just *hog*. I learned later what that meant, but I didn't know at the time it was an A10 Thunderbolt. A mean-ass fucking aircraft designed to wreck tanks and other ground forces. The plane made a few passes, and this time the booms and explosions were way bigger, and we could actually feel the ground shake. What sounded like a giant zipper being zipped up came from the plane's front gun on each pass too. It was beautiful, and when the craft flew back over us, we all cheered.

It was dark, but a full moon gave off tons of light so we weren't blind. Fires in front of us from the bombs and rockets illuminated shadows moving in our direction, but they were still far off. Of course everybody was scared shitless and I thought I could smell the fear. Turns out it wasn't the fear I smelled, it was the dead.

The stench became palpable. It had been weak, but it didn't build gradually, it hit us like a wall. Four out of every ten people (not me) began to retch. Nothing came into view though, at least not for us. A single shot erupted from the tower closest to us, then one of the sniper spotters in the makeshift turret came over the comm net. "Contact front!" Spotters in the other towers began echoing the contact and the snipers engaged.

"Here they come!" screamed a woman in the tower closest to us. Somebody fired a flare and then three more, and then the sky was full of them, floating down to the ground. Everyone grew silent as the flares showed us what was coming. The quiet chatter ceased even if the snipers kept up their firing. The first flare drifted down into the midst of the oncoming swarm and lit them up like the proverbial Christmas tree. It didn't feel like Christmas.

Thousands, tens of thousands of zombies were just outside the fences.

They had been quiet all the way up to us, but apparently the flares or the moon showed us to them as well as them to us, and they began that mournful moan, full of need and iniquity. As I've said before, you can't describe it, you need to hear it for yourself. And we did. We all heard it, and we all knew we were going to die.

I looked at Kat and Ship. "Do either of you have any cookies?"

Kat looked at me, terrified, but the big guy dug into his vest and pulled out one of those little packages of three cookies, the chocolate chip ones with the yellow stripe on it. As he was opening the pack with his knife, gunfire erupted from the front gate area, and then it was chaos.

Some kind of heavy machine gun opened up from one of the towers, and then from another and another. People near us began to shoot, and the soldiers started screaming for them to hold their fire. I thought the soldiers were crazy, but with everybody shooting through the fence, eventually the rounds would tear it open.

I heard FOOM! FOOM! and about another fifty FOOMs, and shit on the other side of the fence, maybe a hundred yards out started blowing up. *Mortars* somebody yelled.

Some kind of officer was standing on bunch of stacked pallets and he was yelling over the moans, "Hold your fire! The mortars and heavy guns will take care of them! Hold your fire or you'll take the fence down!" He was talking to the civilians and mixed military that were with us.

A huge boom sounded off to the left, and fire spewed from some kind of armored vehicle. The dead were swarming the gate.

They had also reached our section of fence, and still that guy on the pallet was screaming for us to hold our fire. The zombies at the front of the horde reached their fingers through the chain link, and many tried to bite it, breaking their teeth, but that didn't last. All their buddies behind them were pushing, and the combined weight turned the vanguard into something resembling strawberry jam. Hundreds of faces and arms were diced into little cubes as their rotten flesh was pushed through the links. The fence, which had already been reinforced, buckled and collapsed in a half mile section almost immediately.

The Bradleys and the LAV raced forward, firing their guns. Body parts and goo flew into the air, and long swaths of infected simply ceased to exist as the guns turned them into a disgusting spray.

The douche on the pallets now screamed at us to fire at will.

And we did. We shot the fuck out of those pus bags, for all the good it did. We fired and fired. I had my M4, Kat had her hunting rifle, and Ship had his HK417. Several thousand other humans threw lead down range with anything that would throw it. My .223 put holes in heads, and I'm happy to say I got my fair share to drop. Ship's big .308 rounds disintegrated heads with a splash. There was nothing left from the upper lip up. A guy in a red Mississippi State ball cap with a bulldog on it ran over to me and handed me several magazines for my M4 and then moved on down the line. Kat ran out of ammo for her rifle, and I noticed that others were calling for ammo too. People were running back and forth distributing magazines, then it turned to ammo cans, and eventually handfuls of rounds. When it got to the cans, the dead surged forward as people reloaded their magazines. Several people picked up mags from the dirt and refilled them. These were the folks whose weapons jammed first.

I heard a guy say "Fuck this," and he chucked something into the dead ranks about a hundred feet away. It blew, and it took out several pus bags, but in the grand scheme it was useless. The LAV and one of the Bradleys ran out of ammo, and they began running into the walls of dead that were approaching. The other Bradley turned on its tracks and zoomed off back toward the base.

It was so incredibly loud with the weapons fire and the moans and the roaring in my ears, that I either didn't hear the screams, or didn't process what they were right away. Ship did. He grabbed me by the shoulder and I looked up at him. Way up. He spun me like a little girl would spin a doll (an exceptionally manly doll, with cut abs), and I could see that while we were dealing with our little portion of fence, the gate section had been totally overrun.

The dead had moved into our ranks from the left flank and were beginning to snack on the unfortunates that hadn't moved with adequate speed. A wall of rot was coming at us from two directions, and that was enough for most of the defenders. In a nanosecond, ninety percent of the living humans, both military and civilian, turned and headed for the hills. Except we were in Mississippi, and there wasn't a God damned hill to be had. It was a slaughter. We couldn't move out fast enough. The guy on the pallets was screaming for us to hold the line, but there was no line to hold. He went down screaming, firing his pistol as his rifle ammo had been expended.

The ammo runners tried to supply us, but they ran into our retreat and then the dead that were hot on our heels, when the runners wouldn't listen to us about what was behind.

I was holding Kat's hand as I didn't want to get separated in the bedlam. You can basically see the Shipster from space, so all I had to do was turn my head to find him. The three of us got to our Hummer and Cartier got there too, but the crowd tore him apart to get the truck. Not the dead, the living. They literally broke him into pieces as they trampled and kicked him when they threw him to the ground. There was so much fighting for the vehicle that it never got the chance to move before the swarm of dead got to it. Most of the dickheads that killed Cartier followed suit quickly. I hope it hurt.

The survivors fanned out and ran to wherever they thought they might be safe. I saw a helicopter take off, then another, then another. Planes were taking off from multiple runways too, until two of them collided and a huge fireball leapt into the sky. I guess nobody was manning the towers to tell them they were going to crash.

We got to the barracks and it was bedlam. Just like the last fenced-in place we were at where zombies invaded, people were tear-assing around, gathering ridiculous items, kids, old folks, and supplies. Several fights broke out, and by the time the three of us had our shit and were out the door, gunshots were coming from inside behind us.

We ran into Alvarez, and he didn't seem to have anything better to do than come with us. He also had a ton of .223 ammo and an extra M4, which he passed to Kat. We ran toward the motor pool, as Ship's plane was in the hangar, and the hangar was on fire.

I saw my first zombie since the fence, and it was pretty gruesome. It was beating the shit out of a very dead man in woodland fatigues on the ground, biting and punching, and you guessed it: it was a Runner. He heard us try to run by and decided that the dead guy wasn't any more fun and gave chase. We ran, but before we turned the corner around a row of housing, I dared glance back to see our pursuer; it was the guy who had given me ammo a couple hours before. He still had his ball cap on.

"Wait," I hissed. The Runner came around the corner too fast and slid a little further than he wanted to going on his ass. I used the time he was taking to right himself, and fire a round into his side. He clutched at it, but when he looked at me I could tell he was more pissed than hurt. It certainly wasn't my intent to anger him, so I shot him in the face as he tried to stand.

Kid was like, twenty two.

Darkness would only be around for another hour or so, and we really liked the cover. We saw several zombies on the way to the motor pool, and when we got there, there were three vehicles left. Two Hummers and a big troop truck. Deuce and a half I believe, the kind with that canvas cover in the back, except this didn't have one, just the little frame for it. One of the Hummers was on blocks, and the other was claimed as the woman who was getting her kids into it pointed a rifle at us when we approached. Apparently, she didn't want to share the ride. Kat and I put our hands up in submission, but Alvarez and Ship wouldn't do it. She aimed at Ship and Alvarez told her she could only get off one shot and she would be dead.

That seemed to fuel her and she tossed her rifle into the vehicle and got in. She sped off, her kids crying. She banged a left, and headed directly toward the front gate and ten thousand dead cannibals. We didn't even have time to tell her before she was gone. I hope they made it.

"We've got to find Reynolds," Alvarez said, and two dead folks sauntered into the vehicle bay. He drilled both of them, and the noise reverberated through the garage resoundingly.

"I like the sarge too," I said, "But how the hell are we going to find him?"

Ship looked about for something, then walked to a small room and kicked open a big door like it was made out of hay, a bullet whizzing past his head fired from within. With a melon the size of a wide screen TV, I have no idea how the person in that room missed him.

Someone screamed in a scared voice, "Say something or I'll fucking shoot you!"

Oh shit.

I don't know, dear reader, if you've picked up on this during your enthralling read of this riveting account of the apocalypse, but Ship can't talk. He can't say anything. At all. Bupkis, nada, niente. Silent as the grave as one might ironically mention.

The person on the other side of the door, the one with the weapon, was not privy to the aforementioned information, and as such was expecting a live person to say something such as *Don't shoot*, or *I'm human*, but no such statements would, or could be issued.

Consequently, in the following nanosecond, even with all or our shouting, the person behind the door shot Ship in the chest. Now we all know that the big guy is just that; big. The shooter couldn't have missed, it wasn't possible. Ship took two rounds in the chest and staggered backwards. This alone would have surprised the average person about six months ago, but today it was commonplace to shoot someone center mass, and not have it affect them in the negative. It was quite obvious to the shooter that my buddy was, in fact, dead and looking for chow.

Ship fell to one knee, and for a second I thought he was done for, then I remembered his body armor.

"He's human," screamed Kat, which probably saved us a Sasquatch.

"Who is it? Who's out there?"

"We're looking for keys to the truck," Alvarez shouted. "I'm coming to check on my friend."

Ship was sitting up and that scared the shit out of Alvarez, who stopped mid stride and raised his rifle, business end toward my colossal comrade.

Jesus, this was fucked up.

Somebody else was *not* going to shoot the Shipster, so I screamed at Alvarez, "Body armor!"

Alvarez lowered his M4 slightly and turned around to face me. His eyes went wild, and suddenly I was looking down the barrel of his rifle. He fired twice, and I heard a thump behind me. An exceptionally torn former human had hit the ground. Sneaky fucker had almost gotten a taste.

"What's that? Who's shooting?" came the voice from the small room.

"We're coming in to get the keys to this truck! There's ten of us and we will kill you if you try to stop us!"

Ship stood and put his hands on his chest, shaking his head.

Alvarez and Ship moved into the room and came out with the keys and an old timer.

"I'm... I'm sorry, I thought you were one of—"

"Forget it," I yelled, "we have bigger problems!" I pointed toward the door

A small crowd of infected had found the motor pool and consequently, dinner. Alvarez leapt forward and up into the truck, which thankfully started immediately. Ship helped the older gentleman into the back, and Kat got into the cab with Alvarez.

I had formed a firing line of one and was dispatching the dead as they stumbled toward me. You know I've got to tell you, a month ago I hadn't really shot any guns. I mean here and there for fun, but never *at* anyone. Living or unliving. I just plinked with buddies or my dad when I was a kid. Two weeks ago, I was shooting at the dead for the first time, and a couple days after that I shot my first live human. Aiming the weapon isn't difficult, but hitting what you're aiming at can be frustrating. Two weeks ago I couldn't hit shit. That night I couldn't fucking miss. In addition, I wasn't the least bit frightened. The infected kept coming and I kept shooting, single shots to the dome each time. Thirty shots, probably thirty kills. I went through the first magazine (they would never be clips again) and performed the tactical magazine (see?) switch that I had been taught in the last few weeks. I felt like a total badass and even began to smile.

Alvarez brought me back to reality when he pulled up next to me and screamed at me to get in. I looked at him, then glanced briefly at the oncoming horde materializing through the smoke outside. Not a small crowd anymore, and then I found out where the fear was stored. My terror storage facility sprung a leak that would make a superfund site jealous. I ran to the back of the truck and Ship helped me in. Alvarez didn't wait and he floored it, crunching the already destroyed and thumping into a dozen or so walkers.

Ship, the old guy, and me slid to the back of the truck and for the briefest of moments I teetered on the edge. Ship grabbed me and I looked behind. There had to be a hundred of them right on top of us, all reaching and hungry. Had I fallen out I doubt I would have had time to scream.

We looked out into the base as we drove. I don't know how the dead bring fire, but they always do. Buildings, vehicles, and even some people were ablaze. Black plumes (it was dark, but it was a greasy smoke) billowed from the control tower. The smoke was thick and choking, and the moans of the dead were grating on my nerves. The old fella had his arm wrapped around one of the canvas frame thingies, but also had his ears covered with his hands and his eyes clamped firmly shut. Everywhere we looked several dead were kneeling and devouring someone.

The truck slid to a stop and began backing up. It whipped to the right, and I saw what Alvarez had seen. A massive swarm of zombies was coming from what had been in front of us. The truck did a three point turn (actually it was like a point and a half) and we booked it out of there to the south. We could hear the thumps as the truck took out stray infected and they seemed to close in behind us as we passed.

A series of huge explosions lit up the night sky behind us and I could see that one of the Bradleys was engaging infected, running them over and firing into the crowds. A camo Chevy pickup truck pulled up alongside us, a man in the back battling two infected that had gotten in with him. The truck veered into us with a screech, then pulled away, its driver side door crumpled a little. The man and one of the infected went over the side, bouncing down the road like ragdolls, but the truck didn't even slow.

Three minutes later, we reached the housing section of the base, and it was chaos as well. The dead hadn't reached here yet, but dozens of folks were throwing supplies into vehicles and bugging out. Most headed south and we tagged along. We heard shots as we drove through. Hopefully people were shooting zombies and not each other.

A few streets down and Alvarez slammed on the brakes and got out, running toward one of the on-base housing units. I screamed at him, but he kept running and didn't look back. I jumped off the side of the truck and stepped up on the passenger's runner. Kat gave a little scream before she realized it was me.

"What the fuck is he doing?" I demanded.

"He's getting Reynolds! He said he wouldn't be more than a couple minutes!"

Reynolds got his own damn house and I had to hot bunk with a gaggle of pigs. Yes, I know a gaggle refers to geese, and a group of pigs is a drove or a herd, but fuck you this is my story. Regardless, it's amazing what you think of in intense pressure situations, and I remember being the slightest bit jealous of the sarge's accommodations.

Shots were ringing out steadily around us now. Screams too.

"We'll be dead in a couple minutes!" I ran back and told Ship what was happening, then moved back to the driver's side and jumped up into the cab shutting the door.

Kat was instantly on the defensive. "What are you doing?"

Huh. Guess my new kid sister had a thing for the army guy.

"I'm not leaving without him if that's what you're asking, but I don't want to be sitting in the back of the truck with no driver if things go bad."

Three figures ran across the street between houses about fifty yards away. I realized that I could see them and that the sun would be up shortly. The darkness was being chased away by dawn, and if I could see them, then zombies could see us.

Fuck.

A group of survivors was heading toward us down one of the side streets. They were moving slow but steady. A few of them broke off and moved to one of the houses, but the majority of them came at us. If they tried to take our truck, there would be a gun battle. As it was there were too many for us to give them all a ride.

I beeped the horn, long and loud. Alvarez was nowhere to be seen.

Double fuck.

A woman came running from one of the houses. She ran up to the group of people that were advancing on us and stopped dead. She screamed and ran back toward our truck. She ran right past us and kept on going, my head following her as she ran past Reynolds exceptionally nice residence. That's when Kat screamed.

A dead thing had climbed up on the runner and smacked its hand against the window. Not only that, but the crowd of survivors had not, in fact, survived. They were dead and they were pissed and they were a hundred yards away.

Suddenly, the zombie trying to eat Kat through the glass was gone. In two seconds, Ship's gigantic mug was staring through the glass, his eyebrows raised expectantly. I raised my palms up in a helpless gesture.

Several other staggering forms were making their way toward us. It was time to go.

"Alvarez! We are leaving right fucking now!"

He came out of the house carrying a rucksack, with two other people, neither of which was the Sarge. He threw the sack in the back, and his buddies climbed in, as did Ship. Alvarez got in on the driver's side and I pushed over.

"Reynolds is dead," was all he said before he threw the big stick shift into first. He let his feet off the clutch and brake, and six of the ten wheels on that truck screeched as we rocketed forward. This truck was in good shape. Gunfire erupted from the rear of the truck and we achieved forty miles per hour in a fifteen mph zone.

"One more stop," the army kid said.

I looked at him like he was crazy, which seemed to me to be the case, and we moved on. He pulled up in front of an identical housing unit as the last one and he jumped out again. One of his buddies followed him, and this time so did I. To the curb, and that was far enough. I stood there, pants-shitting fear clenching my scrotum with gnarled hands, my weapon to my shoulder and tracking.

It was quicker this time, and they came back with another guy, but the dead had found us faster too. Alvarez's other pal shot three of them, and Ship used his machete on the fingers of one who tried to climb up the side of the Deuce. This was getting bad fast. The dead had arrived in force, and they wanted us.

Two more bags got thrown in the back, and I climbed in the back too. Alvarez was about to follow his new buddy into the cab when a bloody hand snaked out from under the truck and grabbed his ankle. He let out a yell, but pulled away and climbed up. We drove off south, five in the back, three in the front, but we had two most unwelcome hitchhikers.

One of them was a putrid, green, very dead, bloated woman with half a face. She growled at me and I kicked the good side of her profile with my boot. The rest of her rotten face scraped away, and I almost went with her when she fell. She slid down the road behind us flopping, grinding her decayed flesh off, and she literally popped with a gooey splash.

The other thing managed to pull itself almost into the truck before one of Alvarez's newbies gave it one, two, three rifle butts. It too fell and tumbled over and over until it came to a stop, motionless.

The five of us in the back of the truck looked at the base as we drove to the southern fence. The old guy was crying. We reached the southern fence and it was down, but there were no infected in sight. Alvarez took a right and we headed off west. We all reloaded our magazines.

I don't know how many rounds were expended that night, maybe a few million, but ultimately it didn't do shit and Keesler, just like every place else we'd been, fell to the dead.

DON OF THE DEAD

They're all dead. Ship, Kat, Alvarez, all the people we picked up at Keesler, all dead and they want me, I can hear them banging at the door in the darkness. The sarge, Ernie, tons of rednecks, Jessup, the old man, Cartier, everybody from my cell block. Even Lynch. I turn around and that damn dead spook is in the room with me. He reaches his rotting hands toward me, smiling, as the door gives way. "Come with us, it's soooo easy…"

"Wake the fuck up," the old timer said and gave me a shove.

Jesus, that damn dream still gives me nightmares. Yes, you can have nightmares of a nightmare, I'm living proof. I remember it like it was last night. Probably because I had it again last night. Fucking vivid, and not the porn.

The first time I had that dream was in the back of the Deuce. Ship, the old timer, and a couple of Alvarez's new pals all staring at me as I woke up from my cat nap. I felt like I was fifteen and my mom had caught me rubbing one out.

"You was screamin'," the white-haired guy said.

I muttered a *sorry* and hunkered down, trying to forget about it, but everybody was still staring at me. Like, really staring. Staring *hard*.

"What?"

"You were saying some weird shit," one of the soldiers said.

"Big shocker there, Audie fucking Murphy, there are dead people trying to eat us. I'm sure *your* dreams are full of roses and unicorns."

The guy was taken aback but his buddy moved up the bench toward me. He looked familiar but I couldn't place him. "Who's Lynch?"

Ship and I looked at each other, then I looked back at the guy. "Nobody."

Guy didn't miss a trick, "Didn't sound like nobody."

"Mind your own fucking busine—"

He interrupted me mid pissy-tirade, "I only ask because there was a guy named Lynch being escorted to the stockade when the base got overrun. I escorted him to Colonel Jessup the day before when he showed up at the front gate." That's where I remembered this guy from, he was one of the guards in Jessup's office when we first showed up.

"Coincidence," I said, my turn to not miss a beat, "what did he want at the jail?"

"Above my pay grade, and I wasn't dumb enough to press, but it wasn't a what, it was a who. Don't know who, but I do know a Company man when I see one." He cocked his head. "I just don't know which company."

"Yeah, well, I don't know who he is."

Guy shifted his gaze and became thoughtful. I didn't like thoughtful, but he didn't say anything else.

We had picked up two other vehicles when we left Keesler and they were following us. We hadn't seen anything other than single zombies, or twos and threes on the road since Keesler, and we traveled until about one in the afternoon.

Swamp. Swamp on both sides of the road, but I'll tell you something for nothing: it was damn beautiful. Big white birds were trying to catch fish or frogs or something, and I distinctly remember they didn't look like they had a care in the world.

Of course they didn't. Damn infected comes to eat it and it can just fly away. I must admit a certain amount of jealousy. Wings might look stupid on me, but if they were functional, I could suffer. 'Course then I got thinking about Victoria's Secret models with angel wings and acquired a monumental stiffy. Those models are probably trying to eat each other right now and not in the good way.

Stiffy eliminated.

We got out of the Deuce and stretched. I moved to the two vehicles behind us, another camo Chevy Blazer, and a Humvee. The fifty cal on top of the Hummer was manned and the guy was swiveling his head constantly, checking the swamp. So were two of his friends with their rifles.

I extended my hand to the driver, who had gotten out when he saw me, and he shook it. "Babe."

"You're not *that* cute," I answered.

Guy actually guffawed. Laughed his ass off so hard he was crying. "My name is Brian Abrams, but everybody calls me Babe," he said as he wiped his eyes.

I shook his hand again, I was smiling too. It was the first time I had smiled in a while. It didn't last.

"Contact, hundred meters left!"

Three stumblers were wading through the knee deep water toward us. "Glad you're with us, Babe." I walked back to the Deuce, Ship, Kat,

Alvarez, and his three soldiers were looking at a map. The old timer was picking his nails with a Swiss Army knife and staring at me.

Ship pointed to something on the map and the soldiers nodded in the negative. "No, we have to assume that airfield is overrun, it's too close to this town." He pointed at the map. "But I have another idea."

Everybody looked at him, so did I, and suddenly I really wanted a beer. Not mass-produced fizzy beer, but something heavier, like a Sam Adams, or a Harpoon.

"We've got company," I said and pointed to the waders.

"Yeah, we heard," said Alvarez, "we'll be out of here soon." He looked at the other kid. "What idea?"

"My brother-in-law works on an oil rig in the gulf. I was thinking we go here," he said, pointing to a spot on the coast, "appropriate a boat, and head for one of the rigs."

Best fucking idea I'd heard since this shit started. Genius. Food for months, maybe years, we could fish, and most of those rigs have desalination plants for fresh water. Plus, the best part of them was that they were not in any way connected to the mainland.

Boom.

I clapped the kid on the shoulder. "That's a great idea!"

Ship looked at me. Stink eye.

WTF? It *was* a great idea! I told the yeti as much.

He shook his head and stormed off, and let me tell you, when this motherfucker storms, the earth shakes. That was just about the time the first shot fired from the truck behind us.

Everybody raised their weapons, but Babe yelled over to us that he had taken care of the situation and all was well. Alvarez packed up the map and told us to saddle up. He was going to talk to the folks in the trucks behind us and see if they wanted to come.

We left a few minutes after that. Ship shuffled down the bench and passed me his book.

Oil rig could be a deathtrap. Trapped if something happens to the boat.

"Yeah, but it's away from all this death, and from them." I pointed to a few of the infected kneeling on the road and hoarking down something that had been wearing boots. "I really don't want to be that guy."

Ship harrumphed and wrote something: *Do you really think we will end up any differently? My estimates are that there are probably almost one hundred of them for each one of us.*

I handed the book back to him. "All the more reason to bug the fuck out yeah?"

We were in New Hampshire. This is Mississippi. It took a month to get here. Do you really think nobody else thought of heading out to an oil rig? Are we going to have to fight off the living as well as the dead? And what if we do secure it? Then we will have to fight off whoever else wants to take it from us.

Damn smarty pants. "So what do we do?"

Stick to the plan. Get away from people. As far away as possible.

"Yeah, I get that, but where do we go? Where can we go that isn't cold and has no people?"

The old guy shifted in his seat. He must have had the dirtiest fingernails on earth, because he was still cleaning them. "The desert," he said without looking away from his hands.

"What's your name, young fella?" I asked him.

"Don." He extended his hand to me, then to Ship. "Sorry I shot you, I was scared."

"Bullets bounce off this giant of a man. He's second cousin is a Bigfoot."

The old timer thought that was hilarious, as did the two soldiers that had been eavesdropping on our conversation. Even Ship smiled, as previously stated, a rare occurrence.

I was killing it today.

So it had to go to shit.

You know, sometimes I think that I'm the plague. I realize that there are dead cannibals trying to munch on humanity, but everywhere I go, there's a nice little bastion or enclave of survivors, and then I show up. Within a few days: boom. Everybody is dead and shit is on fire. Am I a beacon for the undead? Do I light up like a Christmas tree for zombies? Is it fate, luck, or does God just fucking hate me?

Whatever.

Anyway, we're driving along and laughing. Heading, against Ship's wishes, to a boat yard or something to steal somebody's toy or a fishing boat or a God damned overturned cooler to get us to an oil rig.

So what happened?

Fucking rednecks.

One moment we're laughing in this post-apocalyptic undead world and the next we're ducking for cover as a hail of bullets comes our way. One of Alvarez's buddies didn't duck fast enough, and he went tumbling out of the truck. I had never learned his name. The rest of us got down behind the truck slats, under the benches, and shit our collective pants.

We couldn't see our attackers, but apparently they were to our right and in front of us. The Deuce stopped, the riders in the cab exiting through the driver's side. The shots coming at us were from hunting rifles I thought, because there was no automatic fire.

Until we shot back.

I crawled down to the back of the truck, and Alvarez's other pal, Mr. Thoughtful, was calmly pulling something from his load bearing vest. It was a mirror. "Go when I tell you. Get to the other side of the truck, and stand behind the tires, not in the middle or they'll shoot out your knees." Guy had said it like he was ordering his morning coffee. Either this dude was crazy, stupid, or an utter badass.

Redneck dickweeds either hadn't seen or didn't care about the Hummer either, and our guys opened up with the .50 cal. It was loud, so I barely heard Thoughtful yell, "Go! Now!"

He leaned over and began firing at the swamp trees, and I went. When I got down behind the truck, I could see that Alvarez, his buddy, and Kat were already shooting as well, they were shooting forward. I moved to the left and splashed into the stinky water.

There were two police cars across the road in front of us. Cops or not, they were shooting at us, so they could suck it. I moved behind a huge mound of earth, I didn't know what that was doing there, and honestly I didn't care, it was keeping the holes out of me.

I propped up on the side of the dirt mount, and I had a perfect view of a guy with a sheriff's hat and a pretty rifle aiming at my friends.

My M4 had this nifty scope thing on it. Ship called it an ACOG, which then I didn't know meant Advanced Combat Optic Gunsight. It's the best part of the weapon, seriously. There are these three upside down chevrons in there used for aiming, and four times magnification was plenty for me to see that the sheriff wannabe had a big zit on his neck. It was like a fucking target, so I solved his acne issue.

I would like to say that I blew his head off, but in reality, he clutched his throat as he was thrown back from the cop car. I moved on and shot the next guy in line. He had a hat on too, but it was some shitty ball cap. The top of that prick's head did come off in a spray of goo, hat and all.

The other rednecks had no idea I was there, so I moved up a little. Picture me, (in all my awesomeness), standing twenty feet to the right of three assholes all of whom are shooting at my buddies. I could have told them to freeze. I could have told them to lower their weapons.

Nope.

What I did was use my left thumb to flip my selector switch to full auto. Then I fucking mowed them down. Honestly, *mowed them down* is the proper terminology, because they all did a little dance, and then fell to the ground. Mowed.

Sporadic shots were coming weakly from the swamp, but the .50 made them stop in seconds.

I moved to the guys I had shot. I kicked their rifles out of reach. Two were still alive, and I plugged the third in the noggin. "P...please," one of them said clutching his middle. Had to have four holes in him and he was gonna die.

I was disgusted. "Please? Fuck you." I raised my rifle and shot his buddy in the face, then turned the live guy over and pulled his pistol. It was chrome and nice looking. He had nice boots too, but they would be too small for my canoes.

I watched the man take his last breath and I was stunned at my own thoughts. I had thought about taking this dead guy's boots. A dead guy that I had made dead. Granted he was trying to make me dead and I won that coin toss. Regardless, it was right then that I knew nothing would ever be the same. I had held out hope that somebody would rescue us and make all the infected and lawlessness go away, but when that guy's breath let out, so did my hope.

Pretty rich for a guy recently out of prison.

I sighed and drew my knife. I figured I would conserve ammo now that the end of the world was here and hope had abandoned me. Or me it, whatevs.

I dropped to one knee, and drove my knife into that shithead's...well, head, and it bounced right the F off. More like slid off so I sliced divot in his forehead. I went for a softer target and put it through his eye.

Shooting had stopped, so I took the sheriff's hat and stuck it up waving it. Alvarez, Kat, and Ship were there in an instant. "Holy shit, you flanked them?"

I guess I had.

"What about the others from the swamp?" I demanded in a dead voice. Both Ship and Kat looked at me.

Alvarez was looking at the bodies. "Drove em off. We were too much for them."

I spit, my disgust mounting. "Idiots."

I walked back to the Deuce. Mr. Thoughtful was leaning against the back of the truck speaking to Babe from the Hummer and two guys from the Chevy.

"We got two," Thoughtful said, "how many did you bag up front?"

It was like he was talking about deer or trout.

"Five."

Thoughtful nodded and reached into the Deuce for the magazine he had left there. Don grabbed his arm and bit in deeply, pulling his head back and with it a sizable portion of Thoughtful's forearm. Thoughtful pulled him out of the truck and Don went on his chest with a crack of ancient bones. The white-haired old timer was still chewing as he tried to stand. One of the Chevy guys kicked his hand out from under him and the thing that was wearing Don fell on its back. It looked at us and we all shot it.

Other than its head being mostly gone, there were no bullet holes. He must have died of natural causes. He was old.

"Fuck," Thoughtful said, "I'm a damn zombie."

The hole in his arm looked exactly like an apple with a big bite out of it. Not much blood, but all white and different looking. Then it started to bleed. Not a lot like you would think, but a slow ooze from the ruptured capillaries that pooled slowly as he held his arm.

The two guys from the Chevy took a step back each, but Babe and I just looked at Thoughtful. We were helpless, and so was he.

He had three army guys with him, buddies, but he looked right at me. "And I was looking forward to fishing too."

TO THE BOATS!

It took almost nine hours for Thoughtful to die. That was the longest I've ever seen anybody hold out, and it was a while ago. In the end it was the same as all the others. He died with all of us, but he was still alone. Horribly sick, terrified, rambling, and alone. Alvarez used Ship's machete to do the deed before Thoughtful could turn. His name had been Mark something, but it died with him. The last coherent thing he said was to me: "Watch your ass, Lynch means business."

Again, it's funny what you remember and what gets lost in your mental files. I can't for the life of me remember what he looked like, but I remember his name. Usually it's the other way around.

Before he died, I had taken over driving the Deuce, which Alvarez had told me was not, in fact, a Deuce, but an LMTV. Dunno what that is so F it, I'm calling it a Deuce. Alvarez was tired and needed to plan. He also wanted to ride in the back with his dying pal. We dodged some infected and killed some others, but finally made it to the outskirts of Miramar Park in southern Biloxi where we stopped to let Mark die. We couldn't take him with us, and we couldn't leave him, so we waited. It was almost dark by the time we moved into the park

There was a small boat yard to the west, but Interstate Ninety was between us and the yard. As you can probably imagine, the Interstates were one of the worst places to be when the plague struck in earnest: Panicked people getting in their vehicles, bound for anyplace but where they were. All of them trying to go at the same time. That turned the highway into two things; a parking lot and a death trap. There was nowhere to run when the infected came.

So that's what we were looking at. A parking lot full of trapped death. The worse issue was that the road still held the occupants of most of those vehicles. I had thought that all the zombies in Mississippi had attacked Keesler, but I was way wrong. Interstate Ninety absolutely *crawled* with the undead. And walked and stumbled and shuffled and insert any word you can find in Roget's for weird type of walk.

Point is, there were shit-loads of the ambulatory departed between us and our destination. Ship looked disgusted and pointed.

"Yeah, yeah, Big Guy, but now we're committed."

He passed me his book: *You ought to be committed!*

We had some inquisitive visitors that must have heard the Deuce, but we dealt with them quietly while we waited for Mark to go. When it was over, Alvarez handed Ship's gigantic machete back to him and dished out the plan. It was simple really, but I smelled a lot of hope coming off of it.

We go over the interstate about two hundred yards to the west. There was a break in the vehicles, a small hundred or so foot stretch of highway without cars, and more importantly, with minimal infected. We run through that stretch of road, dodge the zombies, and run to the boatyard. We could just see the yard through the coming darkness, and there were three boats left: A big blue and white one with nets and shit all over it, a smaller pleasure craft that was undoubtedly someone's toy, and a fifty foot sail boat.

"So which is it," I demanded, "Forrest Gump, Miami Vice, or Captain Bligh?"

Alvarez hunkered down and looked at each of us as he spoke, "The motorboats are going to make noise when we start them, and we may be on the run anyway so I think the sailboat is our best bet." He looked up, "Who knows how to sail?"

Not a single hand lifted.

"So then it's Miami Vice," I demanded.

"That will have an electronic ignition with an anti-theft device," Alvarez said, "and the shrimp boat will fit us better. It's the Gump."

Kat piped up, "After we get across the zombie-infested interstate, through the boat yard, start the boat, and cast off without getting eaten you mean?"

Alvarez smiled and I wanted to punch him in the face. "Yeah, after all that."

We prepared to leave, and I looked at my colossal comrade. "You're the smartest guy alive, you can fly a plane and field strip an M4 blindfolded. You know every computer thing possible. Your name is *Ship* for fuck's sake and you can't sail?" I shook my head in reproach.

He looked at me helplessly and you know what I did?

Yup.

Stink eye. I had to turn away so he couldn't see my shit-eating grin. I smiled so hard my face hurt. Payback's a bitch.

Once again though, there was a lot of *if* emanating from our plan. We really didn't have much else though. The worst *if* was that if there were thirteen of us, how were we going to sneak anywhere? We had bags of shit, weapons and ammo. We needed to be quiet.

We were. We were like thirteen ninjas, and if there was never a book written with that title, then every now-dead writer can suck it. *Thirteen Ninjas* is the best title for a book in the history of books. When I'm done with this spellbinding tome, that shit is next.

We moved like water flowing around rocks; silent and fluid. I should have used some kind of cork to keep my shit in, but we didn't have any. I was pretty damned scared when we got to within fifty feet of the road or so. There were thousands of these things milling about and they were damn close. By some miracle, none of them were where the gap in the vehicles were. Maybe that was the reason; they were searching for any stray morsels still in the cars.

Suddenly Alvarez stood up and stumbled across the road. He had done it like a zombie would walk, all shuffling and shit, with a fucked up gait, and slow. Not a one of the dead things even glanced at him. A small group of us went next, then Ship and Kat.

I was stunned. I know you want me to tell you that I went last and when I did every single zombie on the entire interstate, not just the ones in Mississippi, but the entire, multi-state length of the road looked at me and chased us. But they didn't.

They didn't so much as shift their gaze. They were a fifty feet from me on either side, dozens, hundreds, and they just couldn't be bothered.

I made it down the embankment to the beach side and joined my friends. We were all as quiet as Ship, probably all stunned. Didn't matter, we made it. A small chain-link fence was on this side of the highway, and it had gotten dark so we couldn't see a break in it even with night vision. Alvarez produced a multi-tool and snipped the bottom link. It sounded like a nuclear warhead went off, but still none of the pus bags caught on. He clipped another, and then another and one of his buddies put his hand on Alvarez's shoulder and pointed back to the road. I glanced back and used the night vision glasses to see that a few of the things had perked up a little, but not enough to come our way. When they went back to not being so perky, Alvarez snipped a couple more links, and his buddy repeated the shoulder touch.

We did this several times, cutting stopping, cutting stopping. We were lined up against the fence, waiting until there was a hole large enough for us to walk through. Alvarez finished, and then motioned us to follow him through.

We never did think to look on the far side of the fence and that was our undoing. A dead man smashed against the other side and began that fucking howl, and it was done. I looked through the night vision back at the highway, and you got your wishes dear reader, every flesh slurping one of them was coming for us.

It suddenly got very loud as well. All the deaders were making like it was Christmas and they were all caroling. I gotta tell you, that's some scary shit, when you know they're right on top of you and it's dark, and you're running.

Alvarez was through the fence first and he dealt with the infected on that side. Problem was, he wasn't alone, and his buddies were coming as fast as they could from all directions. We all hustled through, and for a moment I thought about trying to mend the fence, but I looked at the amount of white figures coming towards my night vision, which was attached to my noggin, and I knew the fence was merely an afterthought to that swarm.

Fucking fences.

Sneaking is tricky for thirteen people loaded with gear. As I've said, I am not a soldier, and never received ninja training, so keeping quiet was tough. We did OK though, and it took at least a solid minute before the shit hit the fan. We were moving past a store with fishing poles in the big glass window when said window crashed outward and two dead dudes grabbed one of the guys from the Chevy. The guy yelped and fired off a quick round from his Berretta into the throat of the first dead guy. Of course, that didn't do shit, and as the thing tried to bite him I hit it in the side of the head with my M4. It slid to the side, but didn't let go of the guy, so I shot it. The guy took care of the second one with a better shot from his M9 to the head.

We had slowed a little to deal with the decaying fisherman, and that was enough for several of the things to get close. We shot them and moved on, weaving in and out of abandoned and parked vehicles, moving toward the dock.

We got to within fifty or so feet of our objective before they caught us again. A small group of them appeared from a bait shop and stumbled right into our path, effectively blocking us. There was nothing for it, so we shot them, Ship using that giant machete to hack up any that got close. More came from the sides, and suddenly there were a lot of them. We hacked and slashed and shot our way to the dock. We must have destroyed twenty of them. One of the dead things managed to latch on to Babe, but he did this underhanded knife thrust thing to the underside of its chin, and it dropped like a rock. Now that was cool shit.

Babe slashed the last one across the eyes and it stumbled back a little, blind but in no way less hungry. The others had closed some distance, and I almost shit myself when I saw how many there were. They had been spread out on the highway, but when they funneled in between the cars and little shops by the docks, they concentrated their numbers and it was terrifying. There must have been hundreds.

Alvarez ran down the dock yelling, "Cover us while we cast off!" He, Kat and a couple others jumped on the shrimping boat, and began to load gear while another couple of guys started to remove the lines securing the boat to the pier.

Ship, Babe, and I took up firing positions at the head of the dock to repel any invaders. Ship stood and Babe and I went to one knee. Two of the guys behind us were fiddling with something on the pier, when one of the Army guys from the Hummer yelled, *Grenade!* and chucked one about fifty feet back behind us into the approaching horde. It almost got me killed. Nobody had taught me not to look at a grenade exploding while wearing night vision goggles. I was totally blinded for a moment, and I stood stumbling sideways, my hand to my eyes. Thank God I didn't get shot.

Course I fell right the F of the dock and into the water. Ship swears up and down he reached for me so I wouldn't go in, but in I went. Guy has arms the length and breadth of Redwood trees, but could he catch me? No. My gear was heavy, and if Ship hadn't grabbed me, I have no doubt I would have drowned. It being dark, and me being all blind and shit, I probably would have swum the wrong way and pounded on the sand until I ran out of breath.

As it was I got my sight back pretty quickly. I felt Ship's massive mitt on my shoulder, and I looked up and grabbed his hand, feeling wet and embarrassed.

"Get him out, they're almost on us," Babe hissed frantically.

Ship started to lift me out, and I just knew I would be fine. There was plenty of time to get on the boat and get away. Plenty of ocean between us and the zombie hordes of North America. Plenty of food and water and beer and tequila and hookers at the paradise we were headed to. Yup, all fantastic, all good. I just needed to get dry and kick my feet up with some of the items I just mentioned. Especially the last one.

If you've never seen the movie Jaws, then you are either A. an asshole or B. a pussy. It is hands down the best movie ever made. The acting, directing, and special effects, are second to none. Hell, even the music is memorable, and it was made in the nineteen seventies. So Quint, the bad-ass shark killer who scraped his fingernails down the chalkboard, and had so many memorable lines? Remember him? Remember the noises he made when he was sliding down the deck toward gigantic toothed maw of the shark? The kicking and screaming and little girl noises he made during the stark raving terror he was feeling as he absolutely knew the jaws of that shark were going to reach him?

Those were the sounds I made, and there was quite a bit of kicking and screaming, not unlike a little girl at all, when the first set of dead hands grabbed my ankle under the water. It wasn't like I had any notions these were the hands of a porn star pulling me to heaven. These were the claws of a demon dragging me to hell.

So there I was, crying like a girl, while Ship and quite possibly a legion of the undead played tug of war for my soul. Ship dropped his HK417 and it hung on his single point sling over the water as he used two hands to pull me from the inky blackness. Babe noticed my yelping and decided to lend a hand as well. So there they are pulling me, with the dead pulling back, and me screaming, and the horde of dead just about reaching the dock, when my buddies finally get me far enough out of the water that they see slimy alabaster hands gripping my clothes and ankles. Ship told me later, and Babe agreed, that there were eight hands on me. My math tells me that was four bad guys against two of my buddies, and I was kicking like hell. Kat and one of the other guys were suddenly there, and they were hacking ever so close to my feet with machetes. It was enough to sever most of the hands, and the others must have lacked the strength when mostly cut, because the living beat the dead and they got me out.

I flopped on the dock like a fish, all of us panting, when the first foot stomped on the wood twenty feet away. As one we snapped our heads up and were able to see the things advancing toward us through the darkness. I got up unbelievably fast with the help of Ship and we all ran. It was maybe two hundred feet to the far end of the dock and that's where we headed. I was last, as I was soaking wet and weighed an extra fifty pounds with my gear saturated. Alvarez's pals were pushing the boat off the dock, and they all jumped in and waited for us. I was about thirty feet behind the other sprinters and I was tired.

My friends in front of me all jumped for the gunwales and made it easily, but by the time I got there the boat had moved a good ten feet away from the dock. I didn't even slow down. I sprinted as fast as my soaking wet, gear-laden ass would go. I didn't make it. Let me tell you, having been in the zombie infested water once was scary. Waiting for those hands to reach up and grab me again totally fucked with my sanity. They never came though. Either there weren't any at this end of the dock, or those dead bastards were reaching and the water was too deep. My friends reached over and pulled my super-heavy ass aboard. Again I flopped like a fish on my back and looked up to the circle of people surrounding me.

"I'm good," I said.

Babe knelt and immediately rolled up my pant leg; I presume he was looking for bite marks. I let him. He moved to the other leg and checked that too. Satisfied, he sat on his ass and let out a heavy sigh.

I sat up and looked at him, "Babe?"

"Yeah?"

"That'll do pig."

AVAST ME HEARTIES!

I love talking like a pirate. It almost got me killed in the joint, but I couldn't help it. Guy had a fucking eye patch, so I called him cap'n, and he tried to shiv me. How was I supposed to know the dude was some kind of Aryan royalty? Actually, now that I think of it, he was covered in Aryan tattoos and I was just a dumbass.

But I digress.

One of the bad parts of our grand plan, something we didn't think of, was starting the boat. There were no keys, and we all kinda stood around until Ship took charge and tried to hotwire it. It would seem that my genius buddy was no criminal. He couldn't hotwire…well…something that could be easily hotwired. Yeah I got nothing.

Anyway, they all looked to me. I *was*, in fact, a criminal. The worst part of it was that I figured it out in about five minutes. Not because I had been in jail, not because I was illicit, or felonious, but because I had been a God damned mechanic.

F you and your thoughts on my past, Dear Reader.

So Ship comes and gets me, (and believe me, I was doing something important) and now instead of being terrified, I'm pissed and full of righteous indignation. And terror. There was terror.

See, this is where the intelligent reader says, "Whoa. Just whoa. Where are my zombies? Weren't they right on top of you? I mean, your criminal enterprises and ability to circumnavigate an electronic ignition not-withstanding, you seem to have misplaced the true antagonist of the tale. Furthermore, everybody knows that old shrimping vessels do not have electronic ignition."

Firstly, Fuck you.

Secondly, Yes, shrimp boats *do* have electronic ignition. The boat was ancient, some might consider it pre-Columbian art. Every piece of equipment on said vessel was brand-spanking-new however. Including the state of the art key hole missing the key (he he) ingredient in starting the boat. The key. Guy must have hit the lottery, and for the life of me I can't figure out why he upgraded the electronics on this tub and just didn't buy a new piece of shit to shrimp with.

Thirdly, and most importantly, I didn't misplace dick. The infected were there and in force. They were itching to dine on us as well, and were pushing each other off of the end of the dock, floundering for a moment, and sinking. I could see them going down, and I would lose sight of them at about fifteen feet or so. They would reach for us all the way down. It scares the shit out of me to think of how many just walked or were pushed off the end of that dock. Hundreds. The line of pus bags went all the way back down the dock, up the gangway, and into the parking lot. It looked like free crock pot day at Walmart, or the line for Space Mountain on a busy Disney afternoon.

Remember five or so paragraphs ago when I said I had been doing something important? Yeah, we had to push off the dock with these huge gaffs because we were drifting back toward the dock which was loaded with infected. What the hell did a shrimp boat have eight six foot gaffs for? I dunno, but that thought kept peeking over the abject terror I was feeling. Picture six of us pushing against the wharf with these poles, keeping the boat just out of reach of several hundred dead hands, while the owners of those hands just kept coming and coming. That boat was fucking *heavy* too.

So there's a six to seven foot gap between the inconveniently un-started boat, and a wall of cannibals incapable of pain or fear. Said cannibals are walking off the end of the pier and beginning to clog that space. Now the dead shit heads are crawling over their struggling buddies, and we can see that all the six foot poles in the world aren't going to stop them from reaching us. In addition, every couple of seconds one of them will grab a pole or get stuck on the gaff, and it's a bitch to get the pole back. We lost two poles in two minutes and were down to four.

It didn't take long for the first dead bastard to crawl across his pals and slap his rotting paw on the gunwale. Kat shot him, and the next ten or twelve dickweeds to follow suit. That's when Ship grabbed me and pulled me toward the ignition. I said it took me five minutes before, but when the living dead are trying to eat you, and people are screaming to hurry up or we're all gonna die, five minutes is a friggin eternity.

There was a toolbox in a crate in the wheelhouse and I used a flathead screwdriver to pry...you know what? F this, I just got it started with a screwdriver and a safety pin. Yup, MacGyver didn't have shit on me. That dude is probably dead too.

The boat started, and I threw the red handle forward from neutral to go. I dunno nautical terms. Drive? Forward? Underway? I had seen enough boats to know that pushing that thing forward meant we were gonna go, and we did. Half a squad of army guys, and possibly the smartest giant on the planet, and I saved everybody's ass.

Almost.

Several dead had managed to get aboard and the guys were fighting them off. I heard three gunshots and Kat scream before I could get back out to help. I couldn't just let the boat sail into the other docks; the channel was narrow, and I had to make sure we wouldn't wreck the boat or get beached or something. Once we were heading out to sea, I hurried.

The dead were all re-killed, but one of the Chevy guys was on his back bleeding out. His hand was on his neck, but there was no saving him. We all knew it and so did he. He tried to stand, and his pals helped him up. Before we could do anything, he shot himself in the dome and toppled over the side. We sailed out to sea watching him float face down like he was playing a game in a pool. I never got his name.

Ship put his hand on my shoulder, and pointed to the wheelhouse. "Fuck if I know how to work this thing," I told him spreading my arms. Everybody was looking at me. A huge blood stain was on the blue deck.

"Shit," I said aloud, "fine, I'm captain. You," I pointed to Babe, "clean that shit up. I dunno if that blood can infect us, but I don't want to find out. Get it off my ship...er boat." I looked at the big guy and gave him *sorry* face.

I grabbed the kid whose idea it had been begin this caper. "So where's this oil rig?"

"Idunno." He said it as one word, that's why I wrote it like that.

"What?"

"How the hell do I know where it is? It's in the gulf someplace."

Fuck.

"So your grand strategy was to get a boat, go out into the gulf, and *look out the fucking window*?" I was incredulous.

"Yeah."

He had me. The little prick had me. We didn't have any living dead to contend with and we had some supplies. The fuel indicators told me we had 2/3 of a tank. We could look for almost a week before we had to abandon the search. That's a week with no dead, and how big could the gulf be? Weren't there tons of oil rigs out here?

I smiled and patted him on the back. "We'll be fine," I said, nodding. "Yeah, fine."

Yeah, so the Gulf of Mexico is friggin big. We lucked out though and found a platform on the first day. It was very small and occupied, and they shot at us so we moved on. We found a few more, most were rusty, dilapidated pieces of shit, not fit to visit. One was a big one, but that had a dozen or so boats tied up to its base. When they didn't answer the radio, we pulled close and I honked the horn. Nobody shot at us. That would normally be a good thing, but the reason they didn't shoot was because they were all dead. The rig was crawling with pus bags.

We moved on again, and found a few more rigs, but they were either useless, hostile, or overrun. There were several of those oil rigs on a ship things too, and one of them, the Ensco DS-5 (stupid name for a ship, I know) took us on for a couple of nights. We traded news and they were a good bunch of men and women. They knew that the US was gone, and didn't want to go back to the mainland, but fuel was going to be a problem over the next year. They were talking about acquiring some type of fuel ship, but that might be a battle as well. The oil produced from the rigs was useless to them until it was refined, so they also talked about snagging a refinery ship, in which case they would have an indefinite amount of fuel.

They fed us and told us to watch out for pirates. Yes, pirates. As in bad guys with boats who want your shit. Probably effing rednecks. Redneck Pirate Zombies. Sounds like a bad comic book.

We wished them luck and they did the same. They also gave us the coordinates of a huge oil and gas platform about two hundred miles south of New Orleans that was accepting survivors. That's where we headed, and it took the better part of the day to get there. It was almost ten at night when we saw the platform off in the distance. It was light up like a Christmas tree, and it was BIG. We hailed them (like on Star Trek) and they told us to come on up and that we wouldn't be fired upon. We would have to be inspected by a doctor and may need to surrender our weapons.

Both of those things filled me with dread, and I not-so-absentmindedly rubbed my collarbone bite. One time I submitted for inspection, I was shot in the dome. Not my favorite. This would be interesting, that's for sure. I didn't think we would part with our weapons, so I didn't know if they would allow us on board anyway.

They did.

We pulled up to the lower docking area, and there were a dozen or so boats there already, including two huge ship oil rigs not unlike the Ensco DS-5. I was to learn later they are called drillships. We were met by some of the oil rig security force, all armed to the teeth. A doctor was there and she inspected all of us for bites. Again, the bite on my collarbone looked like any other boo-boo, as did the one on the back of my shoulder, but the one on my leg screamed zombie bite to everyone who saw it. And see it she did.

"When did this happen?" she asked pointing to it.

"Almost three months ago," I lied.

"Pre-outbreak? Who bit you?"

"Bar fight. I knocked the bastard down and the drunken prick grabbed my leg and gnawed on it."

She furrowed her brow. "Well, it's healing nicely, but human bites can be extremely serious. You're lucky it didn't get infected."

"I think I'm luckier that the guy was alive when he bit me."

She smiled and I was in love, even though I was lying my ass off to her at our first meeting. "Agreed."

She kept looking at me with her gorgeous brown doe eyes, and I swear to Christ my heart skipped a beat. 'Course I was standing in my shorts so I had to spin quickly and get dressed. It had been a long time since I had gone twenty toes, and this chick was hot, so Mr. Happy had come to town. And the little bastard decided to set up shop in my pants. *Little bastard* might not have been the best choice of words to describe my penis. Rest assured, I could beat you to death with it, and we'll leave it at that.

So my stiffy and I left the room, and the doc might have even giggled. Utterly unprofessional and degrading, but holy shit it was cute too.

Then came the bad stuff. The rig security team, which consisted of a couple of marines that had found their way to the rig in small boat, and some roughnecks with guns, demanded that we give up our guns. They were nice about it at first, but when we said no, they flipped the safeties of their weapons. So after all the shit we had been through, we were going to have a firefight on the lower dock of an oil rig.

One of the roughnecks was looking at me with a half-smile, like he really wanted to drill me, but they were all kind of staring at Ship. His size does demand attention. Alvarez stepped forward to try to calm things down, and every one of the rig guys raised their weapons and pointed them at him.

Alvarez had his M4 on a single point sling on the front of him, and he slowly raised his hands.

"We're taking your guns," Half-smile said, "and then we'll decide what to do with you."

This shit was about to get very real.

"If you try to take our shit we're all gonna die," I told him, "all of us, you too."

Mexican standoff. Except we were shit out of Mexicans. Well, Alvarez was of Mexican descent, so I guess he counted.

Half-smile turned into no smile, and I know in my heart of hearts he was about to start a very quick and very deadly gun battle, when one of the roughnecks, a scrawny guy, stepped out from the crowd.

"Greg?" The guy's eyes actually bugged out of his head. He moved past Alvarez, who still had his hands up, and grabbed one of our guys. "Greg!" To my amazement, the guy hugged one of the soldiers and started to cry. Everybody still had their weapons ready, but now nobody seemed to know what to do.

"Hi, Bobby," Greg said.

Bobby backed up a step and said, "Shit! Guys, this is my brother in law! I know him, for Christ's sake put your guns down." They did, and so did we, but Half-smile was pissed about it. One of the marines used his radio to call up to the rig, and in a couple of conversation-filled minutes, some rig royalty showed up. The guy was dressed in jeans and a white T shirt. He walked up to us with his hand outstretched. "Gentlemen, and lady, welcome to Atlantis."

ATLANTIS

It always amazes me what humans, as a species, can accomplish. This structure we were now on was a fucking *marvel*. Firstly, it was big. I mean, huge like a skyscraper huge. Maybe not as tall, but I guarantee you there was just as much space on this rig as in most office buildings. They had thought of everything too. They make their own water, nearly endless supplies of fuel and power. Food for fifty people for a solid year, and not shit food, good food. Really good food. My first meal aboard Atlantis was lasagna that would have made a fat Italian nana soil her granny panties. They even had a movie theater with over a thousand relatively new titles stored on a couple of giant hard drives.

Hot showers, hot meals, a medical staff, an engineering staff, a gym, and plenty of things to do. I always thought roughnecks were all musclebound dumbasses, but every one of them has some kind of degree, and a lot of them are Ship-quality smart. No, not ship like a boat, Ship like my Sasquatch-esque genius pal.

Did you know that a lot of the bigger oil rigs float? They don't sit on giant pilings that are sunk into the ocean floor like I thought. They have those big pilings, but they are just for weight and balance. The actual rig is anchored to the bottom with even bigger weights, with bunches of twelve-inch cables attached to the underside of the pilings extending all the way to those weights I just mentioned.

Genius, I shit you not, there were even plans to get some farms going on the helipad.

Of course, there are the bad things too. There were a hundred and thirty two people now on this rig, and it was made for a crew of seventy. A lot of the original crew left when the last few helicopters or boats took off for the mainland in search of their families. Many of the crew stayed though, and eventually Atlantis started taking on survivors.

There were a few military guys, and a bunch of civilians, even a few kids. All of whom now had important jobs. Some were security, some cooks, and some did whatever they were told. When the elevator to the docks below was locked up, nothing without ninja skills was getting on board either, so defense from bad guys who didn't have flying or floating military vehicles was sound.

There had been an outbreak of the plague in the early days when an older roughneck had had a heart attack, turned, and killed another guy. The two of them were put down fast, and since then steps had been taken to alleviate this problem should it occur again. Not everybody had a weapon, but every door had some type of lock, and if anybody saw an infected, they would start screaming, and someone would set off the fire alarm. When the alarm sounded, everyone was to get to a locked room and get a weapon. Blunt objects, such as wrenches, rebar, pipe, and other heavy tools were everywhere already, so close quarters weapons were prevalent. Security would use the fire location system to see where the fire alarm had been tripped, and ten heavily armed and armored men would be scouring the area inside of two minutes. There hadn't been another death since the first ones, so the system hadn't been tested, but it sounded good to me.

What didn't sound good to me was the math. There was food enough for the crew for a year, but we now had double the capacity that was designed to occupy the rig, so that food supply would go fast. Austin, the guy in charge, said he would not turn away anyone who wasn't infected either, so we had the potential to overfill this place fast should more survivors show up. He did say that we were the first survivors they had seen in two weeks other than the crew from the Ensco DS-5.

The thing that bothered me the most about this place was the name though. I might not be a history buff, but I'm fairly certain that the mythical city or continent of Atlantis fucking sank. What a stupid name for something that is supposed to be sea worthy. It was like naming a jet liner Lynyrd Skynyrd.

All the positives outweighed the negatives, and eventually even Ship had to admit this place was great.

After that great lasagna dinner, our group of twelve was asked to meet with Austin for news of the mainland. All the information that the rig had was from the television, the internet, and survivors. We met and talked, and one of the biggest toughest roughnecks on board cried like a baby when we told them about Keesler. His whole family had been there.

"So it really is all gone then," Austin asked.

"No," I answered, "no, it isn't. We're all alive, and if we do things correctly, we can live a long damn time."

Have you heard the term ear-splitting silence? Yeah. I experienced it first hand for a couple seconds there.

And then everybody clapped and we lived happily ever after.

Yeah, right. Remember when I said I was a magnet for bad shit to happen? It just might be true.

We integrated nicely into the Atlantis family. So much so, that I thought of them as *my* family. Every person on the rig, even Half-smile, who I know you were thinking was going to be a bad guy, and who's name ended up being Ralph, was like a brother or sister or father or mother to me.

We all lived well, ate well, and got along. There weren't any castes or *I'm better than you's*. We initiated trade with four other rigs and some drillships, and soon we had friends all over the gulf. Most of the mechanics on all the ships and rigs had left to go back to the mainland during the initial stages of the outbreak. So when I went on a visit to another rig, the Atwood Condor, I helped repair their forklift and a drive motor on one of their windmills. They had the same type of engineer geniuses, but couldn't figure out the old Cat lift or the mill motor, so I helped them. Word got around, and I became the official mechanic of all the rigs and drillships in our family.

We lived happy and healthy for almost three months. Had plans to go mine some earth to start the farms, and were having a meeting about it when one of the radio operators came down to talk to Austin. He told him he had the *Prague* on the line, and they sounded concerned. *Prague* was another rig a few miles away, far enough that we couldn't see their lights at night. Austin left with Ted (the radio guy), and he came back about twenty minutes later. He sat down, and I could tell he was itching to tell us something.

I interrupted the earth-stealing meeting and asked Austin what was up.

"We may have a concern. Jeff on the *Prague* just told me that a massive container ship, the *Majestik Maersk*, just steamed by them on a heading of one hundred ninety degrees. They tried to contact the ship, and even tried to get aboard, but they couldn't. The vessel is travelling at a speed of six knots, which is too fast for the current, but seemingly very slow for a ship of that size."

"So how does that impact us?" somebody asked.

"One hundred and ninety degrees puts them on a collision course with us." He held his hands up when the room got a little antsy. "Now the odds of this ship hitting us are extremely remote. It's a big ship, yeah, and we're a big stationary target, but it would be exceptionally unlucky for it to come within a mile of us, really."

Fuck.

Exceptionally remote? Extremely unlucky? Do you remember who I am? Fecal attractor. Double fuck.

I truly believe he was going to leave it there, and go back to the meeting, but Ship passed him a sheet of paper, which he read aloud: *I don't do unlucky. We need to get aboard to evaluate that vessel.*

Before Austin could ask how, Ship had scribbled and passed him another note: *The Beaumont has a helicopter. At some point my prestigious comrade here will have to repair it, we borrow it and call it a trade. At the very least the other rigs will want us alive to help if something bad happens, and this vessel could kill us all.*

"He's right," a bunch of folks said at once. Murmurs of assent and worry went around the table, and we shelved the soil appropriations summit for the time being and talked about this possible threat. It never got heated, none of our meetings did. That was how our life was: good.

Things got thrown around and talked about, but it was finally decided that a small team would go aboard the *Majestik Maersk* and see what the hell was happening.

Something I haven't mentioned up to now was that everybody had been calling me Captain. They did this because I was the guy who flew our boat to Atlantis. Jesus, that statement sounded ridiculous… Anyway, they asked me if I could sail or at least stop the Majestic Maersk, and I immediately told them no. One of the drillship captains was visiting, and we brought him into the meeting and told him what was happening. He seemed considerably more alarmed than we did.

"That ship was built this past year," he told us, "and it will have the new course correcting software in the wheelhouse."

We all stared blankly.

He shook his head. "Means that if the course is set for one ninety degrees, that's where she's gonna go. Somebody get me a chart." Two guys ran out for a chart. "The software accounts for moderate weather and current, and will auto correct heading should the need arise. The captain or his designee is still supposed to be in the wheelhouse. Your rig being only five hundred feet wide will probably be enough for her to miss you, but we should still take a look."

Austin asked the captain if he would go with the team to check out the *Majestik*.

"Of course," was all he said.

A kid came running in with a chart, and we spread it out on the table using coffee mugs to hold it straight.

"This is the *Prague*," the captain said pointing at a red dot. He pulled a red grease pencil from thin air and a folding straight edge from his pocket, "and this is Atlantis," he drew a line connecting the dots, "gimme the coordinates of the ship?" The radio guy read off of his piece of paper. The captain found the coordinates on the map and traced a line from them on a one hundred and ninety degree heading. Wouldn't you know it, that fucking greasy red line ran dead across our little red dot.

It just isn't fair.

Austin and the captain assured us that there was no chance this ship could hit us, but I wasn't so sure. Lady luck had abandoned us in the past year and had been replaced by something downright malicious.

The captain pulled out a compass, not one that tells direction, one of the little pointy things that you always see ship captains flipping back and forth on a map in the movies. He did the same thing mumbling something about six knots and then looked at his watch, "Should be able to see her by morning."

The helicopter from the Beaumont arrived just before midnight. A team of twelve of us would go, including the captain, Ship, Babe, Alvarez, Greg, and myself. Ship was an engineer and a computer genius, I was a mechanic, and Alvarez, Babe, and Greg were our muscle, along with five other guys with guns and a medic. Not my doctor hottie. We hit the rack at just before one AM, and were back up by five thirty. I stretched, got my gear and met the fellas at the helipad.

It was absolutely the most beautiful sunrise I had ever seen. The sky looked like it was on fire to the northeast. We were boarding the helicopter when the radio guy came running. He handed something to the pilot, and the pilot looked at his co-pilot like some shit was about to happen. The pilot handed the something, which was a computer readout, to the captain, who then showed it to us.

"This is printout of a reading from the Atlantis Doppler radar. We need to get on that ship soon."

The printout was color, and there was a big fucking green swath coming in our direction. I didn't know what a radar depiction of a hurricane looked like back then, but I sure as shit do now. As it turns out, the weather was the least of our worries with that damn *Majestik Maersk*.

SHIP OF FOOLS

It took thirty minutes to reach the ship. They had painted it a shitty sky-blue, and it had MAERSK LINES on the side in letters you could undoubtedly see from the moon. We circled the ship once in the chopper, and Captain Bob (no shit) pointed out that there were no life boats or those orange floaty circle thingies left on board. There were tents and stuff on the deck, and it looked as if some of the containers had been used as housing, at least from the air. Captain Bob said that there weren't that many containers on board, but there had to be a thousand of them. No people though, and nobody answered the radio even with repeated attempts.

The ship was massive. Much, much bigger than the Atlantis. It was easily a quarter mile long, and tall, really, really tall. We circled a few times, and had the pilot, Billy, called back to Atlantis to get a couple of boats out just in case. Billy looked at the sky and it was black as shit in the distance, but the wind here was light and variable and the waves were almost non-existent. Billy looked nervous and that made me nervous.

Billy brought the bird down on some of the higher containers. There was no place else to set her down. We got out of the helicopter and they took off. They couldn't just hover, it would kill precious fuel, so they headed back to the Atlantis, which was now closer to the *Majestik* than the *Prague* was. They would come get us as soon as we called them, or in two hours, whichever came first. In three hours, the storm would catch the ship, but Bob said that could be a good thing, because severe weather could defeat the course correction software and push this big bitch away from us.

Still, a rogue runaway boat, the size of a small town, was not a nice thing to have running around us or our friends in the gulf, so we had to shut her down. Or take her. If the containers held shit we could use, we would of course pilfer said shit. The water here was too deep to anchor her, but Bob was talking about sea anchors when we began climbing down the containers. It took a few minutes, but we made it to the deck, and I gotta tell you it was creepy in there. It was like being at the bottom of a steep, metal ravine. Everybody was quiet, but our footfalls echoed at each step, and honestly, it was tough to keep our shit together. Even Alvarez, who is normally stoic and tough, was looking a might nervous.

We made it to the tents we had seen from the chopper and my suspicions were confirmed on what had happened here. The tents were torn and bloody, with signs of struggle. Bullet brass and blood was everywhere, as were the tell-tale drag marks of a body being moved across the deck. A stainless steel medical table was overturned and there were medical supplies scattered all over the place. Syringes and unopened gauze and bandages, stainless instruments and even a defibrillator. Steve the medic began to inspect some of the stuff, and pocketed anything not covered in zombie shit.

Other than the sounds of the ship, it was eerily silent. So when one of the container doors moved slightly and squealed, we all spun and faced our weapons toward it. The container was black, and there were three of them. The doors were open, but the boxes were empty. Upon further inspection, the things stank to high heaven. Brown stains covered the floors and walls, and pieces of clothing were here and there. They had been storing their dead in here, or they had been storing *the* dead in here. Either way they were crazy. Why anybody would have a container full of infected is beyond me.

Alvarez, Babe, and Zero, one of the marines, began to confer on what to do. The plan was to run if things got dicey. We would get back to the tops of the containers by any means necessary, and wait for extraction by the helicopter. We did a comms check and we moved on toward the wheelhouse.

We came across the first body lying on its side against one of the containers. It was a torso, and there was barely anything left of it. It was impossible to tell if it had been a man or woman, as there were no features left. It had been dressed in jeans but the shirt, and face, and scalp and every single scrap of flesh and muscle was gone. There were tiny pieces of viscera, but for the most part this was a skeleton that had been picked clean. It looked like the blood on the deck and container had even been lapped at.

So you can imagine how far back we all jumped when the thing shifted its head. The head moved a little, but other than that there was nothing else left to budge, and it couldn't moan as there was nothing below its upper jaw. Zero pulled his knife and jabbed it through the thing's empty eye socket, ending its pathetic imitation of life.

We were all nervous and on edge now. It took a few minutes of frightful meandering through the containers to get to the superstructure of the ship. A really long set of white metal steps went up and up, but there was also a hatch leading inside right where the stairs met the deck. We decided to split up, six up the stairs, and six through the hatch. I was lucky enough to go through the hatch. Alvarez opened it, and it didn't squeak horribly like I thought it would. Eleven firearms lowered when we saw that the inside was totally lit by interior lights, and seemed to be empty, and the stairs-six began their ascent. Ship was the last one through the hatch, and he closed and locked it with those little handles behind him.

A corridor went straight, all the way to the other side of the superstructure, but we wanted the stairwell in front of us. Another body was sitting down in the corner of the first landing, and it opened its eyes and tried to stand as we approached the stairs. It moaned, and Alvarez smoked it with his machete before it could get all the way up. We heard more moaning above us, and shuffling footsteps on the metal.

We were as quiet as possible going up the steps, and our enemy was making as much noise as possible, so when we met, we were surprised that there were only two of them. The guy who had been sitting down was a civilian, but these two were ship workers. They were both wearing what used to be blue jumpsuits with MAERSK on them, and they were absolutely mauled. They came at us, and Alvarez and Zero smoked them with a machete and a combat knife. When the dead were dead again, we listened. We could hear movement above us, and everybody knew what it was. Three landings up, we found it. Again, it was not possible to tell the gender of this one, but it had more to it. No legs and only half of one arm, it was trying to drag its wretched self to us.

What drives these things? Why do they want to eat us? If it's some primal need, then why don't they eat each other? Is it because nobody wants to eat something rotten, or do they consider themselves a different species, and abhor cannibalism?

Alvarez brought one of his size tens down on its noggin a few times and it was finished. We listened again, but couldn't hear anything, so we moved on. There were several hatches on the way up, but they were all closed, and some of them looked to have that gore spatter you see when a group of them have been beating their rotten fists against something. We were smart enough not to open any of them. All we had to do was get to the bridge and turn this big bitch a tiny bit.

We reached the top of the stairs, and there was carnage everywhere. How the hell these things had gotten inside the wheelhouse when there were only a few entrances was beyond me. All the hatches had locking mechanisms, but the port side door was wide open. Why would they open the fucking door with those things pounding on it?

The bridge looked like what I would think a spaceship bridge looked like. There were so many controls and buttons and lights and sticks it was insanity. And it was big. Really big, super wide and if it weren't for the giant broken window, all the blood, and few staggering zombies, it would have looked quite nice up there.

Zero dispatched the first one to come at us with the butt of his rifle. Alvarez got the next one, and Babe and Ship took the last two. All of them were down in under five seconds, and all of them looked like civilians except for one in blue scrubs. She had been a doctor, and she looked fresher than the others. She had a single bite mark on her forearm, even though the front of her scrubs were covered in blood and bits of shit. Although quite infected, she hadn't been mangled like the others we had seen.

Captain Bob moved toward the massive instrument panel and began to search it over, just when the exterior team arrived at the outside hatch. They came in and we were all confused, as they hadn't seen shit. The captain reached for one of the knobs or dials, but Steve, our medic stopped him with a hand on his arm. Steve pointed at all the blood on the panel, and said one word, "Don't."

He opened his pack and fished out a pair of purple examination gloves for Bob, who nodded and put them on. The rest of us searched around for stuff, and the security force began to sweep the giant room and the access points. There wasn't a lot of space to hide, but the first time you don't check, you've got a zombie chewing on your ass, so they checked. With the captain fiddling with his knobs, the heavy hitters securing the perimeter, the medic looking like he was shitting himself, and Ship looking over the computer systems, I had some free time, so I searched for something to do.

I found a black bound notebook and picked it up. It was the captain's private log. I read the last entry, and it was like a fucking horror story.

July 6th

They're at the doors and the stairwell is crawling with them. They can't get in, but we can't get out. We only have a day's rations up here. Eventually we will have to try to escape. My God there are so many. I can see several of my crew members on the deck, feeding on their friends and the civilians we picked up. I've set a course of 190° and a speed of seven knots and turned on the CCS. This should beach the Majestik near the port city of Tampico, Mexico. Seven knots is as slow as I can set her to maintain course, and the CCS will help. I want her to be as slow as possible when she beaches so she doesn't break up. God help anyone left alive in Tampico if the Majestic breaks up and spills her cargo.

If we live through this, I swear to all that is holy I will kill every one of those USAMRIID bastards. That bitch Doctor Callus won't need my wrath, as she was bitten earlier today, and she's already sick. She's killed us all, even herself.

This is the final log of Captain Asmund Pedersen. I hope I see my children again. Jeg elsker deg Hanna. Jeg elsker deg Marit. Jeg elsker deg Jan Egil. Beklager...

I kept reading as I heard the security guys saying *Clear* through the radio. I flipped a few pages back.

June 29th
They dropped off the containers today. Three Sky Cranes plopped them down right on the deck by the tent city that has sprung up there. We had room aft, but Callus demanded we put them immediately in front of the bridge, so they could be monitored from the wheelhouse. My suggestions that these containers be put aft for safety went unheeded, and actually earned me looks of reproach from the soldiers and doctors. I've come to realize that Captain means nothing to these people. I don't run my ship anymore, they do. "A military operation now" is what she said. Those damn containers should not be aboard this vessel with all these survivors on board. They should be doing this elsewhere.

Jarron fixed the electrical issue with the forward boom this morning.

We picked up another eight survivors from the sea as well today. Their boat was taking on water and we were able to get to them before it sunk, but just. They were grateful. One of the children reminds me of Marit, six years old and blonde to the point of blinding me. She is beautiful. I miss my children. I hold no hope that they survived as Trondheim is a large city. Hanna is resourceful though, perhaps they escaped to the sea.

And a few more pages back.

June 23rd
The Majestik received radio contact from the Navy of the United States this morning. We were anchored southwest of Pensacola Florida taking on survivors, when we received a request to weigh anchor and steam southwest further into the gulf. There is a US military ship, the Winston S. Churchill, that has suffered some type of catastrophe, and we have been asked to help.

Forward boom is still giving us some trouble.

Thirty two survivors made it to us today. We are acquiring quite a family here.

June 24ᵗʰ
We now have several doctors and naval sailors on the **Majestik**. *They have brought weapons and medical equipment and supplies from the Churchill. There was an outbreak aboard the Churchill, and they were unable to contain it. Apparently there are dozens of dead confined below decks, but the engine room is overrun and there was a fire. They were dead in the water when we found them. One of the sailors was bitten, and not allowed to come with us. I could hear the dead pounding on the hatches and bulkheads, and apparently so could the sailor, because he took his own life. I don't blame him, nobody survives a bite from one of those things.*

I harrumphed.

When we had moved a kilometer away from the Churchill, one of the sailors triggered something, and there was a huge explosion on the port side. A large fireball leapt from the ship, and she immediately listed to port. She took less than twenty minutes to slip beneath the waves. None of the sailors or doctors would tell us anything other than there was an outbreak and a fire. The lead doctor, a woman named Callus, demanded to see me on the bridge. I think she's a tad intrusive, but she's a doctor, and we need one since Bernhardt died.

June 25ᵗʰ
They have taken my ship. The United States military has taken my ship. I am a puppet, and there are armed guards in my wheelhouse "for my safety." I can't even use the head without armed escort. They are bringing infected aboard for study and examination. That bitch doctor, who is also a colonel in the Army, has told me that this is the best hope for the world. She struts around here like she owns my boat, and with her escorts and their weapons, she might just. Her arrogance would amuse me if not for the fact that she is in charge of me. I requested to evacuate the three hundred civilians aboard, but she said no, stating that the **Majestik** *was safer than anywhere else. Safer until you bring zombies here, stupid woman!*

Three hundred people...plus the crew, plus the soldiers and sailors and doctors. Where the fuck is everybody?

"Contact!"

I had to think it. I just couldn't have kept my mind on what I had been reading, or peanuts or porn stars. I just had to. I put the book in my pack and checked my rifle. Babe had been the one to call out contact and he was pointing down at the deck.

Other than Captain Bob, we all came to those giant windows and looked toward the back of the ship. The containers were stacked a few high, and in between some close to the superstructure stumbled a lone infected. It just milled about, not doing anything scary. Another stumbled into view, then another. They were coming from the rear, and within seconds, the maze of containers was filled with moving bodies.

And they kept coming. They moved in all directions, as long as those directions were forward. Two of them stormed past, pushing the others out of the way. One of the newcomers grabbed a shambler and screamed at it, punching it over and over. The others turned to look, but then moved forward again when the screamer dropped the one it had been striking. Great. Runners. Hadn't seen them in a while.

Once again, I should have kept my big mind shut.

The Runner looked around, then up at us. We didn't think to duck, and we should have, because he screamed, and then fought his way through the crowd to get to the stairwell. The other one did the same, chasing his buddy at top speed, and soon four more were pushing and shoving the slower ones. Then two more, then another. How the hell were there so many runners in one place?

I felt the ship move slightly, and my Ship put his hand on my shoulder. I jumped, and may or may not have given off a quiet manly shriek that only the two of us heard. Ship moved his head in a "let's get the F outa here" motion, and I was on board with that plan. Oh yeah, and it had suddenly gotten very dark outside.

"We need to get out of here before we get trapped!"

The medic looked at me like I was crazy. "They can't get in here, we should wait."

"Yeah, but we can't get out either! After a week up here, you're gonna look mighty tasty dumbass, and I don't mean to the zombies!"

"I'm done," Bob said. "I've set her course for one sixty five, she should miss all the rigs, even the abandoned ones. I'm with him, let's go."

We could hear frantic stamping on the exterior metal stairs. Babe moved to the door and looked down. "Here they come." He slammed the hatch and threw all six hatch locks and the slide bar.

Zero did the same across the wheelhouse. "This side is fucked too," he said calmly and pulled his radio. He called for extraction, and the chopper was on its way.

"Alright," began Alvarez, "we can't get to the roof of this structure, or use the exterior stairs, we have to go down the interior stairwell!"

I shook my head. "By the time we get to the bottom all those pus bags will have reached it."

"Then we use one of the other doors in the stairwell and get into the ship! Now or we die!"

He ran to the door and threw it open, shining his tactical light into the stairwell, "C'mon!" He ran down the stairs and we all followed. I could hear the Runners beating the shit out of the hatches upstairs. Six landings down, Alvarez opened a wooden door and moved in covering the left side, while Babe covered the right.

It was a narrow corridor and we moved into the ship. All the lights were on and it looked comfortable. I realized *I* wasn't comfortable. My belly wasn't feeling so good and I had a lot of spit forming in my mouth. That was when I realized the *Majestik* was starting to move in several directions. It wasn't like being tossed around, more like a slow wave. I looked at Ship, and he nodded, also looking green.

We moved down the corridor, not seeing any evidence of an undead plague. There were stairwells and doors aplenty, but nobody living, dead, or undead to be seen. Still, Alvarez and Babe checked every nook and cranny without opening doors, while Zero covered the rear. Ship stopped and put his massive mitt on one of the bulkheads. You don't call the walls on a boat walls, you call them bulkheads. Fucking stupid, I know, but it sounds cool, and I firmly believe that is why sailors call walls bulkheads, floors decks, ropes lines, and toilets heads. My knowledge of nautical terms notwithstanding, the big guy looked pretty bad off. I stopped and looked at him, and he looked back at me. I saw it coming, and pulled off a ten point zero Louganis to the right, (six point five from the Russian Judge) but he still got me with some of his spatter.

Everybody has to puke on me. Ever since Steven Jordan in the fourth grade, I've been the planet's vomit target, and honestly, I've gotten pretty spry when it comes to dodging. The problem is, sometimes there's no place to go, and in my haste to escape I bounced off of the opposite bulkhead while Ship continued to spray.

Have we covered the fact that Ship is large? We may have gone over that a time or three. So using your Holmsian deductive powers, you've undoubtedly come to the conclusion that big guys supply vastly more spew than smaller guys.

You're correct. It looked like a spilled vat of pork and beans. Same consistency, same texture, same color. I remember this as clear as my own name too; it made me damn hungry for pork and beans. The only difference between Ship's partially digested whatever, and an actual delicious meal, was the smell. That stench wasted no time in assaulting my senses, and as I've previously stated, I wasn't feeling that well myself, so I followed Ship down the toss trail and coated the deck with my own vile liquids.

Everybody was looking at us now, some with the backs of their wrists against their mouths. The problem with everybody looking at us was that nobody was looking at the door (hatch) directly behind my monstrous buddy. It opened, and out strolled a dead guy, bloody and filthy. That damn door had been closed not a nanosecond before, I had watched Babe check it, so it would seem that the dead could open doors now.

What was really weird was that it was holding a gun. A little silver revolver that was pointed nowhere special. It moved toward my colossal comrade, stepped in the puke, slipped, and went on its ass. The revolver went off, pinged off of a bulkhead, and the slug buried itself in some wood paneling down the corridor. Every weapon in our little company pointed at the thing, and I know what you're thinking: The gun? The door? This guy is alive! For fuck's sake, don't shoot him! Someone save this poor troubled soul, who knows what he had to live through on this ghost ship to survive!

Nope. This guy was fucking dead. Or undead, whatever. Half his neck was gone and he had bites all over his bare arms. I probably should have mentioned that three paragraphs ago, but hey, this is my tale. Oops.

Anyway, all the guys would have opened up and turned this thing into Swiss cheese, but we were in a metal can if you remember. We had just seen what a ricochet could do in here, and I didn't want to end up like the paneling, so I screamed for everyone to hold their fire. So did Alvarez and Zero.

It was all moot though, as Ship brought his steel-toed, puke-covered death boot up in a vicious kick that nearly decapitated the thing. With a sickening crunch, the creature's jaw exploded and teeth flew as its head snapped back, snapped being the operative word. It was dead, and now everybody was looking at Ship for a different reason.

And now you want an explanation of how the thing opened the door. That shit is as tough for you now as it was for me then because I have no idea how it did that. There was simply nothing different about that door handle than any other. I realize that this sounds like a copout, but remember, this is an account of the living dead, so deal with it. Insofar as the gun? I've seen those things carrying everything from cigarettes to stuffed animals to hedge clippers, so why not a gun?

We moved on. I was really feeling like shit too, and what little there was left of my stomach contents constantly wanted out. The *Majestik* was moving harder now, and when I looked out a porthole, I could see that the swells had grown and we were looking at maybe six foot seas. Now that might not sound like a lot to you, but if you've ever encountered six foot seas, you know it can be hell. If you haven't gone through that, I only have one recommendation for you: Don't. The only reason we weren't being tossed around like jelly beans in a tin can is because this particular tin can was fucking huge.

Moving deeper into the ship we could only go in one direction: down. I know that might not have been the best idea, but we couldn't get to the exterior decks from where we were. There were just too many zombies. We started seeing signs of struggle as we made our way down too. Blood. A deck of cards all over the floor. Bullet casings and a broken porthole. We saw one more zombie before we entered the door at the bottom of the last stairwell, but it never saw us, and Alvarez took it out with his knife from behind.

I noticed signs for the galley and we followed them. A large barricade had been erected outside the galley doors. Chairs, tables, carts, trays, trash cans, and everything else you can think of had been piled on both sides of the door. A dozen or so bodies were splayed here and there outside the barricade, indicating a big battle had occurred here. The barricade was destroyed and spread out, so it hadn't held.

We heard movement on the other side of the broken door. Babe pulled his inspection mirror and took a peek. The shit got scared out of him exceptionally quickly, and he gave panicked hand motions for us to move back the way we had come. It didn't matter. Something alerted those dead fuckers to our proximity and all hell broke loose.

SEPARATE WAYS

It never ceases to amaze me what people are wearing when they return from the dead seeking the flesh of the living. I guess if you get overwhelmed, or die quickly, then you don't have a chance to change. Or maybe you get too sick, or just don't give a shit. Whatever the case may be, when the plague first struck Boston, it was November, and pretty chilly, although not freezing, so everybody had clothes on.

So when the twenty-something chickie, wearing cut-off jeans and a disgusting halter top that had fallen to about her midsection , came through the door and looked right at me, boobs a-kilter, all I could think of was that she probably looked better in death. Oh, I should have mentioned that she was pushing three bills. Much like the fatties that had tried to eat me on my first day as an escaped convict, this girl was a lot of woman. At least they had been wearing mu mus. In life, this poor girl had thought she was a size six. She wasn't. She was followed by a guy in a brown-stained apron with *Kiss the...* on it. The rest of the verbiage was obscured by those brown stains that were undoubtedly not ketchup. I of course immediately pictured this guy cooking up healthy humans so he and his buddies could eat some livers with fava beans and a nice Chianti. I even pictured a parsley garnish. Hey, it's all about presentation. And if you're inwardly bitching about the word ketchup vs. catsup, I'm a punch you in the face.

Those two were the first through the galley doors, but they were followed by a lot more of their kin. A whole bunch more.

We executed a tactical withdrawal and ran back down the hall (I dunno what the nautical term for hall is) at high speed. The dead folks gave a slow chase, but that slow speed of theirs is nothing if not constant. A couple of twists and turns brought us to a berthing area, and there was blood everywhere. To make matters worse, the power was fluctuating and the lights were flickering. I also realized the Majestic was getting tossed around more than it had before.

My sea-legs abandoned me and I fell to one side into a room with two bunks. One of them held the partial remains of a guy, and he sat up from his nap and looked at me, drooling. I got up quickly and slammed the door. Yeah, it was a door, not a hatch. The thing inside was beating on the portal (do you see what I did there?) in an instant, and suddenly Alvarez was shooting in front of us.

"Contact forward!"

This corridor was much thinner than the others we had been in and I was afraid of ricochets, but as it turned out, I should have been afraid of zombies. The marine in front of me raised his rifle to help Alvarez but the lights flickered, and when they came back on one second later, the marine was gone. Like a total Houdini. I was inwardly *what the fuck*-ing when I heard an "Ahhh shit!" then a suppressed gunshot. The sounds of the rifle shots were deafening in this metal tomb and my ears were ringing. Pity the rifles didn't have suppressors.

I peeked into a room I hadn't seen, and saw the marine holding his neck. "Let me see it," I demanded, "Let me see!"

He brought his palm from his face, and I could see that his earlobe and patch of skin where his jaw met his skull were gone. He looked at the re-killed zombie, then at his bloody palm, then at me, then he shook his head.

"Nope," he said, put the long suppressor under his chin, and blew his head off. The dropped ceiling of the room was sprayed with his goo, and a bullet hole appeared in the now red tile. The Gulf sprayed up on the porthole, and I realized that we were in the midst of the storm now.

I picked up his weapon and closed the door. The whole thing had taken place in about six seconds, but in that precious time, shit had gone from bad to worse. Infected had come from in front of us and we knew that there were dozens behind. Zero was fighting a losing battle to the rear trying to close a hatch with ten dead hands already on it pulling the other way. Alvarez, Babe, and two of the other marines were firing to the front, but the corridor was only about four feet wide and was filling up quickly with infected. The now typical thoughts of "kill one and two take its place" were flying around in everybody's head. Greg was trying to tell Captain Bob and Steve the medic that everything was gonna be OK, and the last marine had checked out and was standing there babbling. Ship was looking green, but had the sense to have his machete ready.

So who do you think stepped the F up? Yeah, dear reader, it was yours truly.

"Ship! Help me!"

The big guy looked at me and we both high-tailed it the sixty feet back to where Zero was about to have the hatch (this was a hatch, not a door) yanked from his mitts. I grabbed a hatch lock and pulled with him. I really wanted Mr. Hulk Hands to start pulling too, but in his smarter-than-everybody way, he diffused the situation. No, he didn't have a cup of tea with the zombies and talk shit out, he used his blade to hack the fingers off of the hands pulling against us. With only a few whacks, he had the digits of those monsters on the deck at our feet. Putting his right hand (the one with the machete) against the bulkhead, he grabbed the hatch handle and pulled that shit closed, amputating a few more fingers. Zero slammed a hatch lock home and I did the same for another. We wasted no time in locking that shit up with all six locks, and I was briefly happy to hear the frustrated and pissed off wails of the dead fuckers on the other side. Yeah, I know they don't get pissed off or frustrated, but I'm using poetic license to amp up the story. I hope it's working.

Zero picked up a woman's finger and smiled. "Now I want sausages."

Ship promptly threw up on him.

Screaming from the front lines interspersed with the shots broke our revelry and I heard Alvarez holler: "Fall back!"

To where? Where were we supposed to fall the fuck back to? We were in a hundred-foot long, four-foot wide steel tube. There were doors on both sides of the tube, one of which contained a living dead guy, and it wouldn't hold very long against an assault by the hands that would be pounding on it. We were well and truly fucked, and in moments we would be hand to hand with these dead assholes.

The pile up of destroyed infected was beginning to hamper the advance of their undead comrades, but not nearly enough. They were climbing over and we were losing ground. The hallway was filled with the hungry ones, but Ship stood on his tip toes, wiping his mouth and pointed. The big guy's noggin was almost touching the deck above us, but he still unceremoniously picked me up like a little kid and raised me high enough to see that the tide of pus bags ended about thirty deep.

"Alvarez," I shouted, "we have to move forward, they're thinning out!"

"Fuck, I'm out!" he yelled, dropped his rifle and pulled his suppressed Sig. He and the marine next to him moved towards the dead, and Babe and the other marine followed. "Reloading," yelled one of the marines. The dead, now only about fifteen feet away, surged forward, tripping over their buddies and themselves.

I ran the thirty feet to our forward line, when the marine that had suffered his momentary breakdown decided it was time to play. We were the third group of two, he and I, but he fought his way forward and brought his shotgun to bear.

"Rafferty! Get back on the fucking line!"

I used to go to a pub named Rafferty's when I wore a younger man's shoes.

The marine, Rafferty, emptied his shotty into the faces of those that would eat him, drawing his M9 pistol and discarding the big gun when it emptied. He took careful aim with the Berretta and fired it until that too was empty. Babe rushed up to join him and the two of them did pretty well until one of the things got past its destroyed pals and bit Babe in the hand. Babe backed up, a little shocked, but the marine went ape shit. He vaulted over the re-killed zombies and entered the fray with his Ka-Bar. If you're unaware what a Ka-Bar is, it's a knife. He destroyed one more of the things before the others tore him to pieces.

That was the impetus we needed to destroy the last vestiges of the undead force in the corridor. Rafferty's sacrifice, if that's what it was, had the dead focused on eating him or trying to eat him, and we took them all down. Babe's last bullet went into Rafferty's mauled face.

There were at least a hundred of these things in the corridor, and it was as blocked for us as it had been for them. We had lost two soldiers, and one was infected. That infected guy was a damn good friend of mine too.

Steve was bandaging Babe's hand when Babe looked up at Zero. "Can they get through there?" He had nodded his head toward the hatch which was undoubtedly covered in zombie shit as they were pounding the fuck out of the other side of it.

"Dunno," Zero answered, "what happened to you?"

Babe held up his now bandaged hand. "I got killed."

"Shit. Sucks." Zero raised his eyebrows. "Wanna butt?"

Zero handed Babe a cigarette. "Might as well take up smokin' now, got a light?"

Alvarez, the two remaining marines, and Greg were clearing a path through the dead, dragging some all the way down the corridor and shoving them against the hatch, which showed no signs of giving under the onslaught of dozens of fists. I pitched in, and so did Bob. Fuckers were heavy. Steve the medic had given us all purple gloves, but the pus bags were still...squishy... I guess is the best word. One of the marines climbed and hopscotched through all the bodies to the far end of the corridor for some recon. "Clear," came through the radio.

Babe was sitting on the deck, coughing up new cigarette smoke and talking to Zero, who had a remarkable calming effect. Steve checked on him constantly, but all of us including Babe knew his game was over.

I grabbed the nasty black hand of one of the more rotten ones and the skin sloughed off. I chucked its hand-rind against a bulkhead, and it stuck like spaghetti. Then the *Majestik* rolled, and I lost balance and almost smacked face first into that black, disgusting thing. My face was about a half inch away and its smell permeated my senses. It was atrocious, and I still remember retching to this day.

Ship was also retching, but it was because the *Majestik* was now pitching and rolling all over the place. Captain Bob was leaning against a bulkhead and looking nervous, so I asked him what was up.

"The course correction software. It can't account for this type of weather. I should be in the wheelhouse."

"Wait, wait, wait, wait, wait," I said, putting my hand up, "you mean we need to go back up there? I don't think that's possible, Captain."

"Then we can't steer into the oncoming swells, and we could get swamped. Worse, we could go way off course and smash into one of the rigs or other boats."

I gave him the *you've got to be fucking shitting me* look and he held up his hands helplessly. "We didn't anticipate the storm catching us so quickly. All we had were a few reports, but usually those rig weather guys are pretty good. Didn't you ever listen to a weather report and have the weatherman be totally wrong?"

"Yeah, but my friggin' life wasn't in the balance!"

"Welcome to the sea my friend."

"Fuck!"

Everyone turned to look at my outburst. Even Babe and Zero looked at us.

Alvarez was immediately suspicious. "What?"

"Captain Bligh here is telling me we might have come for nothing." I chucked a thumb at Bob. I mean I pointed at him with my thumb; I didn't pick up a zombie digit and throw it at him. Why would you think that? Ew.

Bob related what he had just told me to everybody, and they all had the same outburst except for Babe, who stood up.

He looked at Bob. "Tell me how to fix it."

"What?"

"How do I make it so we won't crash into anybody?"

"You can't! You would have to go back to the wheelhouse and…well…steer. But you'll never make it there, there are too many of them."

"Whether they rip me to pieces or I die spitting up my pancreas, it doesn't matter, I'm dead. At least I'll have a chance to stop this fucking tub from killing anybody else if I try."

Wow. Fucking True-Blue Hero. Captain America type stuff. Stupid, but heroic.

"I'll go with him."

I heard it and looked around to see what fucking moron would tag along on that one-way mission.

Everybody was looking at me.

Wait.

Time the fuck out.

Did that shit come out of me?

I sighed, both then and now. Yeah. I said it, but it was such a shock to my own damn system, my psyche must have checked out for a sec.

"I can't get infected," I blurted, and the sea-sick stinkeye I got from Ship almost knocked me over. I hadn't told anyone, not even Alvarez about my immunity. Honestly, it didn't mean anything on the rig. Nobody had to know, and not knowing meant everybody was safer.

"What does that mean?" demanded Alvarez.

I pulled my jeans up and showed him the bite mark on my leg. "That came from one of them a long time ago." I pulled my shirt down exposing my collar bone scar. "This too."

"Bullshit," Greg said.

Ship already had a yellow post it filled out and handed it to Alvarez who read it aloud: *It's true, I saw him get bitten months ago.*

They had all been looking, but now they were all gawking.

Babe stepped up to me. Poor guy already looked sick, but I didn't know if it was from the bite or the *Majestik* chucking us around. "If this is true then there's no fucking way you're coming with me. You need to live. You could be the cure for all of this." He spread his un-bandaged, cigarette -laden hand wide.

"Yeah, I've heard that before, but now it's time for all of you assholes to listen. None of that shit matters if we don't fix this boat. If we crash into something then we'll sink and kill everybody we crash into. If I get bitten on the way back up there, it's no issue. If any of you get bitten, you die. My chances are way better of surviving."

Steve was incredulous. "But you could be torn to pieces!"

"Thanks," Babe said.

Steve was matter-of-fact. "Sorry Babe, but you're already dead. I know that sucks, but even you know it's true. He's important." He pointed at me.

Babe laughed. "Thanks again."

"If anybody goes it should be me," said Bob, "I'm the only one here qualified to pilot this big bitch anyway."

Babe flicked his butt and it hit a dead zombie in the face. "Fuck that, teach me."

"Son, I've been doing this my whole life. I can't teach you everything you'll need to know about steering a quarter of a billion tons of boat through a hurricane in the next ten minutes."

Son of a bitch. The Amazing Super Hero Squad of Super Cool Brave Dudes was on this boat.

A particularly vast portion of the Gulf of Mexico picked that moment to disappear from under the *Majestik Maersk*, and we all had no deck under us for a moment and went sprawling.

Bob actually looked scared. "We need to get up there before the containers break loose! We're side-to!"

I didn't know what the fuck that meant, but it scared the ever-loving shit out of me.

"Right. Babe, me, and Bob are heading back up to the wheelhouse. The rest of you get to safety and wait for the helicopter."

Ship passed me a post-it: *No!*

"Buddy, you're a Double Whopper for these rotten critters. Besides," I said, punching him, "I need you to look after Kat, and you can do that better than me."

He grabbed his post-it from my hand and pointed at it furiously. (That indicated no dear reader.)

"Ship, he's right. I need you with me." It was said in a small voice but we all looked at Alvarez, who put his hand on my shoulder. "I'm sorry."

"My idea. Besides, I'm too cool to die."

I couldn't tell if Ship was hurt or pissed or scared when we split up.

SHIT MAGNET

Holy shit, what the hell was I thinking? They went left, we went right at the end of the corridor. Evidence of undead attacks were everywhere. That classic bloody drag mark. Bloody hand prints on the bulkheads. Broken doors and bullet brass. If all this shit was here, it indicated that there were zombies here too.

We followed the still illuminated exit signs until we came to a closed hatch. The lights were flickering, but the exit signs weren't, the signs being on their own batteries. There was only one hatch lock engaged, but there weren't any windows in any of the hatches, and we couldn't see what was on the other side.

We couldn't go back though. We were close to exiting the interior of the ship and setting foot on open deck. There was an emergency schematic on the bulkhead next to this exit. From here, there was maybe a fifteen-foot stretch of corridor, then another hatch to the open deck. It was all we could do to stand now, the damn boat was rocking so hard. Fifty feet of running would bring us to the steps up to the wheelhouse, and unless these dead bastards had learned to fly or open doors, they couldn't have gotten onto the bridge.

Fifteen feet of corridor we couldn't see. Fifty feet of deck we had to traverse. A hundred feet of steps we had to climb. Less than two hundred feet to our destination, but that could be the longest couple hundred feet in history. Babe looked at me and Bob. We both nodded, weapons ready. Babe moved the hatch lock and pushed the hatch with his foot. The fifteen feet was devoid of anything living, but the far hatch had been left open and the raging seas and rain were pouring in. We couldn't sink because of this, but it was still damn wet. So was the zombie that pitched past the open portal when the ship rolled.

That didn't bode well, but we couldn't do anything about it. Babe's suppressed Sig was ready, but I didn't have one, nor did Bob. I kept my M4 close and Bob had a silver revolver. We moved through the hatch and closed it behind us, sealing it with one lock lever. The ship was rolling badly and we heard the containers creaking against the strain.

Babe moved forward and looked out the hatch left then right. Looking left he should have seen the zombie that had face planted, but if he did he made no mention of it when he waved us forward. Babe made for the wheelhouse and we ran after him.

In ones or twos at a distance, zombies aren't really scary. Fifty of them are scary. One of them that you didn't see that grabs you is fucking terrifying. Two thousand of them is terrifying, I don't care if you're watching them on TV from a lunar station. Yeah, zombies can be scary, but I would be a liar if I didn't tell you that the awe of the sea from my vantage point had me shitting my pants. We were next to containers stacked four high in some places, but when the *Majestik* nosed down, and I could see skyscraper-sized waves in front of me, I almost shit myself, but I kept running. I ran because the hundred or so undead shitheads that were between us and the stairs were strewn about on the deck trying to stand.

Forty eight out of fifty feet to the stairs and the ship took a wicked roll, pitching all three of us to the deck. Do you remember what was on the deck from the end of the last paragraph? Shit yeah. One of the things latched on to my jeans, and two had Babe, but Captain Sea-Legs was up and on the stairs in a nanosecond. He pointed his revolver at one of the things that had Babe and fired. He grazed Babe in the shoulder and the army guy howled. That got the zombies going, and they found their God damned sea-legs. I kicked loose of the one who had me and got to Babe, but a particularly disgusting one of them, all black and bloated and wet and slimy from the rain bit into his calf. The poor kid screamed and I shot the one who had his right arm in the face before it could bite him. He jammed his suppressor into the right eye of the one that had bitten him and pulled the trigger, spraying its brains on the ones behind it. They all started standing, so I grabbed the kid and dragged him to the stairs. Bob was halfway up, and it was friggin' windy.

I made Babe go in front of me, and he was limping badly, crimson dripping on the white steps and being diluted by the rain. We would have been fine, what with the boat rocking and the undead already unsteady on their feet, we should have reached the wheelhouse way before these lurching assholes. Two runners appeared and sprinted at us, and one came from nowhere and leapt on the side of the railing. Babe shot it in the shoulder as it tried to climb over and it fell back on the deck making that shriek that they make. Not dead yet, but fucked.

The other two screamed as well and were on me snapping in an instant. I spun my M4 and flipped to full auto just as one of them was opening its stinking maw to take a nibble. I blasted them both at the same time and made those fuckers dance on the steps. They both fell back into the arms of their dead cousins, soon to join them as a species if you believe in that shit. The dead ones had already started up the stairs.

Babe was bad off. He was in agony and I could see it. A huge swell must have hit us because the whole ship listed to port. An entire contingent of the dead fuckers went over the railing and landed hard on the deck, and it was all I could do to keep Babe and myself from following them over. Bob already had the hatch open and was screaming something at us, but he was a good fifty feet above us, and I couldn't hear him over the wind and rain and the entire Gulf of Mexico that threatened to crash down on us.

I got Babe to the top and we got inside and out of the rain. We were all three of us soaked to the skin. I immediately looked for the first aid kit to staunch the flow of blood from Babe's calf wound while Bob ran to the ship controls. I found it but the fucking thing was empty, not even a band-aid, and I remembered that Steve had raided every first aid kit that he had found on the ship.

Fuck.

I took my sopping wet shirt off and tied it around his wound, but it wasn't a bandage. He bled through my black t-shirt in three seconds, and the *tap-tap- tap* of blood coming from his leg hit the carpeted wheelhouse deck leaving a trail of drops behind. It sounded just like the hard rain outside.

Outside.

I turned and looked through the giant, panoramic windows, and was witness to the full fury of the sea. Fuck Mother Nature. This was all God, and he was pissed. The moving mountains that were out there were complete with snowy caps, and they roiled and crashed everywhere. The bow of the *Majestik* went up and up and up, then it went down, and the whole bow went under the water. I could see the wall of water coming through the containers as I braced myself for the impact. The good thing was that it washed a shit load of those dead fuckers away. A wave of hurricane driven pus bags bounced through the containers with some spilling over the side. The bad thing was the containers that let go up by the bow. As the nose of the ship came back up, a whole wall of the multi-colored shipping containers, with MAERSK on the side broke loose and went into the water. It was loud, and I could hear it over the storm and the sea.

One of the giant steel boxes got caught in a big wave and was thrown end over end against the hull up forward, and came spinning across the tops of the other containers. The screeching metal noise was unbelievably loud, even over the storm. The bow took another dip, and the five thousand pounds or so of metal box (if it were empty) slid forward. We came up the far side of the surge, and that damn thing came shooting across the others right toward the base of the wheelhouse. It must have caught on one of the other containers, because it started flipping again, and suddenly fell into the gap where the tents had been. I felt a small sliver of satisfaction in knowing that those infected that hadn't been washed over, and were hanging around the tents, now resembled something akin to oatmeal.

Captain Bob was having a hard time steering the ship. He called out to me and I left a dry heaving Babe sitting with his back against the command console to go assist Bob. I got to the bridge controls and almost shit. I hadn't seen the ship's steering wheel when we were up in the wheelhouse before, and now that I had seen it…well… I believe I already stated the almost shit thing.

It looked like a steering wheel you'd find in a Lego car. I was expecting a ship's wheel like you see in the movies with the spindles and stuff, which immediately made me feel like a moron. This wheel was missing the top part and was very small. It looked almost like the steering wheel you would see in a race car.

"I need you on the wheel while I…OH SHIT!"

Bob pointed back behind me and I looked across the room into the snarling face of a Runner who had made it to the top of the exterior stairs. She was flailing about and smacking her fist against the hatch porthole. I think she could have smacked it until doomsday…well…a different doomsday, and it wouldn't have given way. We would have to wait for that second doomsday, as with the next loll of the *Majestik* the Runner, who had released a hand rail to pound with both fists, went over the railing and plummeted to the deck. One less Runner, one more pus bag.

"Hold the wheel, keep it turned this way!"

I took the fancy wheel and kept it pinned to the left. Bob moved around pushing buttons and rolling dials for a minute then came back. "Look," he said and pointed out the window. Through the storm I could see that way off in the distance there was blue sky. How the hell did that happen?

I asked Bob.

"I turned us around. We're still in the shit, but the storm is moving south southeast at about forty miles per hour. The worst of it is in front of us and we were going to be running thought it for the better part of a day. This way we'll be out in five hours tops." The screeching of rending metal punctuated his statement . The loose container was still banging around on the forward deck. Bob suddenly had something in his hand. "Atlantis, this is *Majestik Maersk*, do you read?"

Almost instantly, we got a reply, "*Majestik* this is Atlantis, we have you, what's your status over."

"This fucking tub crawls with zombies Atlantis, and *Majestik* is now on a heading of three hundred over."

For the second time today, I felt like a moron. Fucking radios. I had lost mine in the tunnel of death we were in a few hours ago. I asked Bob if he had the wheel OK, and he gave me a thumbs up while he spoke to Jimmy at Atlantis. Apparently, they were getting hammered by the storm as were we. I went to check on Babe.

He was looking at me weird, and he licked his lips when he saw me. He looked hungry. I pointed my M4 at him and he said, "Not yet."

"I need your radio, buddy." He handed it to me. "Do I look tasty yet?"

He smiled. "Gay. I might need you to take care of it, I'm feeling weak."

I wasn't smiling. I really liked this guy. He had saved my ass on several occasions. The ship rolled forward and I fell on him, smacking his wound with my knee. He shrieked and pushed me off, then started laughing uncontrollably.

"I'm gonna fucking die! How funny is that? I'm gonna die because a dead guy bit me...." He started looking in all directions but nowhere special.

I sat up and put my hand on his forehead. I was shirtless and the wind and rain were blowing in through the broken bridge window so I was chilly, not cold mind you, but chilly. The heat coming off this guy could have powered a nuclear submarine.

"Where's Cannonball? Where's my dog?"

"He's right here, pal," I said with tears in my eyes and stood up. "He's outside and barking for you, buddy."

"He took my Frisbee!"

"Dogs do that? Do you want to see him?" I moved Babe's suppressed Sig away from him, then picked it up.

"Yeah! My leg hurts and I want to see my dog. Where's Mom?"

"She has Cannonball, they're outside. I can see them."

I helped him up and we looked out the window. His eyes went wide and he said, "Whoa...." I shot him in the back of the head and he dropped to the floor like a sack of potatoes. I sat down next to him and held his hand while I cried. I took my shirt off his leg and covered what was left of his face.

I used Babe's radio to call Alvarez, but there was no response. We were in a big steel tub with tons of steel between us and he either didn't respond or couldn't respond. I was immediately worried, this was my family now. "I can't raise them."

Bob moved a little to the left and picked up a telephone receiver, wired to the bridge controls, "Alvarez, this is Bob," he said, his voice sounding like it was coming through a far off megaphone, "we've made it to the bridge and we're secure for now. If you can find something that looks like a phone on a wall, that's the intercom system and it will connect you with us. Oh, and to the zombies? Fuck you." Bob hung up. "Intercom system. Oh, the chopper can't come for us until the storm passes."

I nodded. "Tell them," I said, pointing at the intercom. Bob called out again telling our guys that the helicopter was going to be a little late, and we waited.

It was almost dark when the seas had calmed enough for the zombies to make it all the way up the stairwell and start beating on the hatches. They were at the interior hatches too, but they were solid. Just like Captain Pedersen, we were stuck here.

Bob turned us around and we headed back toward the storm, chasing it home. The bridge was lit up like a Christmas tree. I found deck lights and flipped them on. The angry seas hadn't washed away all of the infected, but there were considerably less than there had been. One hundred or five hundred didn't make a difference though, we were still fucked. Alvarez hadn't called either.

"We're about seventy miles further north west than we should be." Bob was looking at a computer screen. " I've laid a course to the southwest of Atlantis, and we should miss all the other rigs and ships if…"

He let that hang. He didn't have to finish… If we got eaten and there was nobody left to steer the ship. He had set it on auto-pilot or whatever the fuck it was called. I was in a shitty mood and looked at my friend's corpse.

Gunshots broke me from my self-loathing. Bob and I ran to the port side rear windows and looked at the rear deck. My group of friends was battling a group of zombies as they ran through the stacks of containers. They couldn't see it, but they were surrounded, and in a minute or two, the infected would be on them in numbers that would overwhelm them.

"Get on that fucking intercom!" I screamed at Bob. Startled, he ran back and picked it up.

"They have to climb! Tell them they have to climb! Big group coming from their left…the starboard side!" (No, I'm not wrong, I was looking toward the rear of the boat, dear smartass reader, it *was* the starboard side). Bob relayed the information and the group of humans moved as one through the containers to my right. They ran up one of the red catwalk thingies between the containers, but a couple of runners were right behind them. Zero and Alvarez dispatched the chasers, but shambling behind them were more of the slow variety, and there were more infected than bullets I was wagering. Captain Pedersen's log said that there were three hundred people aboard, but I was looking at more than three hundred right now and this was only on the rear deck.

Our friends jumped from the catwalk on to an orange MAERSK container. Steve almost fell as he had a huge pack full of medical supplies pilfered from the ship. Zero caught him by the pack strap as he teetered on the edge. He would have fallen fifty feet or so into a horde of hungry dead cannibals. The top of the container was maybe six feet from the catwalk, and soon the catwalk was full to bursting with reaching pus sacks.

Some of the more industrious undead tried to climb over the railings, but they couldn't jump the gap, and fell to the deck like lemmings. I know lemmings don't really do that. Don't be a dick, it was metaphorical.

So there they were, in a light rain, six feet from a few hundred reaching zombies, with zombies surrounding the containers. They took out runners as the runners fought to get to the top of the catwalk, and they were on top of six containers, so they had plenty of room. We were stuck up here on the bridge, no rain but only a half inch of steel and glass between us and more undead.

We sat in relative comfort for eleven hours until I heard the helicopter. It came from a little off our port bow. They had called us a half hour before requesting our coordinates. We could still see the storm, but it was way off to the south. The bird flew in and we told them to get the crew on the container first. Bob had cut the engines when they called us, so they were able to pretty much land on the tops of the containers and they didn't need to drop a line. Good thing too as the post storm static in the air and from the rotors could kill somebody that touched a line.

My friends were on board the chopper and it was our turn. It was when Bob told me he wasn't coming that I wigged out.

"What the hell are you talking about?"

"Well, I've set the course correction software, and everything should be ok, but what if something happens?"

I pointed toward the Runner banging with a renewed fury on the porthole of the port hatch. "Are you fucking certifiable? This is our chance to get off this death tub. Set it and forget it. Let's book!"

"No. No I need to stay. I'll get this bitch past all the rigs, set it on a heading that will beach her someplace in Mexico, then call for a pickup."

There was no talking him out of it. I heard footsteps on the roof of the bridge and knew my guys had arrived. I heard a shot, and that freaked me out a little until they knocked on a roof hatch, and I let Alvarez in.

He was all smiles. "Time to go kids." Then he looked at Babe's covered corpse.

"You lookin' at my smoking hot chest?" I asked flexing my pecs.

"Meh, not bad, but check this out." He flexed his right bicep.

"Gay," we both said at the same time as we burst out laughing and hugged in the most manly of ways.

I looked at our dead friend. "Sorry Babe."

"He would have loved your fucking witty banter," Alvarez said sadly.

In the end, he couldn't convince Bob to come with us either. I left through the hatch in the roof and my guys were all smiles. Babe had been the last to die. Captain Pedersen was up on the roof, tied to a spinning radar mast, twice killed. He did make it out, just not alive. I hope his family made it.

I boarded the helicopter with Alvarez right behind me and we left that fucking death ship behind.

An hour and twenty minutes later, Atlantis was in sight. My home looked no more the worse for wear because of the storm, but there was something new. A big black helicopter, definitely military, was on the eastern helipad. A second bird, also military, came out of nowhere and told us to land as quickly as possible. This one was a gunship. Was the military going to take our home and turn it into another research facility complete with dozens of undead like the *Majestik Maersk*?

We landed on the larger, western helipad and disembarked from the bird. There were armed soldiers there, but they were all smiles and handshakes and their weapons were slung. We walked down the steps to the main deck, toward the galley. I wanted a fucking sandwich.

There were new crates of shrink wrapped food and water and pallets of more shit being moved with a forklift. All the soldiers smiled and waved. We got to the galley and when we entered, Austin and a bunch of the Atlantis brass was on their knees, hands behind their heads with weapons on them. Kat was there too, which I thought was weird.

The smiles on the soldiers vanished and their weapons were on us. We were disarmed, and told to get on our knees as well, where they zip tied our hands behind our backs.

Two minutes later, a small contingent of military came strolling in. One looked like a general, all authoritative and shit. He stood there, hands clasped behind his back, obviously pissed. "Well *hello*!" It hadn't been said by the general, but by somebody else. I knew the voice. I looked left and there he was.

Lynch.

Dude was like herpes: Nasty and pops up when you least expect it.

He strolled over to us and looked at Ship, then at the general. "Ya know, I shot this guy once," he said, thumbing at my buddy, "like our zombie antagonists, he didn't stay down. But everybody knows that's not why we're here." He stood in front of me and pointed at me, but looked at absolutely everyone else. "That's why we're here."

"He's a mechanic," Austin said.

"Au contraire! He's *important*. He's an *important* mechanic, and he has to come with me. Now."

"I'm sorry folks," the general said, "but if what this man," he pointed to Lynch, "says is true, then this man," he pointed at me, "could very well be the most important man on the planet. Sergeant, stand him up please."

One of the buzz-cut douche bags helped me stand and the general told him to raise up my pant leg.

Lynch pointed to my leg bite scar, "Ta-daaaa!" He put his hands up like a ref signaling a touchdown. "Pick six bitches!"

"Son, you're going to have to come with us."

My friends who were not privy to my little secret were astounded. Austin just had to ask, "What the hell is that?"

"That, my friend, is a bite by one of the carriers of this plague. Death to absolutely everyone on earth that we know about except this man. Oh, and I bet he didn't tell you that he's a convict. He would have two years and change left on his sentence if he hadn't escaped."

I harrumphed. "Dick. I didn't escape, I was let out. And any crime I committed is probably not nearly bad as what you did and still do on a daily basis. Douche."

Lynch shook his head and punched me in the stomach. Ship, Alvarez, Kat, Greg, and Zero all tried to stand up, but the soldiers were less than kind to them.

Lynch had hit me hard, and I was unprepared for it so I was heaving. Prick was in good shape and knew how to hit.

"Pussy," he said.

"Fuh…fuck y…"

"Fucky? What the hell is fucky? Doesn't matter. Colonel, should we get this show on the road?"

Yeah, so he was a colonel, not a general. How the hell was I supposed to know?

"Enough. Don't strike him again." He looked around the room. "Anyone trying to interfere will be shot." And with that he just up and walked out with his little security detail.

"C'mon bud," the sergeant said and moved me toward the door. I wanted to hold my aching belly but my hands were tied behind me.

Ship started to stand and one of the soldiers butted him in the noggin with his rifle. Ship shook it off like the Hulk and stood. Every barrel of every gun in the room was instantly on him.

"Ship, don't. I'll be fine. I'll be back soon and these assholes will pay for it." The sergeant raised his eyebrows. "The ride, dumbass."

He smirked. "Let's go."

"Do let's," Lynch agreed. He had his pistol pointed at Ship. "Just one more thing." He raised the weapon, a little higher.

The sergeant put his hand on Lynch's arm roughly and Lynch looked at him sideways. "Not why we're here."

"I need to shoot this asshole to see if the bullet will bounce off."

"Do that and you're dead one second later. We got what we came for. The colonel doesn't need you anymore, and if you hurt anyone else I'll fucking shoot you. If I don't, somebody else will."

Although the guy had a weapon on me, and had me zip tied, I liked him instantly if for no other reason than he pissed all over Lynch.

"We'll re-visit this conversation, Sarge ole sock." He holstered his weapon.

"*Do let's*," the sergeant mocked.

Fifteen minutes later, I was watching my friends assemble on the deck of Atlantis as I was shuttled to who-knows-where in a black helicopter. At least they hadn't killed anybody. Ship had his tree-trunk arms folded and Alvarez had his arm around Kat trying to console her. Before the bird banked and I lost sight of them, I noticed that Kat had a defiant middle finger extended toward the chopper.

Acknowledgments

I would like to thank my family; Donna, my wife, Danielle, my oldest, and my twins, Richy and Chloe, without whom this story would never have been written. I took their daily antics, zombified them, and stuck them in here for you to read.

Thanks Mom and Pops. Mom for her cookies, Dad for his ammo.

Thanks J.R, FF, and Sara. Zombie Fiends for sure.

Thank you, Dawn. You made this better.

Thanks to George. If there were no George, it is likely there would be no flesh eating zombies at all.

Thanks to all the folks who insisted get this book published. Honestly, I wrote it for fun, but their constant pleadings and threats finally got on my nerves so much I sent it off to see if my publisher would like it. Most of these crazy people can be found on zombiefiend.com or homepageofthedead.com.

Also, a big round of applause for you. Yeah, you, reading this right now. I hope you enjoyed reading this story as much as I enjoyed writing it. Without you this whole thing is pointless. Thanks a million.

CHECK OUT OTHER GREAT
ZOMBIE NOVELS

900 MILES
by S. Johnathan Davis

John is a killer, but that wasn't his day job before the Apocalypse.

In a harrowing 900 mile race against time to get to his wife just as the dead begin to rise, John, a business man trapped in New York, soon learns that the zombies are the least of his worries, as he sees first-hand the horror of what man is capable of with no rules, no consequences and death at every turn.

Teaming up with an ex-army pilot named Kyle, they escape New York only to stumble across a man who says that he has the key to a rumored underground stronghold called Avalon..... Will they find safety? Will they make it to Johns wife before it's too late?

Get ready to follow John and Kyle in this fast paced thriller that mixes zombie horror with gladiator style arena action!

WHITE FLAG OF THE DEAD
by Joseph Talluto

Millions died when the Enillo Virus swept the earth. Millions more were lost when the victims of the plague refused to stay dead, instead rising to slaughter and feed on those left alive. For survivors like John Talon and his son Jake, they are faced with a choice: Do they submit to the dead, raising the white flag of surrender? Or do they find the will to fight, to try and hang on to the last shreds or humanity?

CHECK OUT OTHER GREAT ZOMBIE NOVELS

VACCINATION
by Phillip Tomasso

What if the H7N9 vaccination wasn't just a preventative measure against swine flu?

It seemed like the flu came out of nowhere and yet, in no time at all the government manufactured a vaccination. Were lab workers diligent, or could the virus itself have been man-made? Chase McKinney works as a dispatcher at 9-1-1. Taking emergency calls, it becomes immediately obvious that the entire city is infected with the walking dead. His first goal is to reach and save his two children.

Could the walls built by the U.S.A. to keep out illegal aliens, and the fact the Mexican government could not afford to vaccinate their citizens against the flu, make the southern border the only plausible destination for safety?

ZOMBIE, INC
by Chris Dougherty

"WELCOME! To Zombie, Inc. The United Five State Republic's leading manufacturer of zombie defense systems! In business since 2027, Zombie, Inc. puts YOU first. YOUR safety is our MAIN GOAL! Our many home defense options - from Ze Fence® to Ze Popper® to Ze Shed® - fit every need and every budget. Use Scan Code "TELL ME MORE!" for your FREE, in-home*, no obligation consultation! *Schedule your appointment with the confidence that you will NEVER HAVE TO LEAVE YOUR HOME! It isn't safe out there and we know it better than most! Our sales staff is FULLY TRAINED to handle any and all adversarial encounters with the living and the undead". Twenty-five years after the deadly plague, the United Five State Republic's most successful company, Zombie, Inc., is in trouble. Will a simple case of dwindling supply and lessening demand be the end of them or will Zombie, Inc. find a way, however unpalatable, to survive?

CHECK OUT OTHER GREAT ZOMBIE NOVELS

Z BURBIA
by Jake Bible

Whispering Pines is a classic, quiet, private American subdivision on the edge of Asheville, NC, set in the pristine Blue Ridge Mountains. Which is good since the zombie apocalypse has come to Western North Carolina and really put suburban living to the test!

Surrounded by a sea of the undead, the residents of Whispering Pines have adapted their bucolic life of block parties to scavenging parties, common area groundskeeping to immediate area warfare, neighborhood beautification to neighborhood fortification.

But, even in the best of times, suburban living has its ups and downs what with nosy neighbors, a strict Home Owners' Association, and a property management company that believes the words "strict interpretation" are holy words when applied to the HOA covenants. Now with the zombie apocalypse upon them even those innocuous, daily irritations quickly become dramatic struggles for personal identity, family security, and straight up survival.

ZOMBIE RULES
by David Achord

Zach Gunderson's life sucked and then the zombie apocalypse began.

Rick, an aging Vietnam veteran, alcoholic, and prepper, convinces Zach that the apocalypse is on the horizon. The two of them take refuge at a remote farm. As the zombie plague rages, they face a terrifying fight for survival.

They soon learn however that the walking dead are not the only monsters.

www.ingramcontent.com/pod-product-compliance
Lightning Source LLC
Chambersburg PA
CBHW032209170626
46808CB00006B/2392